SOULI

BY MADELINE BROWN

This is a work of fiction. Names, characters, places, and incidents either are the product of the author's imagination or are used fictitiously. Any resemblance to actual persons, living or dead, is entirely coincidental.

First edition July 2020

Illustrations and Design © 2020 BY MADELINE BROWN
ISBN 978-1-8380556-0-8 [paperback]
ISBN 978-1-8380556-1-5 [e-book]

madelinebrownwrites.wordpress.com

We seem to be drifting into unknown places and unknown ways; into a whole world of dark and dreadful things.

\- Bram Stoker, *Dracula (1897)*

Contents

Prologue

[Eris]

"What are you reading?"

That terse voice yanked me out of my stupor. The constant clacks of the train's wheels were as soothing as I had hoped; I might have even been falling asleep. Glancing first at the boy on the other side of the narrow cabin, stood against the wall, then down at my knees, I cleared my throat, stalling.

"It…" I gently turned the cover of the book over, to be sure. "The Definitive Compendium of Espritian Myths: Volume One of Three."

Raised eyebrows informed me that, frankly, he did not share any interest in fiction. He huffed through his nose, and his narrowed eyes flicked away from my hands in favour of the window. They flared amber under the morning sunlight, eerily. An image scratched against the underside of my memory: a flicker of dark hair and shining irises wrapped in a cloak of flames, summoned then by a terror I could not find in him now.

Opening the pages back up in front of me, I began to wonder if a copy of *The Souls and Those Who Wield Them* might have been a better choice. I knew the book like a warm acquaintance, having already rifled through it, filling the margins with pencilled scrawls. It still felt different, somewhere, knowing now that I was one of them—one of those. The fascinated detachment swiftly evaporated. There was a Soul concealed inside me. And I intended to use it to devour down the very thing that had wrenched it to the surface. A part of me believed that to spend time reading up on that was the very least I could do. The very notion grew more laughable the more times I turned it over in my mind.

But then I had already considered this earlier today, under the shelter of the library, balancing precariously on the steps of one of our old rolling ladders. White light was just breaking through the high windows, lifting the gentle veil of dimness from the morning, and allowing jagged shadows to creep out from between the shelves, cases and stairways. Their slow crawl along the floor eventually caught my attention and worked sufficiently to intimidate me down from my perch. Maud still waited, more patiently than usual for me. Such tolerance for my habitual dithering was odd, and in this peculiar situation I perhaps would have appreciated her typical ruthlessness more.

Maud, the old librarian, was by all accounts fastidious and irritable. Nevertheless, she who once lived alone— and perfectly content, she would add—had readily allowed me a place in her musty, heavenly sanctuary. There was much to be said for that. She also possessed a certain air of superior wisdom that I never thought to question. A mutual understanding hung between the pair of us that sustained us like steadfast clockwork.

I could not say how long it took, exactly. Was it a year, or perchance more? One hardly noticed the steady process occur, but after that strange, indistinct length of time, I had successfully become another piece of the furniture in that antique place—but never quite like Maud herself. That was unattainable. Rather fittingly, she was stationed vigil at her oaken desk when I first left, to post to my mother and father, using the new address they included in the last lengthy letter, as they did with each and every one. On occasion my reply covered the ground too slow and found they had already moved on. Strict instruction dictated I was not to attach my own location, so I could only assume they left a faint trail of lost messages behind them, with no place to return to. I had pondered over this one for several days, wondering whether or not it was fair to tell them where I was going, before I remembered the likelihood that the envelope would never reach them anyway. The letter represented, more than anything, one attempt to maintain a semblance of routine. I returned home in a fraction of the time it had taken me to write the thing, and Maud was there, behind her desk. For whatever reason, she didn't so much as glance over her shoulder at me, as I went to linger listlessly in front of our collection simply labelled, "*Souls*".

I'd been there before. All of these covers were marked with my fingerprints. Any question I could think of on that spot, I already had an answer to anyway. Why me? No reason; the distribution of

Souls is entirely random, and you're not superstitious. Why then? You were in danger, obviously. Your Soul protected you. You should consider yourself lucky. So why does that equate to me, shipping myself off to Interieur, with what stragglers remain of its military? You offered yourself up for this. You didn't have to. That was made abundantly clear. Still, here you are, with no particular reasoning, only the awareness of some vague, reconciled feeling that there really was no choice. You are going to kill a monster.

I eventually arrived at: What would have happened to me if my Soul had not surfaced? What if vicious white light had not splintered the air, as it shielded my useless body? What if he had not been there too? What if Kai Hughes' Soul had not emerged in an angry, terrified plume of flames that had, for now, banished the furious beast? I had considered this idea, only briefly, before I decided to stop thinking about it.

In the end, I concluded that reading anything to take my mind away from "what if", even for a moment, was the safer idea. Perhaps I had grasped the wrong end of this particularly thorny stick, and a romance would have worked more efficiently. Something sticky and tooth-rotting from the back end of the library. I shifted a little in my seat, stirring up an aroma from the worn upholstery: aged, almost like home. In reality, I was just barely gone; the train had yet to even cross the border out of the Western District, but it served as a small comfort all the same.

Another familiar occurrence slouched over the cover of yesterday's newspaper in brash black print, folded up and abandoned in the cabin. "*Altairs' Siege of the South Begins*" could be deciphered from where I sat. Looking at it, I felt I had read that particular headline before. I did not doubt the writers had exhausted their supply; news was, these days, frustrating, but never surprising. They'd moved on to the Southern District. Only a matter a time before it would be the West's turn to live with the tired anxiety they brought. That could either take months, or only a matter of weeks: who ever knew? Neither of us touched the paper. Perhaps the Altairs should have played more upon my mind. In ordinary circumstances, they surely would.

The doors of the carriage clattered open about two hours later. My travel partner had fidgeted a little over the journey, sitting down, standing up again, leaning on the window, then the cabin door. His outburst had come a relatively short while after departure, and he'd not said a word since. Our fellow passengers piled off the train as though each one had somewhere they were in a desperate hurry to be. I let all of them go ahead, with him behind me, presumably to his chagrin since I heard him sigh again through his nostrils.

Mindful of the gap between myself and the platform, I hopped out, noticing first the blinding white fog which seemed to swamp my senses. Next were two faces that appeared amongst it. They both must have trodden lightly, the way they appeared to float through the mist, so lightly in fact, that I almost collided with a shoulder. Looking up, I didn't recognise him; his female companion, however, was very familiar to me.

My thoughts were faint and wispy at the time, back in the little street near the library, my recollection of them by this point distorted at best. Nonetheless, three distinct memories managed to stick; these were the same visions as came creeping to visit whenever I might deign to sleep.

Foremost was the image of that dark, vicious fiend, all shadow and snarl and teeth and wrath, bathed in lightning and fire—ours, I had to remember.

Second came Kai Hughes' eyes. They were framed by unruly feathers of hair, and glazed over, in such a way that they seemed to glow red, as if the flames that had burst from the ground at his feet now burned inside his skull. His pupils glanced first over his shoulder, lazily following the fleeing silhouette, before turning back to stare right into my own. The rest of his body remained inert, slumped on the cobbles. He'd been knocked to his knees by the blast, and there he stayed.

Sometime after that appeared a girl's voice, soft in my ears, repeating to me, over and over: "Hey, sweetie, listen. It's okay. See, it's gone. You got it. It's not here. It's not here. Hey. You are okay. You are going to be okay. Hey."

It was her airy chant that I recognised initially, before I was then able to place her tumbling black hair and small, delicate features as well. I remembered thinking, back then, that she was so very pretty.

She was quick to speak up. "Ah—hey, there you are! Eris, Kai, it's me, it's Aria. I'm here to meet you, remember?" She rested one hand on my forearm, the other on Kai's, and gasped loudly. In her enthusiasm she had forgotten herself. "Oh! But—and I am sorry about this—we can't stay here. Tank and Medi are herding up the passengers already, so we have got to grab you two and go, speedy as we can. We will try explaining to you on the way, alright?"

"Come on, we have to go." The young man at Aria's side spoke, already turning to leave, and I noticed Kai had disappeared from my left as well.

Aria gave my wrist a gentle tug to spur me into motion. We were only walking, albeit at an urgent pace, but the wringing sensation in my ribcage and sand at the roof of my mouth more closely resembled wading against a current. I felt the nerves in my feet had shut down; my shoes logically had to be hitting the concrete, but I could scarcely feel it.

"We were stopped on our way over here. There was an unnamed threat detected entering over the border to the city. In such a situation as this one, Aria and, by extension, myself, are under orders from General to act as your escorts, per se," the man continued, raising his voice firmly above the clamour, a sea of footsteps and implacable shouting, made worse by the incessant toll of a bell somewhere outside.

"Eris, Kai, meet Emery. He serves under General Elwin, too," added Aria with a smile, first to us, then shooting another in his direction.

This seemed to catch his attention, and he twisted himself to face us, although still marching ahead. His dull blond ponytail flipped over his shoulder and he volunteered a lopsided smirk of his own, raising his hand in a half-wave.

"You said this threat is unnamed. Tell me exactly what you mean by that." Kai's low drone almost went unnoticed by me; he hadn't spoken in so long. I was hardly one to talk, I soon recalled.

"What I mean is we don't recognise it. Whatever it is, it's not human, or animal," Emery elaborated.

The realisation dawned on me. "So, what you're saying is, this means--?"

"You've barely been here five minutes, and we've probably got the bastard in our sights already."

“Oh, well that’s typical. I gear myself up for this, enough crap to last for weeks, and chances are I’ll be back on *that* train by tomorrow,” Kai snapped.

“Gracious almighty, I apologise for your inconvenience,” I said, out loud apparently, although I didn’t quite register that until Aria’s head whipped around, brow arched at me, presumably in alarm.

They led us out of the station and accelerated to the fastest walk my legs could manage. Aria kept reaching round to pull me along a little, as though as to check I was still, in fact, there and had not absconded. Where she thought I might disappear to was, truthfully, beyond me. They continued making sudden turns, or diving down narrow, dim side streets, which I would ordinarily choose to avoid like a disease. It was clear they knew where we were going, and precisely how they would drag us there. All these roads and buildings looked the same to me. I could be anywhere, and I wouldn’t be able to distinguish it from any other place in this brick wilderness. I was placing my trust, my protection, in the hands of these strangers, like yanking out my heart only to hold it up on a spattered silver dish, in hope.

Now there was a paradox. But there was something else, past that, something off about the whole journey. It escaped me at first, while the situation offered my mind little room to hang back, but upon later reflection I grasped it. There was no strange presence that I’d failed to pin down, but rather an absence. Every door we happened to pass was sealed shut, each street empty, save for us four. Interieur, the bustling capital, had been deserted.

Part 1: Subjection

[Kai]

We had surely traversed a good part of the city already, and with such efficiency that I struggled to trace our position, especially considering we were being dragged along on foot. We were, at least, following the railway, which had suddenly risen above my head, atop numerous bridges and platforms. No wheels rumbled along it now; my stop would be the last until this “unnamed threat” was eliminated. Each district had to react like a refined machine in response to rogue Souls. Experience had taught us how to survive them as well as we did. Even so, I didn’t take long to conclude that the population of Interieur was rather better protected than the outer regions. The bell tower continued to sound for evacuation, insufferably loud at this close proximity.

When Blondie in front of me (whose bizarre accent I still could not place) finally decided to totally and instantly stop—without much consideration for me, following right behind him—he did so before a set of three wide arches. The stone, characteristically dark, cast an equally dismal shadow over the street below. Under the middle archway, there stood a horse, an impressive beast encased in a coat of metal, and raised up on its back a woman, whom I had seen before. She had armour too, on this occasion, visible underneath her elaborate uniform, and a long, narrow blade hanging at her hip. Looking closer, seeing the straight shoulders, hair pulled into a bun at the back of her head, and that emblematic jacket, laced down the spine, I recognised the image of General Elwin.

“They’re here,” I heard her say, before she bellowed, “Tank, Medi, grab those two.”

With barely the pretence of a look back, the two escorts marched towards her, like moths to a beacon. Clearly, they were not “Tank” or “Medi”. I flicked my head around, assuming I’d come face-to-face with those unseen soldiers. As I soon discovered, they were instead behind me.

"Shit," I hissed, as my collar stretched in one hand's vice grip.

"Language, young man," he growled in my ear. I turned and blinked back at him. He couldn't have exceeded my height by much, but he seemed a giant. Everything was designed to appear broad and sturdy. His face, several inches too close to mine, might've been rather pale, if not for the permanent pink blush, and combination of stubble and dirt caked over it. Judging from the rigid twitch at the edge of his mouth, he was making quite the effort not to sneer. I opted to stay put, and quiet, lest he decide to crush my jaw between his fingers.

The other girl, the one from the train, was being held by her shoulders. She had struck me as vaguely familiar when I first saw her standing there, unmoving behind a curtain of crackling white light. But even now, I couldn't remember her name. Beside her, the woman—Medi, by my guess—was not so much restraining her, as holding her upright. Tight brown curls grew from her head in all directions, in the manner of a flower. Her mellow tawny skin wrinkled with concern, just around her eyelids, though in light of what we saw, she remained reasonably calm.

General Elwin galloped past and then away from us, the plates and hinges of the horse's metal shell clattering as it moved. She vanished around the far corner of a narrow-built pub, with a roof that bowed a little towards the middle, aptly signposted "*The Arches*". Its thick, leaden doors were closed. The lingering moment of silence pressed down, making the air viscous, with a stale taste. Then the shattering sound of a gunshot bounded around the empty, open space, followed by another, further away, and muted by the distance. I caught the woman with the flower hair glancing up above the rooftops.

"Tank," she called and, given a second, the man behind me hooted, so loud my eardrums ached with it. I followed the path of her gaze. Above me, the pointed angles of the city's crown were lost, made indistinct by a creeping wall of green mist.

"Here it comes," Tank said, his huge voice effortlessly carrying to Aria and Emery, now stationed beneath the tracks, blind to the sight of the smoke. They nodded, and the former pulled a long weapon off of her back. The pair stood facing away from each other, each poised towards one exit of the towering archway. So, the guns didn't shoot bullets; they fired signals.

A new soldier returned before Elwin did—another on horseback. The man drove on by, with a speed too purposeful to mean anything positive. His brown forehead shone with sweat in the sunlight now blinking above the horizon. Whatever the green smoke implied, it was here.

As if on cue, a second set of hooves rattled from the opposite direction. But the general appeared somewhat diminished now, compared to the creature in front of her. Its shrieking globe of a head rose almost level with the two-storey rooftops, enormous, prehistoric, to the extent that it hovered close to the ground, as though the breadth of its wings couldn't quite lift it any higher. Trying to take in its appearance, my mind immediately jumped to owls, specifically, those that would occasionally perch on a chimney pot and peer inside my window. Buried amongst the mass of feathers, it even had the same shining mirrors for eyes that stared into the back of your head, as if they knew far too much. The round, yellow bulbs glared out from under the gloom of the structure hanging over its head.

The bird, if it could even be called that, was relentlessly pursued by Elwin, but didn't seem to move with any of the primal terror that should leap up, in the chase between hunter and prey. Rather, the soldiers quickly surrounding it were impediments, little more. It rounded the right angle of that street as though it had already been heading this way. I failed to comprehend how it could so gravely misconstrue its current situation; however, that only made it less predictable, and all the more treacherous to deal with. My own head started to sting around my temples, trying to pull me back, by pinching at my skull, back to that first day, to the beginnings of a cataclysm.

Sensing its smaller, decidedly more agile predator closing in behind it, the winged giant reared up with a splitting squeal. In return, Elwin drew the blade from her belt which, almost instantaneously, flew out of her hand and spun through the air, like an invisible foot had kicked it out of her grip. Her horse stumbled, crying in confusion as its knees knocked against the floor. I blinked, and rubbed a hand over my eyes, in case they had deceived me.

"What the hell?" Tank howled over my head, again at an impossible volume.

"General, what was that?" The tall, nameless man, now stationary a little way ahead of me, addressed his commander, but whether in concern, puzzlement or piss-taking, I couldn't tell. His tone was utterly flat, indecipherable. A wide, heavy sword wavered at his side.

"Easy now, love," Medi murmured. She continued to stroke that girl's shoulder, her face twisted into a mild squint as if the movement worried a bruise.

"That thing didn't touch me." General Elwin's voice was amplified by the rounded ceiling above her. She rode to sweep up her lost weapon. Her words were simple, but they said enough. The others all understood that which were tasked with dispatching. This creature had power beyond its freakish size. "Leo and I will keep it cornered. Have at it, you two."

She referred to the pair who had collected me up from the train. They moved silently in the affirmative, positioning themselves either side of their target. Both seemed unfazed by whatever repelling force the creature possessed. Or rather, they fought in spite of it, dancing around one another, swiping for it, constantly pushed back, but ultimately never landing anywhere but on their own feet. Meanwhile, the two on horseback, Elwin and Leo, rode around and around, at opposite ends of a perfect circle they had formed. Together, with the great arches above holding the railway tracks aloft, they created an arena, from which their enemy clearly saw little chance for escape. It was obvious to me, if the giant flapped its great wingspan fast enough, timed its charge well, it could have slipped through their formation with no trouble but, for the first time, it was panicked. Instead, it flitted back and forth almost aimlessly, grappling in the empty space for the nearest living being in sight.

The young woman, who had called herself Aria, wielded a spear as tall as she stood, in long, sweeping arcs around her body. The seamless flow of her movement, her weapon like a fluid, organic extension of her body, was impressive, hypnotic even, but nonetheless, it couldn't reach the creature's wings. It appeared as though each strand of a feather exerted the same obscure, opposing force in equal measure. Aria's partner flew in step with her, a long, silver knife in each hand. He tried throwing one once. I thought it the most idiotic possible decision, although, when it suddenly came looping back through the air at him, he raised his arm and caught it in his fingers. He could have been testing his opponent, perhaps, but surely, he presumed that this would happen, the poser.

Yet somehow, I briefly failed to notice when, amid the shade, he moved behind the creature and seemingly ceased to exist. He vanished without a trace; no-one stopped to search after him, not even me. It could have been that he was never there, if not for Aria struggling harder to keep up, effectively on her own. She could no longer afford to waste effort on attacking the target, but instead skipped backwards, as was necessary to evade its snatching talons. Her lance now existed purely to maintain the distance between herself and her foe, not to close it. Neither Leo nor the general thought to move in on their horse and rescue her. It seemed they saw their own role, being to sprint endlessly around in circuits, as far too instrumental to the plan. All the time, the huge soldier held his grasp my shoulder. I couldn't go anywhere. I was a meaningless observer, trapped on the outside of their tightly closed circle.

I felt a tiny ball of anticipation begin to shudder against the walls of my chest. In those days after my Soul surfaced, I noticed I became acutely aware of the tiniest sensations, right down to my nerves. I was watching, waiting to stop something permanently on the edge of breaking out.

This situation was hopeless. The creature would bear down upon this little human obstruction to no end, until she expended herself and could run no further. There was nothing to be done, if Aria wouldn't try harder to get away.

Such appeared true, at least, before the thing dropped abruptly to the floor, in a mass of bluish feathers. It tried to leap forth and snap at her with its beak, in an unusual change of tactics. But I noted a particular ungainliness in its actions, and that moment, of either inattention or fatigue, permitted Aria to swipe her blade in front of herself, making a clean, horizontal slice across its legs.

It stumbled, obviously unsure whether to plant its feet, or just let the rest of its body hit the ground. Still it held its gaze on Aria, assuming she presented the greatest immediate threat. It must not have imagined, nor even sensed that which rained down from up above. I only caught sight of it for a fraction of a second, the figure plummeting head-first onto the beast, and the two slithers of silver, one for each hand. I flinched, and while my eyelids flickered, it was finished. In a single false step, that giant had walked to its death. My hand moved to pad at the back of my neck, and I realised that my skin was hot, almost enough to burn. Now, through the gap severed between the creature's head and body, I thought my vacant stare happened to meet Emery's, as he glanced to check what damage he had done.

I couldn't be sure though, because as suddenly as he had fallen—though never hit the ground—he vanished again, back into the air. My more conscious instinct taught me to follow the man, properly this time, and in doing so I saw he was not actually able to fly, as my mind had first tried to convince me. He was propelled up with distinct, elastic buoyancy, before slowing to a halt, over and over, each time a few metres closer to the ground. No foreign powers were at work here, but real, far more inspiring skill. I knew exactly what he was.

Somewhere under the standard uniform of shirt and jacket, Emery had to be sporting some variety of harness. And attached to it, a cable hung down from one of the tall arches, right above where Aria had been conveniently leading his prey for him. Just as I attempted to examine the little hook lodged between two joists, it suddenly detached from the cable, the metal bouncing against the pavement with a reverberating ring. The cord itself snaked towards Emery like a drawn-out rubber band, hastily retreating back to its owner.

He finally landed on the pavestones with only a slight scuff of his shoes. Aria raced towards him, offering up a hand, which he took out of politeness; I was more or less certain he didn't need it. She licked her thumb, scrubbed something dark off her forehead, then her sleeve. Afterward they returned their attentions to the spot on the ground where a broken, feathery corpse should have lain. Only nothing was there, save for the last powdery flecks of dust, settling atop a dark heap. It could have been ash, from where I stood, more alike to the remains of a campfire than a monster of its great, grotesque stature.

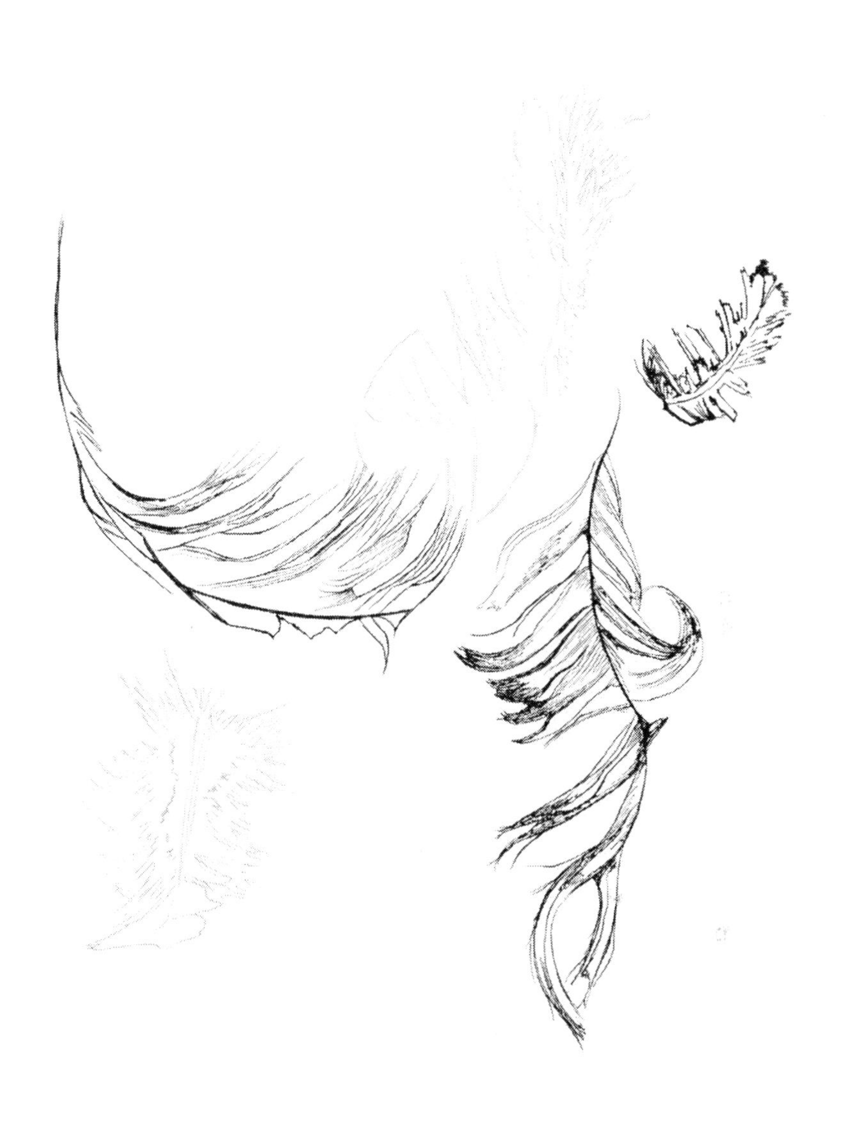

[Eris]

I never told anyone what I'd felt, nagging in my chest, just for a moment before the dread properly settled in. They would condemn me, I believed, if they knew I was sorry for the creature, as I watched it disintegrate into a heap of dust. The fear came after. It only took a few words. General, the grand lady who had come to see us in Flodside after the attack, now approached to look down on me from atop her mount. I could hardly recall what she had said to me before, but her voice had a stoic sound that plucked at my brain.

"Was that the beast you fought?"

"Fought" seemed a strange choice of verb. I didn't consider myself as having "fought" at all. That vile thing had paraded into my home, destroyed as it went, and moved on when it happened to make a wrong turn. For what it was worth, I was merely a vessel for a Soul, a product of forces beyond my control. That was not me. I was simply fortunate. I evaded death.

And here I had brushed shoulders with it again. A waking dream washed through my head, of yellow eyes glaring through the mess of light and smoke and infuriated screeching. Hesitantly, I glanced at the remains on the pavement. That one had yellow eyes too. If I said yes, then my enemy and that pile on the floor would become one and the same. Was that it? The strange entity I so feared had been reduced to that?

"No." Another voice, Kai's voice, echoed from behind my back, stole the word out of my throat. He snatched it from me, before I could decide whether or not to use it. I noticed him stride up towards General Elwin; he narrowed his eyes at me, as if to scold me for my negligence. He had to look down on me too, I stood so small.

General stared past the top of his head, still awaiting a response from the mute. "Would you agree? Are they not the same?" she said.

I hung my head and swayed it slowly from side to side. "No…No, that was different." I berated myself for the way I spoke, like a blubbering child, trying to make excuses for knowing no better.

We received nothing in reply for a while, besides her turning her back on us, as she lowered herself down off of her saddle. She wanted to examine the remains for herself. I could understand that—not trusting, the adamant need to *see*. Leading her horse behind her,

I saw her crouch to the pavement. She ran a finger through the soot, leaving a shallow valley in the heap, otherwise untouched, like black snow. Then she brushed and clapped her hands together, ridding herself of a dusty fingerprint.

Distant by a few feet, and more than that, Kai fidgeted in front of me, shifting his weight from one foot to the other, and every so often unfurling his arms from across his chest to cross them behind him, and vice versa.

"Lieutenant, Songbird, are you both fit to walk with these two?" General called, before acknowledging the pair of us. "We'll bring you both back, for now at least. To headquarters, I mean." She must have noticed the immediate drooping of my spine. "I'm sorry it isn't your home. But it is mine."

And I wouldn't be given any chance to protest, even if I could have gathered the will to try, as I was swiftly swept up by another careful pair of hands, leading me away to my fate. Needles grew up under my skin, surely piercing Aria's fingers. She seemed so calm, following her orders; her partner too, who loomed at Kai's heels. They soon let go of us, once we'd escaped the scrutiny of General Elwin. They both marched on, with tranquil faces that elegantly, but quite deliberately, avoided our eyes. Their figures could have been immortalised on a tapestry: two different faces of the grim reaper, more beautiful than a phantom cloaked in shade, but mercenaries of some higher power nonetheless. This was a hideously unfair comparison, however. After all, Lieutenant and Songbird did not bring me to this place; I'd taken the six o'clock train.

"It will be fine; no need to worry, honey," Aria said, intermittently. Even while we loitered on the front steps, apparently waiting for our belongings to be brought from the station, she paced back and forth, touching the top of my head as she passed. "It will be fine." In between her determined mantra, she sung in time with her otherwise silent footsteps. A simple tune, quite subtle, but her voice was the clear inspiration for her title, so effortless and gentle on the sprits it felt—like a lark's, I thought.

Emery sat hunched over, not so much to recover from his bout of flight, but instead to tighten a bandage, which covered his whole forearm underneath his sleeve. I hadn't noticed it before. I watched the young man, careful to avoid being too conspicuous, at least until he rose to his feet. This was in response to General Elwin, who appeared on the other side of the building's own square. He moved to follow Aria inside, but first paused between Kai and me.

"Songbird doesn't only say that for her own benefit," he said. "She won't let anything happen to you…and nor will I." He turned to acknowledge the woman at the foot of the steps, before retreating. There resided some additional meaning in the glance they briefly shared, which I could not profess to understand.

"Thank you, Lieutenant."

It wasn't my home, but it was hers. And yet, in spite of General Elwin's words, as I was led throughout that maze, I couldn't shake a nagging awareness of the place's emptiness. Some corridors echoed louder than others, but wherever I went, there seemed to be ghost rooms, closed up for lack of use, somewhere within my sight. Living quarters, offices, meeting rooms, training halls or storage cupboards? I couldn't tell what shells lay behind those impassive wooden doors. As far as could be discerned, by someone who never saw them, only the holding cells underground were still kept in their entirety.

I found myself weighed down by the urge to make a mad dash from door to door, opening each one, just to know. But we continually moved on, along to the next corridor, which would inevitably feel twice too long. Perhaps if it had been a stately mansion instead, the sheer extent of pointless space would have been merely superfluous—ostentatious. Instead, the proud military base was abandoned and sad, locked in hollow stone. Wandering its halls seemed akin to creeping around a church: cold, lonely, and haunted by a grander past now lost. It followed you, like an intruder entreating upon its final resting place.

Of all the rooms I entered, none assailed me in such a profound way as the dining hall. It was the tables. Their lengths stretched from wall to wall, so that one had to shuffle around the short ends to reach the other side. They looked old, well-used, once. Sixty men could fit along the benches of one, and this room housed three. Doubtless, the group of soldiers left behind would never appear so scarily tiny as when we scattered ourselves across those tables at mealtimes. We were as fleas, crawling on a dead dog's back.

They frightened me, I realised; those virtuous men of the past frightened the breath out of my lungs.

General didn't look around though, only ahead. Her stern, steady footsteps did not hesitate for us. She knew where she was, where she would go; the walls bent under her command. This belonged to her. To me, she was imposing, indeed, unreachable, but as I unravelled, her presence provided a curious amount of relief.

[Leo]

Tank sauntered into the office several minutes late. General met my eyes from behind her desk for a split second, as the door swung open before him. She watched him trundle to my side and drop to his knee in salute.

"At ease, Colonel," she said, resting her chin on the platform of her delicately crossed fingers. "You can likely guess why I summoned the both of you here."

"It'll either be the huge fuck-off bird, or the kids; I'm not convinced which is worse, to be fair."

"You're off to a flying start, Tank," I interrupted, through my teeth.

"Don't mind me. Carry on, General."

"It's both, in a sense," she continued, her eyes flitting between the two of us. "Kai Hughes and Eris Rayne are in my care now. Their Souls have only just surfaced. I want them both looked after carefully, especially now we know the…extent of the situation. Therefore, I am assigning each of them one of my trusted soldiers, to prepare them for what is to come. Like a retainer, if you will."

"Oh, no," he piped up again.

"Leo, you'll see to Hughes."

"Understood," I said, with a firm nod. This could be interesting, to say the least. I'd taken a glance at the kid earlier. They were all engineers of some ilk, the Hughes family; the mind was forged in the blood. So, to me, the calculating glare, under which everything had to be verified, immediately made sense. The biting attitude, though, would be something new.

Tank, on the other hand, practically whimpered. "You're givin' me the library girl, aren't you, ma'am?"

"That's right."

"And you're sure this ain't just a recipe for disaster, ma'am?"

She came awfully close to rolling her eyes. "I'd like to think it's not, Colonel. I've given them both rooms on the third floor, and they are currently waiting for you there. Oh, but before you go, I should let you know something." That prompted us to raise our heads. "I found the titles of their respective Souls, based on what has been described to me. Hughes has Initiative."

Tank and I gave a similar amused noise. “Back for another go, eh? I wondered how soon it’d be, before it cropped up,” mumbled his voice beside me.

“Miss Rayne is interesting, though. She’s got Fortitude, if you’ve already read of that one’s capabilities.”

“Only vaguely, I have to admit.” I looked to Tank as I spoke. He quirked his brow and shrugged.

“Yeah, I know the one,” he confirmed.

General hummed to herself, rising up out of her chair. “Fine. You two should get going, then,” she said, gesturing us out of the room. “Good luck.”

[Eris]

The dull thumps of my boots travelled far in the cool air. So too, I noticed, did the muted gasp I produced once I caught sight of the city's outline, sprawling past the rooftop's edge. Warm blood lurched up to my cheeks, and my throat dried out, despite there being no-one else around to embarrass me. I took a few extra steps to dislodge the feeling. The resulting view was magnetic; the paved streets, high spewing chimneys and glowing windows were smaller, but the labyrinth no less complex, the scene no less splendid. Stray strands of hair tickled at my face in the breeze. There was a hint of refreshing moisture to the air, and my eyes closed against it, as though as to absorb it through my skin. On a far ledge, a pair of crows shuffled from side to side, keeping their beaks pointed at the terrace below.

Naturally, the moment of peace was temporary. I started at the creak of a door handle, whirling my head around towards the movement across the roof. My fingers and toes crackled with an electric twinge—my Soul stirring.

The young man, Emery's head appeared in the blank space, followed by the rest of him. He had to duck a little to get through, his eyes already searching my face.

"Oh, sorry," I stuttered, "I didn't realise anyone else would be coming out here now, I don't know why, really… I'll move out of your way."

A mild, breathy laugh and outstretched hands halted me in my tracks. "Hey, calm down. This isn't my roof; you can stay up here if you want. I don't bite, I swear."

He seemed to glide when he walked, making his way beside me, but not uncomfortably close, his hands still resting in his trouser pockets. I decided that he reminded me of a deer.

He reached to adjust his ponytail, which had transmuted into a neat braid at the back of his head. "Oh, I didn't do that—Aria," he said, seeing that I had noticed. He hinted to the sky. "I like this place. Come up here most days now. The open air, the height, it helps me clear my head. And it's so much quieter…"

"Like I said, if I'm disturbing you, I can always—"

"Seriously, you're not bothering me. Great minds think alike, as they say around here. If anything, I feel bad for crashing in on you—thought you were going to take off, you jumped so quickly. I don't think I've *really* introduced myself: Emery Altair." He bowed at the waist, enough to reach my eye-level, and lingered there, expectantly.

"Eris—Eris Rayne." I mustered a half-smile for his courtesy.

"Good to meet you—properly, at least." Emery gave a nod, before turning back to the sprawling horizon, and I followed him there, silently.

Altair.

I recognised that name, as well as anyone. *"Prideful cowards"; "Arrogant bastards"; "A whole rotten brood of them"; "Murderers".*

This one particular rumour had grown so comprehensive over time, that even I had come to accept it. But until Emery Altair had appeared in the train's steam at Interieur, I had never seen, with my own eyes, the prize son and heir who had supposedly turned traitor. This was the one who betrayed his clan, and all for what little survived of Esprit's military. Their prescribed punishment for such an act was brutal and hideous, so the remains suggested. The idea was incomprehensible to me. It was not until I recalled his figure falling from the ceiling, coasting through the air just as if he belonged there (in the way only one of them could), that I truly believed it. And although I had tended to take the more tasteless remarks about this hypothetical man with a pinch of salt in the past, the image in my mind still was not remotely close to the reality I saw standing beside me.

The tales compared them to predatory birds, hawks disguised as men.

I remembered the way his vicious blades had descended—reduced that creature to dust. Perhaps the metaphor persisted, in a sense, still true of Emery. I, however, maintained that he was more akin to the woodland stag, unorthodox though the opinion might have been.

I contemplated if mine matched the typical train of thought he expected of people, considered the slight wince he'd made when he spat the name off his tongue. As if he fully believed I would have jumped off of that rooftop in fear of the sound of it. I felt a twinge of guilt begin to knot itself in my insides, because it seemed I was not afraid of him. I appreciated his sincerity. In fact, I was comparatively at ease. My two crows suddenly took off, disappearing below the wall. Emery's rigid hazel stare continued to track them, even though they were well beyond my sight. I thought of raising a different subject.

"You and Aria are based here in Interieur, then?"

"That's right. This is where I ran to, where General Elwin dragged me off of the cobbles. I know these streets better than my own face in a mirror. Aria's been here her whole life. She's got stories to tell, some of them passed all the way down from her grandparents. They migrated to Esprit shortly after they married. That was…before General—ah, sorry, I'm giving everything away. You should ask Aria, if you get the chance," he said, turning his head with a tinge of a smile. A better result than I had expected.

I nodded, tucking my hair behind my ears. "Alright then, maybe. So, what were you both doing in Flodside when you found us?"

"We were taking our leave actually," he chuckled. "The idea was to get out of the city for a little while, see some trees. That'll have to be scrapped, for now."

"Oh no, so just to top it all off, I took away your holiday too."

"Never mind that. It's just all the more reason to destroy them, the way I see it."

"Them…I see. You believe that there are more of these things."

"Maybe I do. I've seen animals with unruly Souls, but nothing like that." He grimaced. "What're you going to do? General spoke with you?"

"Yes, she saw to Kai first, and then me. She told me everything, the same as the first time: that I didn't have to fight; I could go home, and stay there, where I would be safe. It was my choice. She reminded me I could be here for some time. She doesn't have enough information to say for sure, barely even enough to report to Governance."

"She's right, of course. And have you decided?"

"I'm going to stay."

I could not explain it; I didn't have Kai Hughes' livid determination. I didn't feel like a soldier. But there lived a Soul imprisoned within me, and that had to mean something. The scythe looked beyond my reach, but I would do something. My hands could linger behind, hold the basket.

They would later be given a name: Soulless. That was a powerful notion, finally having a name for something; it made them so much easier to hate.

[Kai]

Following my first meeting with the soldier, Leo—who, it seemed, would be hovering around me on a permanent basis—I had specifically requested to be taken to the lake, which I knew to be some half a mile away from the military base. My plan was decided, and my mind couldn't be changed. Once I had explained my reasoning, and insisted several times over, he eventually conceded, directed me through the streets, and promptly discarded me at the lakeside, telling me to be finished in a couple of hours.

Now I stood alone, surveying the expanse before me. Although I could not see it from my low vantage point, I knew the botanical garden had to be close, hidden somewhere behind the hissing belt of leaves. There was only one green spot growing out of this stone crater. Of course, the presence of nature failed to comfort me much in this case. On the contrary, a sudden, unreasonably violent splashing amongst the mass of reeds to my left—which slid a chain of silvery bands across the lake's surface—seemed to mock me.

Abandoning my shoes in the long grass, socks stuffed inside, I took a first step out into the water. It was not as icy cold as I somehow remembered it being. I made my way deeper, until it lapped around my chin, almost the bottom of my ears, decided that may be too far, and took a few paces backward.

I refused to venture further, isolated enough now that any stray flames should be contained within the banks, extinguished well before they could become a threat to anything other than a particularly brave fish.

So, what now?

I had prepared only about this far. I knew that Leo would be returning for me in a matter of hours, which I hoped would be enough time to at least start to figure this out. But how did one even begin practising producing fire with a hardly sentient power source that I couldn't just bloody-well force into doing what I wanted?

That was, unless I could. I embodied only another machine, of an odd sort, missing the right mechanism to make it work—a connection. Needless to say, I had no idea what component fit.

I tried focusing my thoughts. My Soul, wherever the thing actually resided inside me, was wired to my nervous system, thus, my brain. Hence, I figured that this solution would be the simplest. I conjured up words, concentrated on repeating them over and over, until they all fell apart and ceased to sound real: Soul, fire, help, fear, useless. No reaction.

Instead, with my eyes closed, I tried building an image upon the dark void at the back of them. I pictured flames licking anxiously around my legs, through the gaps between my fingers, gulping at the air I breathed, listened for the low, admonishing hiss, imagined that scent of charred cotton and the rush of heat pricking at my skin. Alas.

I opened my eyes, took a breath—in and out—and tried again. The water didn't even change temperature slightly. It took at least ten attempts before I accepted that this idea carried me nowhere. Or maybe it was closer to twenty? It hardly mattered now. Next.

I needed something more tangible. What about a physical action instead, a coaxing movement to lure the Soul out? No, all flailing my arms ultimately awarded me was an appearance even more asinine, to anyone who hypothetically saw me standing, by myself, in the middle of a lake at that time of day.

Straightening out again, my gaze fell on the agitated surface of the water. It seemed to wink at me. In that fleeting moment of frustrated resolution, my legs curled up to my stomach and I plunged my head below the rippling surface. As my ears flooded and my vision blurred into an indefinite mess, an invisible force pressed down on my neck and whatever oxygen I fought to hold in my lungs felt far too heavy. If only I could have grasped that water in my fists, held it and burned it to death. It certainly was not inclined to hesitate before it drowned me.

My arms started waving in little windmills, though whether these sought to go back up or stay down I could not determine. Instead I was trapped there. My chest suddenly constricting in urgency, I felt a desperate gasp mounting, rising. I noticed the heat first. It began at my fingertips, fluttering in the murk, and reached around me in a familiar embrace. The light came after; an orange deluge in amongst the grey—the colour seemed to creep like ink bleeding through paper.

In a single, clumsy movement, I pulled myself up through the broken surface, kneading the excess moisture from my eyes just in time to see the last remnants of steam fade.

I shouted, mostly out of relief. Though broken up by my hoarse panting, it cut triumphantly through the chill in the air. Giving myself respite with which to recover from the aching in my sides, I threaded my fingers through my hair and over my head, brushing away the clumps sticking to my face.

The water had barely cooled around me when I decided to try again. Though far from ideal, these conditions presented potentially my only option and were, invariably, better than nothing. I clamped my mouth shut and submerged myself before I had time to waver. I must have been a little more graceful about it this time, too, since the crashing sound above me reduced to a spatter. Perhaps I imagined it. I tried not to struggle, so much at least, and to concentrate on the Soul. The flames needed to materialise again. That way I could be sure.

A stream of bubbles rose from my nostrils as I thrust my arms forward, both hands reaching out in either a weighty command, or a desperate request. Whichever being true, there was an answer; the amber flare flowed weaker than before, and it did not stretch as far through the hazy water. Nevertheless, it existed for a short time, before it died. It seemed to burst out from my palms, as though I had thrown it. I raised my head, and my toes thumped against the mud. Not bothering to rearrange my hair, I allowed my cheeks to quirk upward into a smile. I'd found it.

I had slipped—grown slightly too eager to be under the lake for own liking—by now. My mind buzzed instead of thinking, and I presumed that to be the reason for which I failed all successive attempts.

As I surfaced for the final time, the bell tower's bass ring called over the high roofs of the city. It struck half-past eight, which handily explained why the sky overhead had mutated into such a deep purple shade. It also alluded to Leo's return—my stint was up for today. As expected, he latched himself to time, punctual to the minute. Once the chime's echo had faded, another low, piercing voice replaced it.

"Hughes! That's enough for today; get back over here." He made a few strides closer to the bank and stopped to peer down into the undergrowth. "And pick up your shoes!"

Only once I began wading laboriously out of the shallows did I notice the chill of autumn slinking into the air. My nose fizzed, and my clothes stuck uncomfortably to my skin. The dirt and grass glued to the dampness of my toes with each step. I would have to carry my shoes.

Although that observation gave me pause. I put them back down on the ground, causing Leo to stop in his tracks and direct a questioning squint.

"What?" he said.

"Go ahead, I'll be a moment. I want to try something."

He didn't, instead opting to cross his hands behind his back coolly, side-eyeing me over his broad shoulder, a silent instruction to get on with it, then. I turned away in some effort to ignore his presence. Returning to dry, solid land felt, on one hand, like a boon, and yet necessity called for the watery ordeal. Aware of the trench of squandered time already carving itself out between us, and ever more so of Leo's acute stare, I could not spend long faltering. I repeated, in the most embodied sense I thought possible, the moment before I sank below the surface, raising my chin, arms hovering out from my sides, and took in a long, deep breath through my mouth (gaping it a little less wide this time, only so it looked somewhat less ridiculous). This could work; I knew it. I had seen it work. And the flames were not particularly necessary anymore, just some heat. I preferred not to set off any explosions. I could almost feel it, pressure welling up, scratching at my skin; it shivered. But nothing blossomed out from my palms.

I cracked one eye open, then the other. I was about to let go, begrudgingly accepting this attempt would be just that, when my sight started to fog over with heavy, stifling moisture. I tilted my head down. Pale mist seeped from my clothes, my bare feet and even, from the feeling of it, my hair, the way it gradually became lighter and brushed against my forehead.

"Huh." Leo's terse voice cut over the whispering sound. I whirled around, my eyes narrowed, to look at the veteran's face: steady, unchanging. "That was quick. You're sharp, kid; must be a Hughes thing. Now put your shoes on. Let's go." As he moved off, with me hopping on one foot some way behind him, he paused. "And you should realise, Hughes," he said, "that I wasn't trying to stop you coming this way. It seemed a perfectly logical decision to me. You only needed to mention you hadn't a clue where you were going."

[Eris]

"Here, put this on. Tie it round your eyes; don't panic, it doesn't smell or nothin'," Tank said, pushing a wool scarf into my hands. "And don't gawp at me with that face. I'm pretty sure I know what I'm doin' here, better than you, anyway."

I had to restrain a shake of the head as the scarf covered my face and the world grew immediately claustrophobic. Illogically, maybe, I found being shut in a dark room somehow more rattling than simply closing one's eyes. That blindness felt different, forced. It was just the same here.

"Nice job on my part," he added, as I tied a knot at the back of my head. "Look at that. Green's your colour."

"If you say so."

My words seemed to soar over his head. "Hey, it'll keep your ears warm in this bitter wind, think about it like that. Right, this is the idea. You strike me as not trustin' your Soul that much."

"How could you tell?"

"Listen, I watched you with Medi under the arches, looking at the psychic-bird go nuts. So, I want you to see somethin'. I'll wander off this way and take a run up. Then I'll make a swing, try my best not to clout you. Got it?" He didn't wait for an answer. "Alright, here I come." I heard the clamour of heavy, armoured feet getting closer, and closer, within metres.

I had almost forgotten what it felt like. The bizarre pulse jumped through my veins, like they were flooded with angry water that reached through every cell in my body, dispersed to each tiny capillary and lingered there for a second. At the same time, a vicious crack split the intangible air some distance from me, loud enough that I almost didn't hear the shout above it. It sounded painful. And yet I felt nothing of the sort but a vague throbbing in my temple.

My fingers crept up to the scarf, and slowly lifted it to my forehead, raising the veil on a scene I should've already known to expect. Latent arcs of static still flickered from Tank's right hand and forearm, although the way he was violently shaking it made it difficult to see. Once he noticed me removing the blindfold from my face, he barked from his position, but did not move just yet.

"Hell! You threw that up quick!"

I let my rigid shoulders drop a little. Of course I did.

"I'm so sorry. I'm afraid that I am beyond a little bit jumpy." I tilted my gaze vaguely towards his arm, which now rested sluggishly in the opposite hand.

"You're tellin' me! You've got good instincts for someone most of the way asleep, and that there's a Soul-and-a-half to boot. We can work with this." He nodded, mostly to himself, evidently satisfied with his experiment. "Take a bloody breath girl, for goodness sake!"

I did as I was told, albeit with effort, and tried loosening my stance to make it more convincing. Although Tank's pounding voice most likely could have knocked the air back into me on its own, a strangely reassuring thought. I hoped it was with some visible resolution that I turned the rough fabric over in my fingers, folding it into a neat square, before extending it towards Tank, in an invitation, or perhaps a request.

"Where should I start?"

His face turned up in a smile momentarily as he took the square into his hand, which measured twice the size of my own. "In an ideal world, we'd start right at the very basics: work on your physical strength, stamina, speed, anythin' an' everythin' we could, see, but…"

"There's no time for that."

"Exactly, we don't know when another one of those things'll show up, so for now I'm trustin' you to work on that stuff on your own, as you see fit. Although, and uh, don't get offended, but there's probably not a whole lot of point. Luckily for us, you've got a hell of a Soul in there," he said, uncrossing his arms to point at my head. "So, our top priority is to get you knowin' how to use it. And on that note, let's get a few things clear. General assigned you to me for a reason. We are human shields, you and I. Built for a head-on defensive fight; no sneaky skippin' around here." He raised his chin firmly and puffed out his chest, as if he needed to appear any more imposing.

I may have opened my mouth to interject but—

"However! My job is to protect these people: be their extra armour, if you will, and their batterin' ram half the time, but that's not important. There more than one way to succeed 'gainst your enemies. Your job, before anythin' else, is to keep yourself safe. You and Hughes, you focus on takin' care of that, and each other if you must. Our endgame is to beat the ever-loving crap out of that Soulless, but if you've got to run first, you run. Ain't no shame in it. If you're still standin', that'll do for now."

"Ah, right."

"Honestly, from what I've seen, and felt, your Soul's already pretty capable of that. I'm already gettin' ideas for tricks you can pull off with this. Counterattack's your main mission, I reckon. Oh heck, they'll hate you," he added, taking another glance at his right wrist.

"Hm, odd, I kind of like the sound of that."

He smiled again, but this one quickly faded into something far more severe. He ducked his head to meet my eyes. "One more thing, Sparks. And you could well know this already, but I'm about to say it anyway. You're one of a random few folks to get one of these Souls. Blessin' or curse, whatever you want to call it, yours is bound to do everythin' in its power to protect you. Any threat you sense, even if you can't see it, your Soul is *there*. 'Cause from now on, you and it are linked like that." He crossed his fingers in front of his face, as he continued. "You could say it's a part of you. No-one can just keep on fightin' forever, and neither can it. You conk out, so does your Soul. I guess what I'm gettin' at is…" He looked down, as if searching for a way to finish his lecture. He found one. "…Be careful."

I nodded hastily, and kept my head down, feeling suddenly guilty. My hand reached up to tease a knot out of my hair. Tank had neglected to mention the mess of strands floating out in odd directions like a dandelion tuft. I tried to pat them down, to little avail. Wonderful.

[Kai]

It had been days, at least, since I first climbed those stone steps. Faces I had assumed would remain familiar seemed to be replaced by new ones. Emery and Aria did manage to push their way into my room once, carrying a desk between the two of them. They said General Elwin had sent them with it. I could put it wherever I needed.

In fact, Emery knocked at my door every other evening, for a while, to check how I had made use of their donation. Aria, however, seemed to disappear. Her presence, before me at least, was usually limited to mealtimes. She looked as bright in the face as ever, while she skipped away on her toes, but hardly spoke. The person who had met my arrival with such fervour perhaps caught on to my general disposition the earliest, ultimately deciding to leave me be entirely.

The desk had been sitting forgotten in a room somewhere. A layer of dust and grit coated almost every surface, which took two scrubs with a damp cloth to remove. It left me with something else to do, I figured. I kept the thing empty for a couple of days, my belongings stacked on top. But no word on the Soulless came to justify delaying the inevitable. Eventually, I had to resign myself to my fate, and went about filling the drawers with the contents of my second suitcase: as many tools as I could fit in it, plus a few small projects to waste away the time. I hoped that a broken watch, a wind-up music box and a small motor would be sufficient to keep me sane. From time to time, Emery, having noticed the change, tried directing me towards old storage rooms that I might ransack for bits and pieces to "borrow". The man desperately wanted my trust. He once tried to tell me who he was or, rather, he wondered if I'd already figured it out. I reminded him that he had made it blatantly obvious.

The soles of my feet ached constantly, an angry sting creeping up through my toes with each step. I waited for the unfortunate moment that my knees would give way underneath me.

[Eris]

Prior to my brief escapades with them, I knew very little of the watchmen. I couldn't claim to know much even afterwards. They were a group of at least five strong—presumably more, though I would never find out—who were stationed at neat intervals along the circulatory Interieur Wall. Their collective task was to detect and send early warning of threats attempting to enter the city, which from now on would include the Soulless. They were the silent, invisible eyes, watching over our fortress from their little high towers.

On one occasion, as an alternative to my usual daily exercise (although, in hindsight, probably more so that he could use the precious time at his leisure), Tank sent me off to merge among their ranks. The idea disconcerted me considerably, given that I hadn't so much as caught a glimpse of these mysterious sentries before; I could not be sure even as to their titles. What was I to say to them? However, Tank assured me that this would not be an issue—they would be perfectly willing to have me. And so, I went, out of a combination of both compliance and plain curiosity.

Admittedly, none of them objected to my presence exactly, although, to my distress, I found myself being passed around the group in the manner of a carrier pigeon. I therefore felt more like an inconvenience upon their territory, than any sort of help. And while my long-winded strolls along the Wall, alone in the mild breeze, with the most marvellous view over the piled slopes and steps and narrow valleys of the streets below, did indeed make my journeys between towers very pleasurable, in actuality they achieved very little.

Of course, I did not blame them for this. These were individuals who each were experienced, to an expert degree, at spending days with only themselves for company, and were not fettered by that fact at all. The most dealings they possibly had would have been with each other. One must have a particular frame of mind for such a task, as I understood, and I did nothing but disturb it.

Keys was the youngest of the five from what I could discern. She was quite the severe-looking woman, and proud of the fact too, guessing from the state of her fair hair, firmly scraped back to show off her more aggressive features. Though, at one point, she still could not resist tugging out a blond strand to absently twirl between her fingers. Her ability to maintain a constant atmosphere of threat about her was particularly impressive. Watching her, I wondered why we didn't simply set Keys upon the Soulless and call it good.

Gate looked nearly as youthful as her, and much softer, courtesy of the bright gleam in his warm, round eyes and curling hair. He sprawled back, swinging around lazily on the legs of his chair. This room I judged the most agreeable to pass the time in. He ignored me like an unassuming insect on the windowsill, and he possessed a rather charming singing voice, worthy of its lofty height. I lamented that such a restful man should forever hence be doomed to comparison with Aria, the lovely, remote songbird. Perhaps he hid himself away in his lonely room for that very reason. Here, his music would not be heard, could never be made to fade under the girl's angelic fanfares. It was a merry purgatory.

There was something unsettling about Ward. He sported a pair of expensive spectacles, which framed an icy, shrewd stare that could presumably see straight through mere mortals such as myself. That stare flitted meticulously over the horizon, entirely disconnected from his hands, which furiously juggled a peculiar cube-like contraption: a puzzle of some description, which he appeared to be solving without even glancing at the thing. And, though this was fascinating to watch for the short time it lasted (I could understand how my childishly avid interest became annoying very quickly), I grew increasingly tainted by thoughts of bitter jealousy towards the haughty man.

Motte must have been middle-aged, but looked older, and he knew perfectly well what he was doing, until I showed up. He stood as the perfect embodiment of my fears before coming here. The poor man shuffled and fidgeted, feeling obliged to house me, to find me something to busy myself with, when in plain reality there was nothing. Heavy with empathy, I volunteered to leave him to his work, as it presented no trouble to me. He accepted my invitation hastily, but with a tinge of something like guilt. And as soon as I excused myself, the shift in Motte's demeanour seemed nothing short of instantaneous. I chanced a hopeful look over my shoulder after I passed the threshold, and there he was, posed perfectly, one foot resting on his other knee, leaning on the back of his hand like a marble statue.

River was the kindliest face among them, despite sharing the same characteristic beady eyes as the others. Rosy-cheeked, she gazed out wistfully from under a bundled scarf that seemed somewhat excessive for the weather. Her voice quavered, low and tentative, as if she were perpetually close to giving some bad news. To her credit, she made several attempts at light conversation during my stay but, through my own fault, these petered out without success. Several times I longed for a book in my hand to accompany me. I soon batted the thought away, however, out of shame, when I remembered that these workers were granted no such luxuries.

Still, I managed to make myself unbearable to this unfortunate character as well. Kind River smoothly recommended I didn't return for another try, as the job of watchman was evidently "not my calling". I imagined this occurred to her fairly soon after I went to sound the emergency alarm, at the decidedly petrifying sight of an oncoming pigeon. I apologised profusely, but the damage had been done. Not my calling indeed.

As I wandered back, useless and reconciled, wasting as much time on walking as I could, I found myself running my fingers along the Wall. I could peer almost straight down into the circular pit below. Thoughts slithered into mind such as, say, what might occur if I were to conveniently trip, or just happen to leap from that edge. They horrified me. I almost physically felt the sensation of shoving the notion out of my thick, bleeding skull while I continued to step onward with tremors in my legs, bits of brain splattered all over the pavement.

[Emery]

I sought out Aria on the rooftop. Tank had made the questionable decision to send Eris out on an errand on the Wall, and Kai had once again carted Leo down to the lake. Neither of the two apprentices were here so, from what I had observed, there was a good chance Aria would be.

As I thought, I found her sat on the stone floor, arms resting on the ledge, looking over it with a distant glaze over her eyes.

“Ah, Emery. Is everything alright?” she said, not budging.

I walked over slowly, taking time to compose what I had to say, and crouched next to her. I did not touch her yet. Evidently, she sensed something strange in my demeanour, since she suddenly turned and stared into my face with weary eyes.

“What is it?” she whispered, as if she already knew.

“I’ve noticed how you’re treating the newcomers, ever since they arrived here.”

“Kai and Eris, you mean. Now, I do not think I have been speaking with them any differently, have I?”

“No, when you’re made to speak with them at all. You have been looking past them, though. I’ve seen you, leaving rooms when they come in—you do so very politely, I’ll give you that. But you still do it. You won’t dare come up here unless they’re both gone, and you haven’t once checked up on either of them from what I’ve seen. I would guess that you aren’t even sure how they’re doing at all. You’re blanking them, Aria.”

“Or, maybe, I simply have not had the chance, what with Tank and Leo minding them constantly, plus the library, and that enormous desk we lugged up the stairs. One hardly crosses paths with either, so how could you know that I have been ignoring them, as you say?”

“Do you remember the boy you used to tell fairy tales to, by heart, in the early hours of almost every morning? You would drag him by the underarms into your bedroom on the bad nights, while you swapped for the armchair—against your mother’s will, I might add. And he knows full well that you couldn’t have cared less about having to carry that table. I know when you’re being deliberately obtuse.”

She sighed and dropped her hands into her lap, with a frustrated thump. “I don’t want to be unkind, I just…It is just that, up to now, I have worked, so much, to reach the point that I could fight under mama. You know that better than anyone. Eventually, I always thought I would match her, and that everything would be worth it. I could be truly proud of my service.”

“I wouldn’t measure a child based on where they stand in their parent’s shadow.”

“I know you don’t, Emery.” She offered a transient smile.

“You’re going to be the finest soldier I’ve ever known. I mean, you’re already—” I halted there, because her face fell again as I spoke.

“It still feels so pointless sometimes, you know, fighting so hard, in the light of these crazy powerful kids, who have their abilities served up to them on a platter, without even trying.”

“Exactly, they didn’t try at all. They never asked for this. I’m sure that, right now, they’d rather be at home, safe, with their families, never having possessed a Soul at all. And still they chose to stay and fight for us; that’s not a selfish thing to do. We owe them all the help we can offer, but you want me to be honest? I can’t do much. They need you around, Aria. We need your heart. You’re hiding from them, avoiding them, sure—but you can’t bring yourself to condemn them really, can you?” I thumbed away the tears threatening to crawl down her cheeks. “That’s not you. You help people. Don’t betray yourself like this, for an idea that’s not even true.”

She nodded frantically, taking one of my hands in both of hers. “Yes…Yes, I know. I shall start afresh right away.” She paused. “How are you always right? What is your secret?”

“I’m not.”

She giggled, and slung an arm around my neck, pulling me tight to her.

“We look after each other; it’s what I do,” I added.

“Always, yes?” She glanced away to think. “Have I told you that you are wonderful, Emery?”

I smiled at the familiarity of those words, in her slightly nervous tone. “On quite a few occasions, yes.”

"I do wonder sometimes…Oh!" Aria jumped back, noticing the time on her wrist. "I'm on watch in a bit. I should go and put Medi out of her misery. Would you let me know if the young ones are back when I finish, please?"

She bustled past me and through the iron door before I could reply in the affirmative. I assumed she never truly needed me to.

"*Take care of my daughter: protect her; question her; hear what she has to say. She will do the same—I do not get to dictate that. You are to serve her, but you are not her servant. You will be loyal to her alone, do you understand? You will keep her safe, always.*" Such were the orders under which I was saved. I think Aria knew from the beginning. She had not been present, so she never heard it, and yet she knew somehow. She made it obvious, to me, that for her there existed no want of a right-hand, a criminal under her command like I had thought: cold, detached and employed. She wanted her friend, the strange, ragged boy who appeared in the street one day, and who liked to hear her songs. She alone commanded my fidelity. And through my service to her I came to realise the tasks assigned to me by the two women were not so irreconcilable. Subordinate, companion, I could be both and neither. Simply, every scrap left of me was hers.

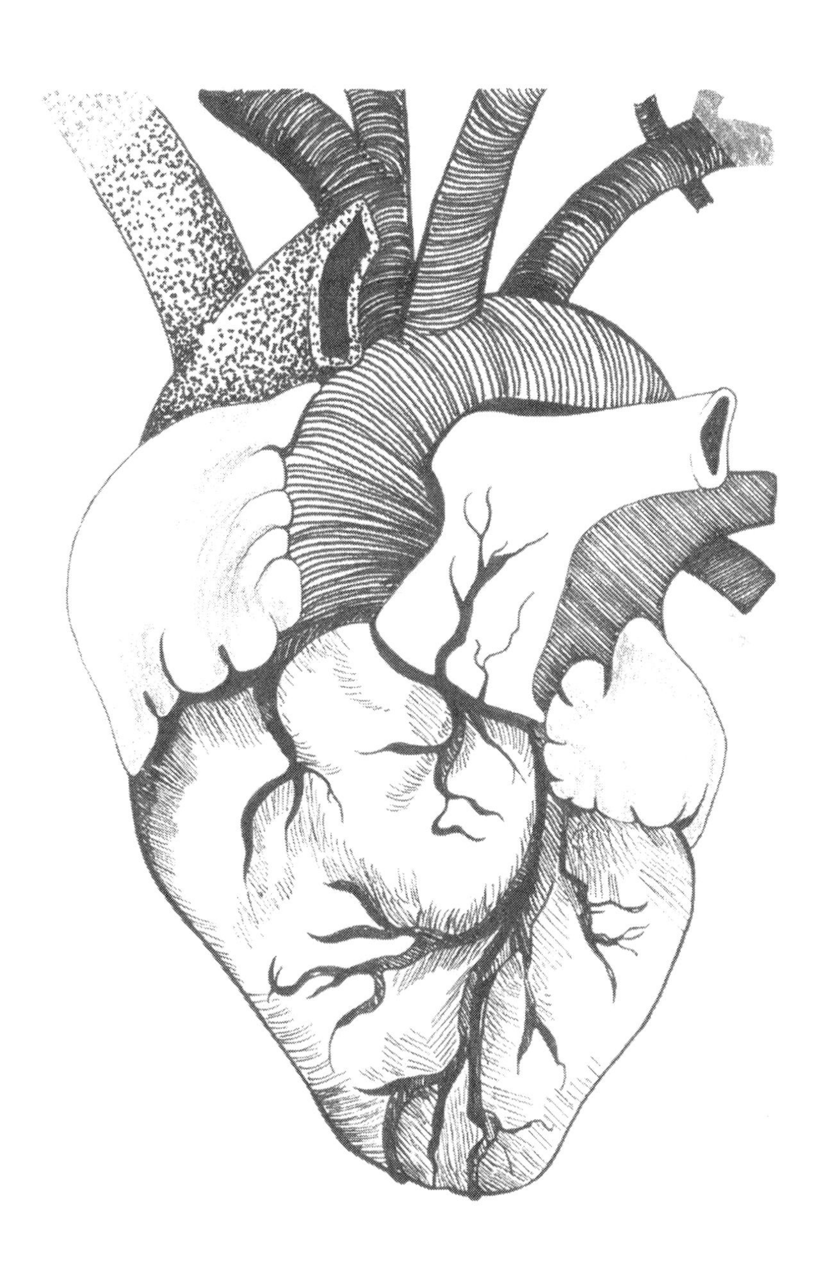

[Eris]

In the wake of the day's unmitigated disaster, I'd retreated to the rooftop with a drink that had still been slightly too hot and burned on my tongue. At this juncture, I could not remember what I had expected. The day simply insisted on being this way. Besides, coffee at this time of the evening was never a healthy idea, but the mug sat empty on the floor beside me anyway.

Looking out over the great Wall glowing, as it seemed to in the dusk sunset, it moved me, in a strange, sideways direction, to imagine that I had been over there. I located each of the turrets I had reached to, trying to visualise the lives that still rolled on by inside them. They looked like little rooms in a dollhouse from this distance.

Too sleepy to jump at the abrupt noise, I simply listened to the door whine as it opened, immediately smothered under a chirpy voice.

"Aha, here you are, Eris! I have been searching for you. Oh, goodness, is something wrong?"

"Not at all. Why?" I replied, already unable to keep up with Aria's unearthly supply of energy. I had simply assumed she was already exhausted of me, given the distance she had, rather tactfully, maintained until now. It would hardly surprise me.

"You look very thoughtful, that's all."

"Oh, that's just my face; it does that. I'm probably dozing off too. I've been out on the Wall all day. Tank fancied a break from me, I guess."

She sniggered, pushing the last stub of a liquorice pencil into her cheek. "You're fine, I'm sure. Tank just has his own unique way of doing things. I wouldn't try too hard to understand how it works. Can I sit?"

"Sure, this isn't my roof," I said. Aria smiled still, though she let out a loud sigh through it. "Emery told me you might be up here. He's rather a lot better than me at keeping an eye on things, so much better at watching over people than he thinks." Her eyes squeezed with an unthinking fondness as she mumbled, suddenly steady and musing.

"You two are very sweet," I said, desperately hoping I had not grossly misjudged the both of them.

"As a dutiful soldier, devoted entirely to the cause, I have no idea what you are talking about." She stifled another laugh. "Do you have anyone back home, Eris?"

"You mean at the library? Maud?" I tried to deflect the question I thought I detected.

"No, you know what I mean." She winked, leaning slightly in my direction.

My whole body deflated with a sigh. "Ah, I see. I don't, no. Sorry."

"Oh." A concerned tone trickled into her voice. After a few seconds of thought, she asked, "Do you wish to?"

"One day, maybe, of course. It's just that I…" A hesitant noise rumbled in my throat. It almost stopped me short. But Aria's questioning look made me feel as though she found me transparent anyway. "I simply fear I'll never have the chance, at this rate."

"Whatever do you mean by that?"

"How do I explain it? I think I want a relationship. I've spent a lot of time thinking about it actually, what that person would be like. But I have never felt that…physical draw to anyone. And, come to think of it, if I go back to daydreaming, nothing of the sort ever comes up."

'So, what about…' Aria leaned closer, the inquiring word shaped almost silently on her lips, '…sex?'

I shrugged, amused. 'Not for me, I suppose. The fabled loin-burning still eludes me.'

'I see.' Her eyes wandered down to her feet, which fidgeted. She tried to laugh at my flippant sarcasm. I could sense more came to her mind, which she pondered, but could not speak of.

"From what I can piece together, when you meet someone, you are meant to feel something, in your head, your bones, I cannot say for sure, but it's instinctive. You *know*. Me, I have never found that, not with anyone. Or maybe I did and now I can't remember. Honestly, though, that's okay. You needn't look at me quite like that. I don't feel lonely at all, just like I'm missing a trick here. That part of my brain is switched off, like a light bulb without the wire. I'm sorry, that doesn't make much sense, does it?"

"I would not be so sure, sweetie. I think I understand you fine; you are very eloquent. If I could make one suggestion, that desire you describe is not always quite so…instant, necessarily, at least not in my experience."

I realised, then, that she had been attempting to lean gently into another conversation, about herself, for which I had now broadcast myself as largely unhelpful.

"I was exaggerating a little there, wasn't I?" I gave a chuckle, dry, more than reassuring. "Perhaps it's for the best. I mean, look at me. I'm so difficult that I can't even shake someone's hand properly, let alone—"

"Up," Aria suddenly piped up, one finger pointing at my nose, "I won't hear any of that! What does it matter? Maybe you will feel different about all that one day," she continued, waving her hands dramatically in front of her face, "or maybe you won't! You know yourself, and you must be given the upmost respect for that. Send anyone who says otherwise in my direction. So long as you wish for it, there will be someone who adores you just as you are. You make yourself sound like a broken bulb, when you are simply a different shape. Get it?"

"Hm, I get it." I hoped my smile was convincing enough.

"And they will treat your metaphors much better than I can."

"But, still, I don't see how—"

"I, for one, think you are quite lovely." Her hand fell lightly on my shoulder. "And since we know I am always right about these sorts of things, no more fretting, alright?"

"Alright. I am sorry for all of that. Yes or no probably would have sufficed, right?"

"Ah, but far less interesting, do you not think so? I like this." She gestured to a black ribbon around my neck. "Your tie."

"This? I hardly realised I had it on. Force of habit, it seems."

"At least one of us is allowed to have some fashion sense."

"Oh, I can't make any claims to *fashion*. Or sense."

She hopped up from her perch, hand outstretched. "Here," she said, "I am going to grab something sweet to eat, if you want to join me. You don't even have to stop for long, I promise."

I wondered how this young woman still owned all of her teeth (I asked Emery later, to which he laughed, and said yes, she definitely did), what with the amount of sugar she seemed to consume in a day.

“Actually, now that you mention it, I’ve been drinking too much coffee on an empty stomach,” I said, glancing down to my shuddering fingertips. “Yes, oh dear. Thank you.”

[General]
Giving Eris the library was one of my best decisions. I felt that within myself, anyway.

She kept to her assigned schedule without fail: two hours in there each evening after the army grouped for supper. Somehow, her retainer seemed to do well by her presence, too. I heard that Tank appreciated the opportunity for a nap. This, naturally, meant ignoring that sleeping was the precise opposite of what he had been tasked with. I might have hoped for different, though I could hardly claim I expected it.

On one occasion, my curiosity got the better of me, and I took a detour to check on the pair of them.

"How is progress, Miss Rayne?" I asked, swinging open the heavy, antique doors.

I found Tank, lounging on a precarious-looking desk chair, arms folded over his chest. The man yawned as Eris added a couple of tomes—or crumbling pieces of—to a tidy mound she looked to be accumulating on a table. A distinct, musty smell of age clogged the air. Since the velvety purple curtains had been flung to the side of the window, I could see endless tiny flecks floating in the air, shifting direction with the slightest movement, searching for new ground upon which to settle.

As soon as she heard my voice, Eris leaped away from the pile of books as if someone had ordered her not to touch them.

"Bored are we, General?" Tank jibed.

"Watch yourself, Colonel. Go ahead young lady."

"Ah, yes, of course," she stumbled. "I've finished sifting through the cases on this side; I thought I would work through the oldest volumes first. They aren't in good shape, although I could revive a lot of them, for now, at least."

"And the pile you have there?"

"These ones will take some more work, should you wish to keep them, I'm afraid. They can definitely be repaired, but not here, with what little tools I have to hand."

Tank started drumming his knuckles on the table.

"So, you could do it?" I said.

"Could I restore these?"

"Yes."

"Well, of course, I'd be quite happy to." A trace of fulfilment passed briefly over her expression. "But there is all manner of bits and pieces I would need. If I were home, even if I could just get at the things there, then I certainly could. But, as I say, there is not much I can do right now. Still, I thought I might separate them, perhaps for future reference for you, ma'am." Her eyes darted left and right constantly, seeming to look everywhere but directly into my face, though not for want of trying.

"I see. Well then, I should leave you to the remainder of your work. Thank you, Miss Rayne."

I stepped back through the door, to an offended "um" from Tank.

"Colonel," I added, tipping my head ever so slightly in his direction.

[Eris]

"Ah," I heard.

General Elwin suddenly reappeared in the doorway, and surveyed me up and down, with an unusual look on her face. Unaccustomed to such an inspection, I could not decide how to react suitably, even if I dared.

Her attention lingered around my face for a few seconds, before she said: "You have an old soul."

If I had been blind, and only able to hear her voice, I would have guessed she had smiled, although I must have simply appeared confused to her.

"Apologies," she added. "It's an old phrase, well before my time even, hardly makes sense in this day and age. You simply brought it to mind."

"It's quite alright ma'am; it is only rather archaic, so it caught me unawares."

She once again dipped her head slightly, and Tank and I watched her disappear down the corridor.

It was bizarre; I struggled to relate the two events in any significant way. But something about that brief conversation launched me back, years and years, back to when I was still a girl. I recall being in a melancholy, not particularly unusual state, chewing my lip and prodding my face to save the embarrassment of dewy eyes. We happened to be leaving a quaint town in the Western District, and would not be returning for some time, if at all. I hadn't a clue where we were going next.

"You'll have your library one day, love," a woman said. She was my mother. That promise captured the clearest memory I still had of her real voice. Remembering seemed much harder than it used to be. I wondered, when the realisation arose, why it did not cause me more discomfort.

[Tank]

It wasn't often that Sparks would drop—or rather, gently set aside—whatever work had seized her, just to let herself get distracted for a bit. It was hard going enough, to get her to stop and move one of her chess pieces. Supposedly, she didn't realise that she only acted to make my inevitable defeat a very slow one. Haven't played before, my arse.

She coped perfectly fine with procrastinating, though, once she got to some loose papers, lying among piles upon piles on an upper shelf. They were arranged into folders at one point, presumably; who knows where they went. She grumbled in her usual disapproval, while she made an effort to flip through, and begin organising them into her sort of order. That was, until she stopped, and actually started reading a tattered-looking, handwritten page.

"What you got there?" I asked.

"It looks to me," she said, without looking up, "like an original copy of some of Morrigan Larsen's research notes."

"Larsen? Haven't you dug through loads of her stuff already?"

"Oh, yes, all of her published works, even piles of drafts and notes written in her hand. Right there, between Kristian and Lawrence." She pointed. "But all of them are from post-War. After that, the law was finally implemented to stop those with Souls being automatically forced into the armed forces, around the same time as the Esprit went through its demilitarisation. Once they stopped being seen as living weapons of war, academics could start looking at Souls differently—or it would be more reasonable to say they could freely make such views public. It was in the same period that Larsen made the greatest strides in her theories around the Source—probably because much of the work she had already done. This, looking at the date on it, she wrote this before the end of the War. But here, she has already listed the idea of an extraneous entity creating the Souls, although she is still questioning that hypothesis. I suppose her notion of the Source was not too outrageous, even for the time, but it being scattered in the same atmosphere we breathe was another matter. And yet now, broadly speaking, her system is the accepted one. She was a remarkably persistent lady."

She knew more about these scientists than I could recount. Why I realised so with such surprise, I couldn't say; clearly, she lived for this stuff. The girl fell quiet, but kept stroking that paper, as if pre-emptively grieving for the moment she would have to let go of it, to stick it in a file with the others.

There were two things I remembered about Larsen: first being that one colour photograph of her that everyone and their cat could recognise. She was real pretty, like a doll—a redhead, with big blue eyes. The second was my old nan and grandpa, telling us stories about the day she disappeared. They had really believed for a while that she'd come back, that they'd catch her eventually. No-one even knew how she died, in the end. Apparently, they never found a body.

Crept me out of my skin, it did.

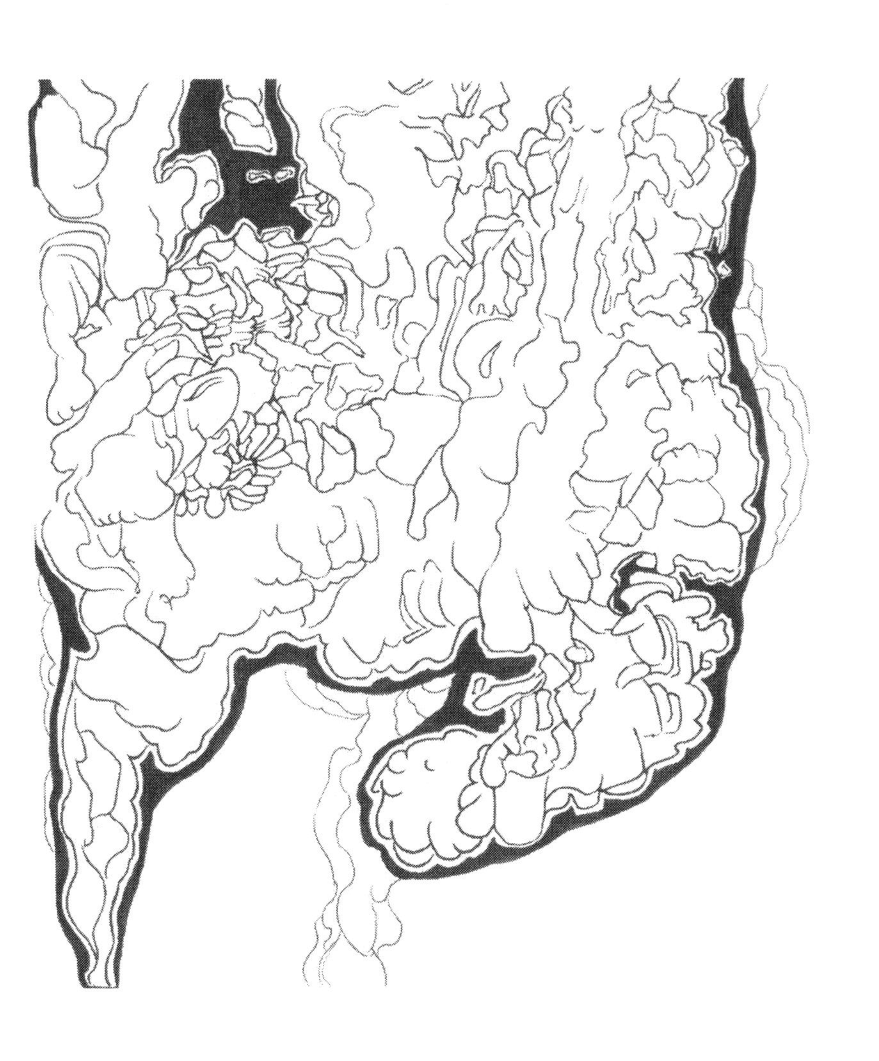

Part 2: Treason

[Aria]
Bells…I woke to the chime of the bell tower. It made such lovely music, I felt as though I still slept yet, that I was still rising through an airy dream. I blinked slowly, in time with each great, undulating clang that arrived at my window from the monument's giant stone throat.

The lack of light in my room confused me most, at first. I sat up onto my knees and pulled my hair into a tighter knot. Looking out of the window, the only glow came from a few lit squares in the distance, and further on, the early-morning sun, barely emerging from behind the boundaries of the city. I pressed my palms hard over my ears, and then lifted them. The bells rang.

Before another wasted second passed, I leaped from my bed, and snatched yesterday's trousers from the bedside. As I tucked in my crumpled shirt, I felt a faint breeze and heard the wooden groan of the door swinging open. I turned to Emery. He peered up at me from under his crossed brow and flung my jacket over from the hook on the wall.

"It woke you too," he said, watching down the hallway. Hurried footsteps could be heard somewhere near the stairs.

"Where to with us, do you think, out of the side door?" I asked. He paused for a beat, before nodding once. I laid a swift hand on his back as I slipped through the doorway, and we followed each other down two floors, already breaking into an impatient gallop by the time we reached the first flight of stairs.

We located General lingering outside her office, tapping her fingertips together behind her back, while she waited for someone to appear before her. We were satisfactory enough, the shift in her stance suggested, and she led us outside. The horses were growing restless.

"Have you received word from the watchmen?"

“Yes. Get rid of your harness, Lieutenant; I want you both with your mounts.” Her reluctance to say anything more, as yet, led me to think we had no time for hearing news twice.

Medi quickly caught up to assist the three of us with preparing enough mounts—Eris and Kai would have to rise with their retainers. Their group of four arrived slightly later. The young apprentices were, clearly, taken aback in one way or another. If they were not being pushed along by hunched shoulders, I doubted their stubborn legs would have moved at all. I wondered if Tank and Leo had literally dragged them from their beds, or if they had been awoken by the chiming too. The sound still vibrated over the rooftops; I felt both indebted and terribly sorry for the individual who had tasked themselves with ringing the bell.

The veterans saluted to announce their presence. However, young Kai glared straight into the nearest empty space, his jaw deceptively level. Eris made that same, steadfast look, only down at the floor. General Elwin would not stand for that.

“Are you set?” she demanded from them, lifting the girl’s head with her gaze.

They made an indistinct noise each, though a few extra seconds of sustained eye contact seemed enough to convince her.

She continued: “I’ve just heard from the Wall, not with good news. They have detected a very large unknown body headed straight toward the western side, at some pace. We can be fairly certain it is another Soulless. Our one advantage is we should have enough time to intercept as it breaks through, then trap it before it makes it very far. That is, if we leave immediately.” She spoke with such clarity, without a pause to think. This particular trait of hers I could never find in myself to understand. Nonetheless, in spite of her tone, there were several glaring faults in her speech, which the others declared with vague sideways glances and shuffling of feet.

Leo proved brave enough to actually raise his voice. “Our equipment isn’t that advanced, to pick it up so quickly. You say this is a Soulless; General, just how vast is this creature?”

“Small enough,” was all she offered in response, disregarding us in favour of her hulking white stallion observing from over her shoulder. As she heaved herself onto its back, Leo brushed past to follow in step, taking the calm mare with the gorgeous feathery socks over her feet. Emery and I interpreted this as a prompt, to lead our own mounts out into the open. My little girl was a lanky and fidgety thing, apparently of the ghostly white stallion's progeny, though she clearly did not take after her father's disposition. Even still, I found her overly fretful on this particular occasion, like she could feel the enemy's giant footsteps through her shoes. I massaged between her fluttering ears, but it did not seem to ease her nerves at all. In contrast, Emery's mount moved by with barely a sound. I gave a quiet sigh. The two of them could make a formidable partnership; he flaunted so much skill when he rode, if only he had not been so content feeling the ground with his own two feet.

Kai's low voice sounded over the top of the commotion. He had to look up at us now. "Am I supposed to use one of those things?"

General quickly turned around, making sure he had not already tried it. "Absolutely not," she said. "Tank, Leo, you'll be responsible for keeping this pair safe for now."

Medi hung back to give Eris a leg up onto the enormous brute given to Tank, a poor choice for the unfortunate girl, whose head did not even come level with its back. She appeared quite unsure what to do. Tank, apparently not unaware of the mismatch, immediately held both the reins and Eris's wrists in the same iron grip round his front. Meanwhile, Leo simply lugged the taller boy up behind him with one arm. After a moment watching them, I realised, in their own fashions, neither seemed to fear the wrath of their protégé's practically new-born Soul. But in my temporary distraction, I jolted at General's call, and almost missed her moving off.

"With all speed," she commanded, "we make for the basilica."

The ruins of the great church—built in lost days, intended for the worship of Souls as gifts, granted by the wise deity—struck me as far from a suitable place to corner a creature of the size her instructions implied. Before preservation of the ancient monument was put in place, a good part of the roof had already fallen in, and fabulous though the sandy brick might have been to admire, I somehow imagined it would provide little resistance against the brute force of a Soulless.

It took a little time before I remembered, that an idea of great importance equated to a building of great scale, which would make the basilica the largest this city had at its disposal. Furthermore, the stern pillars, which made up the arches encircling the whole structure, fell in a particular vertical, orderly manner. Contrary to the roof, most of them still stood to remarkable height. Not unlike the bars of a cell, I thought. If the target were to be lured inside, with the right placement of our men, it would indeed be maddening for the creature to seek an escape. And the site also stood fairly close to the border. So long as we succeeded, the people would be safe.

We spent around fifteen minutes, by Emery's watch, traversing straight through the middle of the city in almost complete silence, waiting for the next order to be passed.

"Leo and Tank, you're going to divert onto a direct route to the basilica. The rest of us will catch the target at the Wall and take advantage, so anticipate our arrival. I summoned a couple of cars to arrive as well, when the dust settles. Keep an eye out."

"General," they both grunted in confirmation. As their horses peeled away from the group, disappearing down a side street, we continued our march into the mouth of the enemy.

Faced with the height of the Wall so close in front of me, I began to debate how great a hole this giant could make in the Interieur's most reassuring line of defence. It had always stood here; I found it hopeless to imagine otherwise. We soon trotted to an uncertain halt before it, and General sent up a green signal to declare our position to the watchmen. We waited. It took until then for the idea to cement itself in my mind, that this was truly about to happen.

"This is the position the watchmen gave me," General muttered, glancing down the curved road, running parallel to the foot of the Wall, first left, then right. The timing of the first crack came close to being comical.

The ground shook with the impact, causing the startled animals to toss their heads and kicking their feet beneath us. Even those already at the basilica would have heard the awful noise. And it only got louder, as the unnamed Soulless tried again, and again, each thump knocking out billows of dust, and maybe a brick or several. General slowly backed us away, seemingly expecting the structure to fail with the next couple of blows. The Soulless must have known it too; once the end of its snout finally reached through an opening, it flung its jaw open, letting out a savage wail that brought the rest of the stone down with it.

Before the Wall crumbled, the creature had been not only without a name, but without a face. I had assumed I would prefer seeing what my enemy looked like. Not knowing always seemed so much worse. My mind threw doubt on such presumptions now. Oh, it truly was a gigantic beast; each individual scale that covered its body must have equalled the size of my face. However, the size of it alone did not slide an enfeebling tremble under my skin. Rather, it had a lizard's head, stuck on the end of its neck, long and full of teeth, with a mouth that stretched past all of its eyes. I counted them: a total of six, three on each side—all yellow, save for the tiny black pinpricks in the centre. Its limbs were strange to watch, crooked and lumbering, and while its legs were like trunks of Northern pines, the meagre, skeletal branches extending out from its shoulders framed a papery membrane. Perhaps they were wings. Yet I was not convinced of how far this giant would fly if it tried to use them. I might have argued that, instead, they functioned simply to make it appear even larger. Only in hindsight did I notice the total, eerie lack of a tail to balance the, presumably disproportionate, weight of its skull. The creature was a towering error of nature.

I caught a tiny movement from metres away: a silver knife, one from Emery's arsenal, soaring towards the Soulless's face, before lodging itself between the grooves around its nostril. It simply flicked its eyes to glare at him, much like one would jump in irritation, to examine a bee sting.

"It—General!" Emery managed to keep his voice at his usual, steadfast tone, right up until that last syllable, which leaped up a key.

Medi was not nearly as reserved in situations like these: "What are we doing, ma'am?" she cried, already turned around in the opposite direction.

"Not going that way," she replied firmly. "We're going to have to take the widest streets we can."

As she corrected us, she had to yank the reins quickly to the right, to rescue her stallion from the Soulless, which veered to snap at his feet.

"Down here, let's go," she urged, herding us past the gaping cavity in the Wall, down the gently curving road, past the wheelwright's and, I hoped, in the direction of our comrades.

The giant screeched again, furious with us. Emery's head flicked around to check behind, ensuring that it still pursued us. He tipped his head, and his eyes lingered around me, unblinking before General called upon him.

"Lieutenant, are we still good?"

"It is right at your heels, if that's what you mean."

She did not react to that, instead opting for, "Right at the next junction."

[Leo]

These kids brought a challenge for Tank and me in that, appreciative or not, they relied on us. Right now, daunted by this deserted strip of rubble, they required us to place them in a very specific position: far enough apart that they were not a liability to each other when their Souls inevitably went berserk, but also within reach, such that they could be both protected and useful at once. I knew they were both too naive to understand the delicacy of the process. That was not their fault. Tank deposited Rayne right in front of a weathered stump, where one column had collapsed into two great pieces—on the opposite end from which General would enter, with the Soulless in tow. We agreed that Hughes should dismount around halfway along the floor's length, which he managed rather more elegantly.

If we were honest with ourselves, we could not be sure of our decision until the first crash came. The city seemed to shudder with it. As the boy's hand flew over his head, the two of us charged away from him and the plume of fire and smoke, which grew from the ground in a circle around him. My eyes darted to the girl, who kicked up dust with her toes, a freakish blankness on her face. Tiny white sprites bounced frantically about her feet for a second, then disappeared.

Tank counted each hit, out loud, as he heard them, and as each wave of heat brushed round our necks. He still lost track, though, as soon as he realised the wall had ruptured. We heard the low sound, dull, and distinct from the rest; it could not have signified anything else. It sounded as though an immense hole had opened up in the earth itself, and the whole city was falling in on its knees. Awaiting the rattle of hooves, I pulled my sword from my back.

No amount of imagination could have led me to conjure an image of that creature in my mind, what with its huge head, even a pair of wings, stacked impossibly upon two legs. Not scales, but rather row upon row of tapered razor blades lined every fold of its body. From where I stood, I could only trust that four horses made it inside before the thing exploded through the largest of the archways, in a shower of stone fragments, and that they, like us, managed to narrowly evade the wall of fire that came to meet them. In truth, my attentions were mostly fixated upon this foreign creature over our heads.

Tank seized the opportunity to speak, before General delivered her next instructions. "Shitting bloody hell."

I was inclined to agree with him.

"Fan out," she said as she skidded to a standstill nearby. "Don't let it escape now."

"Just try not to get toasted alive, yeah?" Tank said.

"By either of these kids," I suddenly felt a necessary addition, before he ran off too satisfied with himself. But I was interrupted by a vastly approaching shadow. I pointed my sword ineffectually at its foot, all I could conceive to do as I fled.

Fire erupted from the Soulless's scaled side, sending it into a slow, backward stumble—if such a colossal movement could even be called that. My eyes flicked to Hughes. He had, at least, stuck to the outer walls like I told him to. However, my gaze trailing back to the giant's twisted, wrinkling shape in the centre of the basilica, I caught a glimpse of someone else instead. She stood alone, and completely out of place. I recognised Songbird's plume of hair trailing down her back, as she craned her neck to meet the goliath bending its gaze down upon her.

Time seemed to shrink, but only for myself; I shrivelled into a spectator to the unthinkable playing out just beyond my control. My feet seemed to weigh the same as the giant's head as it plunged towards Songbird. Foolishly, but predictably, she had released her mount, letting it gallop away, screeching and circling in panic. She was trapped under the stare of half a dozen yellow eyes. Not one person could reach her. She deftly managed to avoid its closing jaw—but only to be caught instead by one of the creature's feet. A single talon running with scarlet lifted over her head, flinging her to the floor a few metres away. Her lance clattered onto the stone with her. She didn't get up. For a second it stopped, twisting its neck to examine the girl's body, as though she were laid out on display for its enlightenment.

"This one is yours, is she not?" I imagined it thinking. *"What would you do if I killed her?"*

I chanced a rushed glance back to the kids. It had finished them. Hughes stood by one of the gaping arches, holding his spindly knees, and straining to hold up his head. His face and hands were blotted with patches of charred black. And the girl, Rayne, stayed a little further into the monument, looking ahead inertly. I could see even from my distance that she struggled to take shallow breaths, swaying precariously on her feet. Tank hovered near her, sharing his hasty looks between her, General, and Songbird on the ground, unsure of whom he should leave behind, in favour of another. Where was the excusable sacrifice?

My attention suddenly veered to General, at the left side of me. She made to launch herself forward, but her horse could find no way through the creature's flailing limbs. She did not believe the animal at first, kicking the stallion in its sides and striking it savagely between the shoulders. When it refused, she leaped from its back onto the ground. I followed her, throwing an arm around her, confining her against my chest. General's face became a blank slate, much too perfectly still. Only her pupils darted around, from side to side, while her wrist jerked erratically, desperate to react, but with no move prepared to make. If she could have grabbed hold of her blade, she would have stabbed me. And I would only have forgiven her. She didn't make a sound, though I did not think it necessary, not to me. The image had already presented itself at the front of my mind, one of my baby girls, in Aria's place. That nightmarish fancy would never quite leave.

In her absence, the sound of Lieutenant's voice overpowered us both. The first faltered a little, drooping tentatively as though, in a lapse, he had forgotten the correct word. Then, after a whimper of epiphany, he screamed the girl's name until the stone walls echoed it back to him in communal despair. General recognised in that instant what he was about to do, from the way she turned her head. Yet her mouth still would not expel any proper speech. Instead she continued to hit me in the side with the heel of her hand. His own horse, void of its master, marched a few hesitant steps in pursuit, and surrendered just as quickly.

[Emery]

I ran into the giant's shadow. One foot landed somewhere to my left. Perhaps the thing intended to crush me. I cared little for it. I could have easily thrown a dagger or pivoted on the spot and stabbed it in its heel, but I didn't think to do it. I simply chose not to think, not while she lay there, sprawled on the ground, and everyone else just watched her fold her limbs around herself in agony. I failed to understand why they all refused to act, but it did not matter. I would go for her, alone.

I fell down beside her, pulling her into my lap. She weighed lighter, felt smaller than she should have been. Her blood seeped through my shirt, sticking warm against my skin. Its colour crawled up the fabric, appearing black under the shade. My hand pressed over the tear in her side. I couldn't stop it; I wouldn't be enough. I was choking, drowning in Aria's blood.

She watched over my shoulder, almost as if I did not exist, to her mind. I heard the Soulless behind me as it crashed and bellowed, trying to manoeuvre in this close space, and now and then, the faint sense of sharp edges slicing into my clothes and my flesh. No matter: that sort of superficial pain meant nothing. This—this was wrong.

My eyelids clenched shut against a stinging concoction of dust, blood and sweat. But I forced them open at the sensation of her hand, cutting my arm in a strange, deathlike grip. Her face creased tight in agony, but those green eyes swam with terrifying conviction. I already knew what she would now try to say, and I was sickened. Not at her, but at what this creature had managed to make her do. It would be so like her.

"You need to go with the others. Hurry," she managed.

"Like hell."

She worked to take a breath, so that she could continue: "That wasn't a request, Emery. Leave me, go, now."

"Never."

My voice struggled against the dryness coating my mouth and throat. Like her, I spoke without words, but through that which she could see. Her eyes would meet their match in mine. Her will struggled relentlessly, yet her blinks grew longer and longer as sleep began to engulf her. While her grip failed, sliding slowly down my wrist, I sensed the air surrounded us shifted. Death, being upon us, finally began its downward plummet, as I understood. This would be my punishment: execution. I lowered my head, ready, resting against hers. So, this was marriage.

I waited and waited to be taken, listening to an agonising wail enfolding me. Only when I raised my gaze in resignation, could I see, at the edge of my vision, a smaller, swifter figure than the one I had envisioned, and so dark it could barely be distinguished from the shadows it cast, an apparition. I tried, deliriously, to follow it; it took the shape of a dog but seemed at least twice the size of any hound in the wild. It charged away from us with a rasping scream, untouched by fear, towards the towering Soulless. It forcefully drew closer, under the still, uncomprehending eyes, snapping its teeth, until the giant wheeled around, tearing up the stone floor beneath it. The earth trembled under their thunderous footsteps. I couldn't be mistaken. The monster had overwhelmed us, but now it looked to be retreating, through a cascade of falling dust, framed by one of the basilica's great archways.

The Soulless feared the lesser creature. At least, it feared enough to flee, for the time being. Tracing our saviour's silhouette moving between the pillars, it occurred to me why its form had seemed so familiar. It belonged to no predator of the Soulless; those two beasts were of the same kind. Unless, of course, I had hallucinated the entire scene. I felt my head floating, detached from my body.

Aria's pulse still thumped, determined against my fingertips despite her wilting body. I pulled her closer.

A blaring voice vibrated in my ear. "Lieutenant, we need to take her, now."

[Medi]
"Lieutenant," I pleaded.

The sound of General's command had only caused him to collect Songbird tighter to his chest, glaring up into his superior's face. I saw an unsettling fearlessness in those eyes, such that I hesitated, voice snared in my chest, before repeating myself. The blood drying around his face and neck didn't help the effect. I had no option, though. At the current rate, he would need my Soul even more than she did.

"Lieutenant, I can't heal her like this. Emery, please, let me help Aria."

He seemed to rouse at the mention of his name. And at hers, he carefully lowered the girl into my arms. General immediately dropped down at my side, resting her daughter's head on her knees. I prodded the pads on my gloves, and a pair of needles pricked into my palms, stirring up my Soul. I looked down at her face; she took a few, rapid blinks, otherwise staring blankly at the ceiling. Poor girl, she knew more pain was coming. I obeyed my own rule and looked past her, well before I tucked her shirt out of the way and pressed my hands onto the wound in her side.

The flow of blood slowed, and I felt the laceration begin to stitch together under my fingers. After a minute or so, all that remained was a thin white line, usually surrounded by a light pink blotch, to my experience. The dark wash over her drenched skin made it difficult to tell right now. I straightened her clothes for her, although these were unlikely to be ever worn again. But her breathing had gradually begun to even out, the best I could hope for so soon. She would be alright. I nodded to General, who held onto Songbird by the shoulders as the latter tried to sit up.

"She's safe, ma'am," I said.

"Thank you so much, Merida."

"Thank you, Medi," Songbird mumbled.

With a long breath, I pushed myself off my knees to treat Lieutenant, only to find he had vanished.

"General," I called in a steady voice. She crouched on the floor behind me.

"What is it Medi?"

"I'm missing Lieutenant."

"What?" She suddenly rose up.

I searched over the ground of the basilica. From the crimson-stained spot where he and Songbird both lay just minutes ago, a faint trail of shoeprints stepped out, towards one of the archways leading outside.

"Oh, hell," I muttered.

At the opposite end of the floor, Tank's voice boomed, "Ah, they're here!" He announced the timely arrival of the cars.

General collected herself before she gave her instructions. "Tank, get those two into the car," she started, referring to Eris and Kai, both currently collapsed on top of a scrunched jacket each, "then Songbird. And quickly—we're looking for Lieutenant. I'll need your hands."

[Emery]

"Hey."

I found him just outside the shelter of the monument, gazing after the tracks left by the other Soulless. "Shelter" was a loose term; anyone would have been a fool not to question the bricks' integrity now. His eyes turned to look over his shoulder at me. Like the others', his gleamed yellow.

"Was that you?"

I had to ask, simply because what stood before me now was no animal, but a man. Pallid in every feature, but more glaring than that, I noticed the slightness of his frame, hardly indicative of a creature that could shake the ground beneath its feet.

Wordlessly, he held an arm out, and watched my face, impassive, as though anticipating a certain reaction. At first, I assumed I had failed to see whatever he referred to, until I caught sight of the white skin crawling with a foreign, charcoal substance. The greyish film spread over the entire limb, although my eyes were drawn to his fingernails, which visibly grew into five vicious claws. Meanwhile, a hideous sound, like scraping metal, cut the air. This formed his answer.

"You are the Soulless, then."

"Is that what you people call me?"

"And you have a voice," I noted to myself.

Making an unsuspecting glance up to his face, a shiver racked my shoulders. Everything above his nose remained the same, unlike his mouth, which appeared to stretch wider, what with the several extra teeth protruding from his cheeks like broken bones. More exhibition, I realised.

"Turn your back on me now, and I won't finish the slaughter Wyvern started," he said.

I shook my head slowly. "I don't think you'll do that. You saved us."

"The fact that I attacked her does not mean I intend to take your side."

"But you did. What's your name?"

His brow narrowed in suspicion, although he still replied. "I was given the name Fenrir. It is the only one I know."

“Okay then, Fenrir, it’s time for you to make a decision. Right now, you are hovering in the middle of a war, to which the end can only come when one army or the other is destroyed. Consider this: you’ve already shown that you see more than a single path ahead of you—you have been gifted with a choice. But I’m afraid you have got to make it now, because neither our side nor theirs can afford to relent for your sake. Your indecision will get you killed in the end, which helps no-one, does it?”

My words sounded like an ineffectual drawl to my ears. I took a step forward, which grew into an unnerving struggle all of a sudden, and I stretched out an open hand.

My vision swam, blending the scene before me with a view of a street, taken from a gutter flooded with spring rain. I found myself in two places at once. Floating beside Fenrir’s body, as it shed tiny flakes of grey skin, I also conjured the shape of a young girl, proudly sporting a wooden lance on her back. Holding a weapon, yes, but she wore none of their armour; the soldiers, my brothers and sisters, all were alike in hunting me down, but she looked strange. She crouched, neat black braids falling over her knees, as she reached forward with open palms.

“Here, look, you can be safe now. I’m Aria—what is your name?” she said, before she disappeared.

“My name’s Emery,” I uttered, as Fenrir’s hand, stony, but definitely organic again, fell into mine.

“I would advise you stop fixating on me for a second,” he said bluntly, “and turn yourself in to your medic.”

His hold on me loosened, and with it I felt my knees began to tremble almost as violently as my sight. My body slumped into a squirming heap propped up by a pair of hands, which I found to be Medi’s. She yelled for Tank’s sturdier arms.

I had not felt it before then, that unique searing pain of fresh wounds, which caused my back to constrict, only serving to make the sensation worse. The familiar rattle of unsheathed blades brought me back to consciousness enough to grind out a few words.

“Stay your swords! He’s a friend.”

A pause followed.

"I thought as much. Fine, I will heed your word for now, Lieutenant. But I don't trust it here unaccompanied. We will take it with us. Leo?"

On General's order, I was carried away.

[Aria]

I watched from the car, which I had been hauled into with the poor apprentices. Both lay on their backs, unable to move, but Kai kept his eyes pried open to stay awake and listen. I could not let my gaze move away from Emery's face, knotted and halfway hidden behind his shaking hands as Medi worked tirelessly to repair the damage. I had cared for him injured, sick, and crying, but had never been made to watch him hurt in this way.

He had to wobble to his feet, literally as soon as he mustered the self-possession, in order to face Leo, who brought with him a young man I did not recognise, save for his bright yellow eyes. I did not consider that they could look like people too. Metal bangles hung heavy chains from both of its wrists; it truly looked a prisoner. General stood between them, addressing Emery. This is where he had vanished to.

"Lieutenant, you mean to suggest this Soulless is not our enemy?"

"I do. Fenrir, and the animal that attacked our true enemy, are one and the same. His power allows him to change shape, from man to hound."

"It's true," the Soulless said, in flat, unaffected mumble.

"We lost this fight," Emery continued. "Fenrir saved us from it. You have to admit that."

"And your conclusion is that I should take it into our ranks?"

"I see no better alternative, General."

"Right. And if it decides to turn again, and returns to destroying us, what will you do then?"

Before she could reach the end of her question, he lunged forward. The Soulless tipped its head back, inching away from the knife grazing its white throat. General did not flinch. Emery gave her a purposeful look askance, which she acknowledged by turning to Leo.

"Very well: Leo, you and Tank will form a convoy to transport the Soulless back to base. Lieutenant, your ride back is waiting over there. Go."

Emery made an effort to salute, before he followed her direction to the car. On his way, he abruptly halted in his tracks, clutching his stomach and pressing his lips together, as if about to vomit. He took another, tentative step, though, managing to hold together his composure before the host of dissecting eyes. Lowering himself down opposite me, he refused to look at my face despite all my efforts. A bead of sweat fell from the end of his nose. I noticed, as he leaned his head down, that his long hair had been hacked away at an awkward angle, just above his shoulder line. Medi had returned his shirt and jacket to him once his wounds were closed but, like my own, there remained little of them worth keeping. He wrenched his hands together in his lap, watching Eris and Kai lying on the parallel benches beside us. Having both given up, they were sound asleep. The pair looked in dire need of rest; maybe the Souls knew what they were doing by forcing it upon them. Much better than we did.

I compelled myself to speak first. "Do you remember when we were younger, still in training? Or I still was, anyway. You gave me a shove, right here, with your foot. I lost my balance so badly I fell flat on my back." I stroked my elbows, almost feeling the round, green bruises which had lingered there for two weeks. You did it to teach me lesson. You said: 'It doesn't matter how good you are, never let anything bigger than you strike you. Avoid them above all else, otherwise they will knock you down, or worse, disarm you.' And then you handed me back my lance. I had thought it awfully strange, you know, appearing outside with your bare feet."

I sniggered at the slightly embarrassing memory. He made a tired sound in reply, slowly shaking his head. For a second, he held his breath, about to say something, before we were interrupted by Medi hopping over our feet and sitting down, exhausted, at the head of the car, as the wheels rattled into motion.

"What is in the trailer behind us then?" I queried.

Medi opened her eyes to answer. "Whatever pieces are left of his horse," she said.

[Medi]

I added the last letter to my report in a juddering hand, while hooves clattered up to the front entrance. As we rolled to a halt, I folded the paper in half, and turned my attention to the tired young spirits still curled uncomfortably on the wooden floor.

General was evidently preoccupied with our new, impromptu "ally" (I hung back with my scepticism, as yet), so I waited until the morning to drop it onto her desk:

"*Medic's Report*

Name: Merida Grieve

Date: XX/XX/XX Time: 1533

Mission failed.

I write from the seat of the trailer that is carrying Songbird, Lieutenant, Hellhound, Garrison and myself, back to safety.

Songbird and Lieutenant both exhausted. Have sustained blood loss and lost consciousness briefly but are now stable. The former was gashed once below the ribs; the latter suffered numerous lacerations across the back and shoulders. Injuries of both, and any additional, more minor wounds of others, were able to be mended in due time by my Soul (Empathy). Possibly require antibiotics.

Garrison and Hellhound currently lie asleep at my feet. They, like the aforementioned two, for the moment require a bath, a filling meal, and copious rest.

As for the exact status of the Soulless we are bringing with us, I cannot say for certain. However, I saw no visible injury and it looked to be walking without hindrance."

[General]

"The hawk looked to its bloodied wings and thought itself an angel."

It was far from the first time we had returned to the base to find such accusations scrawled over my walls. His presence materialised a certain denial, a fracture, to be acknowledged with anything from mild discomfort to aggression. But on this particular occasion, the crude paintwork seemed to seep out from the surface of the bricks like fresh blood.

The culprit's timing proved impeccable. Now my own failure surrounded me in all directions.

I avoided looking directly at the car, but I watched Emery at the edge of my sight. He fixated briefly on the message, before his head dropped back below his shoulders. He was stained crimson. The boy was in tatters. Two children probably still lay sleeping, robbed of their strength, just across from him. Medi had stationed herself at the front of the car. I imagined her careful eyes watching over them.

Leo and Tank lagged behind, left to escort the rogue Soulless. The creature had fought off our enemy when I had been helpless, to what end I could not say. As far as I could discern, Fenrir and the animal that had attacked the Western District were the very same creature. Yet already a small degree of faith dangled between it and Emery, and I knew what I had witnessed. Once the pair arrived, they would leave the question of how to proceed to my own judgement.

The cars slowed. Aria rose up from her seat; she no longer held the dark bloom across her middle, but the look of agony contorting her face had been seared onto the backs of my eyes.

I dismounted, recalling the way Emery had curled his body around hers instinctively, when I tried to take her from his arms. He had said nothing, but the shift in his countenance spoke for him; he was shielding her from me. Merida still reached her in time, and I still knelt at her side when she stirred, but it occurred to me that I had acted in no way to stop him.

I would have killed him, without a pang of regret when I first found him, soaked through on the pavement like refuse. Aria had insisted on following us, when she overheard the report: Altairs, three of them, wandering the streets of Interieur. And still, somehow, she had managed to slip from under all of us, the moment at which my brain flipped over—perhaps it had not been right from the start. She was not ready; I didn't care what she believed, these were monsters she could never survive, playing dress-up as she did, in our uniform. I rounded a corner, and he sat there, laying his hand on Aria. My blade bore into his throat. Only the little wooden stick, clutched in my daughter's hands, stopped it from bursting open his jugular.

"No, mama! I will not let you. Emery is my friend."

"You don't understand Aria. This is not your friend. This is a demon. This is danger."

"I am not that stupid. Just because I find words difficult, I am not stupid."

"Aria—"

"I know what that thing on his arm means. But I will not let you. You want to kill him, but I will not let you. It is you who is a monster, not him, you!"

"Do it." A small croak came from his mouth, barely louder than the rain. *"You're right."*

I remember glancing away from the metal tip of my weapon, for a second, and seeing his face. His eyes might have been green, but they were flooded and bloodshot. His body shuddered under his own weight, and his filthy hair knotted up in his teeth, yet he would not stop staring at me. I thought he wanted to die.

"It is cold out here, mama. He is not well."

His name was Emery. He was fourteen years old, and he had a terrible case of the flu.

The sword fell to my side. I wanted to throw it, but General Elwin had clawed her way back to the surface, and stopped me. Aria forgot about her little lance, throwing her heart at the boy, struggling to pull him onto his feet by herself. The other two Altairs had been out to murder him too. His father sent them to ruin him, for daring to run. They both escaped us in the end.

Unable to resist the stinging urge, I lingered for a moment as I passed the car, only to see her again. When she felt my presence there, she smiled down at me, a perfect fairy.

"I'm alright mama, see?" she whispered, clutching my hand. "I can still fight. We do still have to fight them, right?"

“I do,” I corrected her. “I have to do better, Aria, for the people whose battle this is *not*.”

“We will be better, don’t worry,” she nodded, probably unaware that she asked the impossible from me. I squeezed my daughter’s hand before she let go, to crouch down and help Medi shake the unconscious pair awake. Exactly as I went to leave, I heard another voice.

“General.”

“What is it Lieutenant?” I replied.

“I will wait here for the convoy and bring Fenrir to you.” I recognised his tone of voice, too carefully measured; he was hiding. “After that, I’ll get rid of that mess.”

Aria sighed, her gaze drifting to the defaced wall.

“No, Lieutenant,” I countered, “I will clean this up myself. You were severely injured today, don’t forget. Keep to your rooms tonight, the both of you.” Without waiting for a protest, I gave my thanks to the driver, and promptly led my own horse away, calling as I marched: “It will not get away again.”

[Emery]

I reached for the nail brush again and ran a fresh basin of water.

The messages didn't get much more poetic than that. So, I persisted as some sort of false deity now, did I? I wondered whom this ingenious idea belonged to: my siblings maybe, or one of the eight different concubines that might have been my mother, or simply some disparaging teenager with too much time on their hands? The blood on my wings made for a particularly effective stab; I couldn't seem to be able to scrape these traces of red out of the creases in my fingers.

Perhaps it was the sovereign himself. Perhaps Lester Altair finally fostered more than pure, blinkered hatred for his defect son. He appeared to have concluded that, even if he couldn't bring me death, he would bring me hell.

I continued to scour at my hands. Was this mine, or Aria's? I had not seen her since we walked up the stairs together, at the same sluggish pace. We had retreated to our own rooms without a word. Both of us had witnessed the ruin of the other, but to spectate the task of fixing ourselves, as best we could, seemed just too much to endure. A lifeless body with her face on it kept crawling into my mind.

Moving away from the bathroom, I took a glance out of the window, the drips from my skin leaving a shameful trail over the floor. Sure enough, the wall outside was soaked, and the paint gone. A stream of dyed water trickled between the paving stones.

[Aria]

"There, all done," I said, brushing the last hairs from Emery's shoulders, and discarding the cuttings in my hand.

He curiously rubbed the back of his neck, which he now found bare. A couple of hours passed by, at most, before I had to get up and find him. I caught him in the process of tying a clean bandage over his tattoo. Years ago, when a fumbled exchange between my blade and his forearm left a short, clean slice beheading the distinctive black hawk, he had specifically appealed for Medi to leave it alone—so that the mark would remain, he told me. Yet he continued to insist on concealing it himself, like a filthy stain.

He had sat there in silence. His palms were still inflamed where he had been furiously scrubbing at his skin, and his hair looked somehow even worse for wear, having been cleaned. It gifted me with the perfect reason to drag him out of there.

"What do you think?"

"It's…different," he noted, and met my eyes, enquiring.

"Very handsome," I assured him, before I shooed him from the chair and busied myself with tidying away the clutter, leaving Emery to pace around the little room.

He passed by the window several times, but I did not see him pause even once to look at his reflection. By the time I finished, he had finally stopped across from me, arms folded across his chest. He seemed to sense what was coming.

"What happened to you?" I asked, shaking my head, trying to recall more than mere brief flashes of memory.

"I'm alright," he lied.

"Can you show me?"

"No, you don't need to see."

"Yes, I do. Please."

Emery did not say a word, only sighed. He sat himself down on the edge of my mattress, unbuttoning his shirt, his back turned to me. Slowly, carefully, he slid the sleeve from his arm and let it fall, revealing one shoulder. I groaned at what I saw, but he stayed quiet. He simply bowed his head and, after a moment of hesitation, removed the defensive hand from the space next to him. It opened up, a wordless offering.

I crept over beside him. Moving the limp fabric aside showed that the scars spread to the bottom of his back. The dim red light left from the sunset grazed over the pale criss-crosses that Medi's power had not quite been able to erase. My eyes stung, as my fingertips found each raised line that marked his skin. He tried to breathe slowly.

"You made a promise to General Elwin. Is that why you let that—that evil brute do this to you?" I asked him.

He brought his hand over his shoulder, like doing so could erase it from my sight.

"To me? Look at what it did to you," he scoffed. "What it could have done. Think about that for a second."

"I am okay, remember? I am here; I am safe, because of you." My wrist froze. "But this…I told you to leave me."

He flinched against my touch. "Never."

"Because of my mother?" I demanded.

His simple reply was to slowly turn his head and glare. All I could see were his eyes, shuddering from behind a blond veil, but it said enough.

"Then why?"

"You know exactly why, Aria," he snapped.

"I know what I would like to think. But that scares me."

"Are you going to try and tell me never to do this again?"

"I want to, but I shan't. Because I know that, if it had been you lying there," I said, as my palm landed on the spot where my own, faded blemish remained, "I would have done the same thing. I cannot lose you, Emery. I will not."

I winced at the idea. Simply having to admit the possibility of it, out loud, left a cruel, sick feeling in my stomach. I became so agitated by it that, for a second, I did not notice Emery finally turn to face me.

"I'm safe. I'm here, and I'm okay, alright? Because of you," he said in a low shaking hum. "And, I'm scared too."

I could not say for sure which of us took hold of the other first. I had kissed him before, of course, hiding up on the rooftop, charming, moreish little experiments that gradually settled in, grew into a habit, like common knowledge. But this arose as though fashioned, or rather compelled, somehow a different thing.

Perhaps it was not as pretty. It started raw, aching, and terribly untidy. There were emotions behind it of the desperate kind neither of us dared try to put into plain words. No, instead such things passed between the both of us, unspoken, with every shared breath, each brush of a thumb across a cheek, or the little bones at the top of one's spine. Our confession fell from us easier, clearer, this way, whatever we had left.

From thoughtless drifting, as I reached over to untangle Emery from his other, rather uncomfortable sleeve, my mind lurched in horror. My knuckle grazed over one of the scars. But then he laughed, in a tentative sort of giggle, the one which brought those lovely little wrinkles at the corner of his eyes. He laughed at himself, pointing to this strange simmering daze, which had also dawned on him. Still, when I caught myself, pinching the hem of my own blouse between my bumbling fingers in a return gesture, I stopped, and looked to him. He scanned my face, left to right and right to left—working his way around what I seemed to mean by it. That was okay, then; it was okay to be a little bewildered.

"Are you sure?" he said, slowly, in his quiet, wise voice.

I could have torn my brain into pieces attempting to reconstruct myself into something at all sure. The last few hours had presented me with an awful lot to think through. I knew he did not refer to past events, not in that instant. My answer to his question flew forth, refreshingly straightforward. This situation surfaced not as I had kept it, ready and rehearsed in my head, nor even as it had slyly crept into my dreams. But still, I smiled, and replied with what I knew for sure.

"We would have died today, and—"

I searched around for a word, before cutting myself off, nodding anxiously instead. There were so many things that fitted onto the end of that sentence—too many. I could not think, could not choose.

"Yeah," he said, plainly, and carefully helped with my collar, which had somehow gotten stuck around my ears. I noted the slight tremble in his hands as he lifted them over my head. He let out a long, measured breath.

When I moved the mess of hair from my face, I noticed him, gently flattening and folding my shirt, unlike his own, which he had immediately thrown at a wall in annoyance. Strange, how it had always happened in a different room before, one with smooth wallpaper, and a carpet. We had also been, through some sorcery, proactively undressed, I realised as I fretted over my own socks. Under our feet, the floor claimed a wonderfully jumbled mess. I turned his face up towards me, a fluttery laugh stirring in my stomach.

I would have died today. But that did not matter now. It would tomorrow. But for now, there was no Soulless, no duty, no blood-stained clothes.

Only him.

[Fenrir]
Immediately upon arriving at their building, which turned out to be quite the impressive-looking den, for a force of its meagre size. The woman from earlier, their leader, met me at the top of a short flight of steps. She was the one who, ultimately, chose to keep me alive. They called her "*General*".

"Let's go," she ordered.

She had the same commanding attitude, wordlessly striding a step ahead of me, down a path of stone passages, as came naturally to her. Seeing how she moved, how she held herself, I tried to find something of my master—former master, I reminded myself—in her guise. I wondered how they might appear, standing before each other.

She sent me into her office first, then took up her chair, gesturing to the one across from her desk.

"So…"

She wanted everything from my name—again—to where I came from, who I served, how many of us existed, what my purpose had been. Occasionally, she returned to a previous question, presumably to check that repeated pressure would not somehow pry out an answer I did not have. In fact, through this tedious exercise, I began to see how little I ever actually knew in the first place. At the end of it, my thoughts were so clogged by a series of disconnected pieces of fact that I could not tell whether my actions made more sense, or less.

I noticed, despite the rest of her probing, she never questioned what reason I had for turning, so suddenly and violently, to her side. At least she spared me from that. Perhaps she saw no palpable import in it.

They placed me in a room, basically furnished, with a bed, a set of drawers with a tin lamp on top, and a washroom tucked in a little annex off to the side. It lay in a fairly central position, within sight and earshot of several other occupied rooms, presumably living quarters or offices. Any route out to the terrace required I pass some of those doors, and there were no windows inside. I hadn't failed to notice the locks either. The window had been firmly blocked off, setting the room in darkness. No doubt, General had selected this room carefully, with a strategy in mind. She led me into the room, closed the door and left me. I did not see anyone else that night. The young man—Emery, he said his name was—had disappeared, as hardly surprised me, given the state he ended up in.

He reappeared in the morning (judging from the clock), though it took me a few extra blinks to recognise his image, which now lacked blood, gashes, or hint of any pained, decipherable expression on his face from before. The sight of him induced the memory of a metal edge, cleaving the air by my neck.

He brought with him some words of warning. "I think you've figured out the arrangement. This room is given to you, specifically, for a reason. Here, we can survey you. You can also be trapped. This door will have to be locked from outside, for now, same time every night. And there will, as always, be someone awake at every hour, so I wouldn't try to be clever, if you're that way inclined."

"You suspect me already?" I contested.

"Me? No. No, quite the opposite. I owe you my life. I'm certain she feels the same, too." Emery paused, examining the floor, leaving me to mull over that for a moment, before he spoke again. "Being watched like this, having eyes on you every minute, it can wear on your nerve. But it will pass. Your strength is welcome, friend. Breakfast will be taken on the hour; you might like to join us."

At that, he walked out, leaving the door ajar. I would not go to breakfast. There was no need.

Instead, I used this time to map the rest of my surroundings. I did not bother venturing into any of the rooms to my sides, but preferred to at least learn the stretches of halls and stairways. After making a dash past the exposed dining hall, I found myself outside the closed-off walls of the main building, walking out onto a stone terrace.

I noted the smooth, chequered surface and low wall, this being the place from which I had been received by General Elwin. She had proven an immediate improvement, admittedly. My pair of escorts had spent the entire, torturously slow journey muttering to each other over my head. And they were accompanied by horses, who clearly did not approve of me. The act of the exchange seemed significant, as though, at that moment, I had crossed over a threshold from which there could be no return.

"Fenrir." Emery again; I had been followed.

"Don't hurry, I'm not going anywhere," I assured him.

He stood beside me, only barely outside the door. I continued to look straight ahead.

"I know," he said. "Although, trying to sneak by us like that won't do much to lower suspicions. What were you so fearful of?"

"Fearful? What?"

"Ah, my mistake. Still, you didn't come to breakfast."

"You never suggested it would be compulsory."

"No, you're right, I suppose I didn't. You know, by all means, you need not stop. Most of us just sit down to eat then go."

"Exactly, I don't eat. So why would I attend your meal meetings, when there is no point?" I explained plainly.

There was a short silence, during which his face twisted upwards, either in surprise, or amusement, or both. "Do you plan to continue on in isolation like this?" he asked.

"I suppose so, why?"

"Being honest, I wouldn't recommend it. It always sounds safer, simpler, I suppose, but…I don't know. It's up to you."

"Then, unless that fact somehow changes, you may rest assured I shall fare just fine where I am."

"Maybe. Give it time."

"I don't understand," I admitted, "what you think you're going to gain by talking to me."

He hummed quietly and tossed his head to the side. "What do I *gain*? That is a curious question, if a bit sceptical."

I peered over when I saw him move his hand to his sleeve. As I thought, he pulled out a small-handled knife. He held it loosely, and as he looked down at it, the blade pointing at his own chest. I heard him gasp in air.

"I get that," he said. "I only hope that you can learn to trust—not even me, just someone.

[General]

"You continually refer to her, your progenitor, this "master" you speak of. And yet, you have remembered scant considering that, until now, you have been, as you say, following her will. But you must have her name."

"Morrigan," the Soulless had replied, its face inscrutably even.

"Is that true?"

"I might be lacking in truths, but I do not lie."

I had anticipated something of a haughty smirk on its face as it spoke those words, but there was nothing. It continued to look straight ahead, hands crossed in front of it, as if the irons attached to its wrists still bound them together. In fact, the creature stood so still that the dangling chains did not make so much as a sound. The borrowed clothing it wore hung away from it, obviously too big, the trousers held up by braces over its shoulders, which were swallowed up by a white shirt with rolled sleeves. But I could not escape from how uncannily human this one looked now. There remained no trace of the earlier chaos on its body, save for its left palm blotted with blood, presumably Lieutenant's. First an Altair, now this creature on the other side of my desk. Why? It occurred to me that I must have inherited, from somewhere, a masochistic craving for the inevitable sacks of shit raining down from the mouth of Governance. I blinked and returned to the keys at my fingers.

Morrigan. It felt strange, tapping out the letters, right at the foot of the report. Even having yanked the finished page out of the typewriter, I found myself stuck staring at the name, fixed there in black print. I had naturally expected something more unearthly, but that was not the issue. To steal not only the name of a woman long dead, but *hers*, seemed so fundamentally perverted that it became ironic. Fenrir told me that his kind were being sent for the two with Souls, the ones from the West, plus anyone else who got in their way. I would protect them from it; I owed them that much. And the monster called itself Morrigan. It mutated into a cruel joke, as if the word crawled off of the paper, onto my shoulders, whispering, "I know you, General".

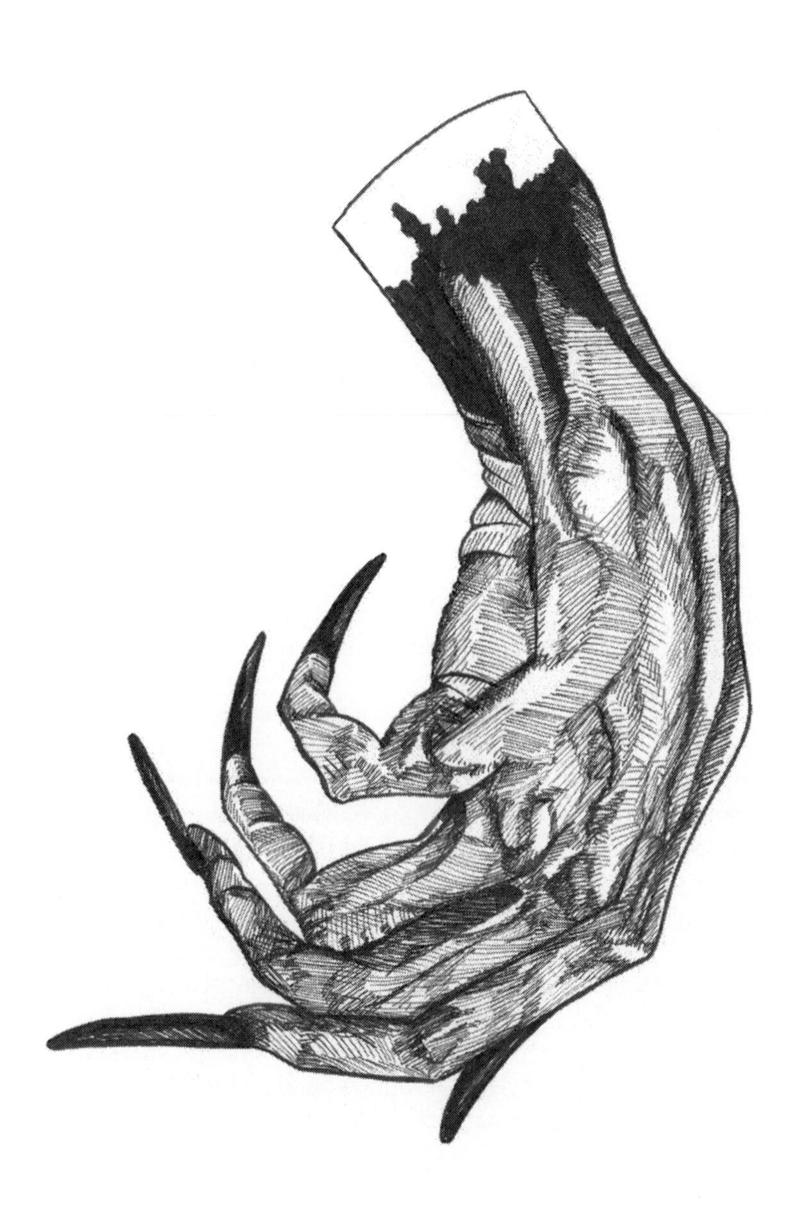

[Eris]

Of all the books in the library, I found one particular set to be much better kept than the rest, albeit this did not signify a terribly significant accomplishment. Each volume from the *Official Archive of Souls* grew dustier with age, forming a sort of hoary gradient along the shelf but, inside and out, the books were well-made, and had been looked after to a certain extent.

Wiping over the covers with a scrap of cotton, I had a sudden, pestering thought I could not resist entertaining. My Soul was Fortitude. I picked out the earliest volume and aimed to flip through to the appropriate section. Following a couple of failed, rather confused attempts, I eventually realised that Fortitude did not exist as far back as the initial records. In fact, it would presently be called a relatively "young" Soul, first mentioned just under half a century ago. I found the page, already folded into a small triangle in the corner.

Scanning the information next to its title, I found a brief description of the Soul's capabilities, followed by a short list of its previous wielders. My predecessors, according to this book, were an infantryman, a schoolteacher and, for a short period, a sheepdog. I wondered what these people, who felt a little closer than mere strangers, would think of me, reading their names off a list like this. How did I compare?

Out of curiosity, I searched through the books for Initiative as well. By contrast, Kai's Soul had pages of names associated with it, stretching back as far as the earliest dates being, most likely, one of the Souls that had surfaced long before records even began. Many of them, I noticed, were soldiers, particularly around the time of the War. I took a breath, rubbing a knuckle against my forehead. Those poor men were made hardly men at all, reduced to nothing but their fire—by this place.

These lists however, while enlightening, were not to be taken as reliable. Each book even included a highlighted notice on the first page warning that, while all information included in these archives remained correct, the record as a whole should be considered inaccurate by omission. Countless Souls were taken in by wild animals, such that each settlement in Esprit had mitigation plans prepared and practised, in the event that one went berserk. Some names were inevitably lost in combat, others to rural communities, probably more still in the midst of the Altair Clan's rumoured enterprises in Soul trafficking. There were countless reasons why a name might end up missing from these huge, heavy tomes, which were thereby, for the most part, unfit for purpose.

As I absentmindedly dusted the shelf, I considered whether our own names would appear here, in this library, or vanish into obscurity. *Eris Rayne, 19 years old: just a librarian, who foolishly wandered into something bigger than she was.*

[Leo]

The low hiss of heavy rain echoed through the halls. Above us loomed the densest cloud in some time, and the whole building turned dimmer and ran colder than usual. I rubbed my palms together. The higher the floor, the worse it seemed to become.

"Up you get, Hughes. It's that time of day again," I called, rapping on the door.

I heard clattering on the other side, before he appeared, silently meeting my eyes. His stance struck me as slightly off, until I caught sight of a shining edge glancing at his side.

"What's that in your hand?" I raised an eyebrow at it. He pulled the sword round in front of him, backing up slightly into the room, unfamiliar and slightly wary of it. But he made no attempt to hide it from me. This was his, and he intended to take it with him.

At a glance, it looked like a double-edged short sword, designed for close combat. It had the characteristic sheen of new, clean steel. I couldn't see much of it, but the glimpse of the hilt I made out from between his fingers looked rather ornate. He flipped the grip around in his hand, feeling around its weight and the shape. Up until this point, I had devoted myself to keeping the kid as far out of the Soulless's reach as he could get. I figured he would manage fine, given his Soul blistered so mightily even from a distance, but watching him now, I felt my efforts soar out of the window. To his credit, he had forged himself a fine blade. He pointed the weapon before him, looking down its edge, at the metal gliding through the empty space. His wrist was too tight, but that only meant a simple fix. I did notice something clearly missing, however.

"I feel you've forgotten a piece. You'll need a proper scabbard for that, you know," I said.

Immediately, he wavered, looking at me, and then at the floor. He deflated, taking the blade out of the air, and burrowing the tip straight down between two floorboards. Standing stock still like that, he appeared far more like the mythical Roman emperor than when he waved his weapon around like a fly swat.

"What's its name?" I asked, "I presume you've come up with one by now."

"I'm calling it Van Helsing."

“It’s a lofty title. The man himself lived a tad, ah, eccentrically, but nonetheless…I’ll see if you stand up to it.”

Turning around to set the weapon down on the desk behind him, he answered, “What’s yours?”

He referred to my own blade, slung faithfully across my back as it was, like a weary friend, or game tied up by its legs. “It’s Castelle,” I said.

“What, you mean you named it after yourself?”

“It’s my family name, yes.” I tugged at the belt, sitting tight against my chest. “One day, this will be in the hands of my boy. That is, so long as one of his little sisters doesn’t snatch it first.”

“You have children?” he exclaimed, though why exactly he looked so surprised I could not tell.

“I sure do; but they’re all still young. This thing is too heavy for them yet.” I clapped a hand against the doorframe. “Let’s go. I want to get out before it stops raining. I suppose I had better teach you how to use that thing too. Bring it along with you.”

Part 3: Fallacy

[Eris]
He suffered strange dreams in the night, I thought. They started not even a week after our journey on the train.

The old walls were thick, and though I gained the impression neither me nor Kai spoke much on either side, I would not hear him anyway, not while our two doors both remained closed. Still, every other night, almost, a blunt slam vibrated through the bricks, followed by a brief, muted yell. The shimmering city beneath us never felt truly silent. Even under the cover of darkness, a low hum would constantly float up to my window from there. But it failed to smother the noise breaking through from the next room.

Traipsing into the dining hall the next morning, always slightly later than everyone else, Kai would drop into a seat, nursing a spot on his foot or across his hand. Tired, purple blemishes emerged out of the corner of each eye.

In the back of my mind, the boy brought around memories of my old tabby cat, Enobarbus, who I had left behind at the library. I entrusted Maud with his care, though, really, it had always been him having to look after me. But he would act like this too. Very often, he fell into deep, quiet slumber, before he would jolt, first an ear, then his feet, until he shook himself awake with dark, round eyes.

In this way, Kai probably drained himself almost entirely, and the following evening he could sleep undisturbed enough that no sound made it through the bricks. It offered a stretch of refuge, in exchange for hours of waiting and frustration that began as soon as the moon reappeared over our heads. But how selfish of me it was, I knew, to keep building this torturous idea around myself.

All that time, I grew more aware—or I had some egotistic suspicion, at least—and I did nothing. I heard his shout, every time, became so accustomed that I could sit on my bed, back leaning against the wall, waiting for it. My weight sank to my legs, and my brain emptied like water streaming down a drain. I would stare at the door, as though the handle might twist itself open if only I wished it hard enough. And it went on, the continuous cycle of anxiety and temporary respite, spun between the two of us, unspoken and so blatantly unacknowledged for so long that it only brought me grief.

Alternatively, I could have been wrong—completely and utterly mistaken. That seemed more likely. Kai Hughes, with his burning eyes and furious Soul, was fine. The bruising meant for me alone, it was punishment, punishment for tending to ideas beyond my station. But still I kept them, held on, or rather I could not stop it from murmuring away, burrowed somewhere deep in my ear.

[General]
I managed to catch Tank before he made it to Eris's quarters. He faltered at the sight of me lurking pre-emptively around the door. It did not take him long, to realise I had come here in search of him.

"What can I do for you, General?" He held his voice low, wary of the block of wood separating us from his new student. It seemed he immediately assumed I had some terrible message to give. Unsurprising, since I usually did.

"Are you taking her out for some exercise?"

"I was about to."

"Don't worry; I just want you to pass this on to her." I held out the sheath before him, and he held it aloft, clutched between his thumb and forefinger. "Leo told me that the boy has practically fashioned his own weapon," I explained. "I don't know what I think to that yet, but I can hardly confiscate it from him, nor can I let her continue to go on with nothing."

"But this is just a little knife." He removed it from its casing, examined it, still dangling it in front of his face. "I'd peel potatoes with this."

"That is precisely my point. It's simple."

From my experience, in terms of a tool, simplicity was never a drawback. Simple was easy. I would have expected the young Hughes to choose a sword, given the option. The artistry of the weapon probably appealed to him more than practicality. Swords—like any sharp edge, really—would be formidable, in time. But they took extra practice to be able to wield anything near effectively. I delegated that responsibility to Leo now, and he would carry it out, but such an approach would not befit Eris. She needed something to pick up, strap to her side, and know it was there.

"And these as well." I passed over a pair of black gloves, tightly folded in my hand.

"On the contrary, these look new and flash. But what for?" he asked.

"I had them made up for her; they're insulated on the inside. They should, with luck, make her feel she has a degree of control over what her Soul's doing, at least. She just has to wear them. Still, I will need you to talk her through using that," I added, referring to the knife.

"Like, this is the handle to hold it with, this is the pointy end. You mean that?"

"Basically. Can you?"

He clicked his tongue. "Sure, I can. Somethin' tiny and old-age like this, she'll probably think it fits her nicely."

"We'll see. She is in your hands, Colonel."

Tank may have been right. I later heard from him that she had named the dagger, as soldiers traditionally did their most prized weaponry. I let out a small chuckle, when he mentioned she'd christened it "*Dorian*".

[Tank]
General hauled us together in the early morning on urgent grounds, with news from the watchmen.

"I've just received notice from the Wall," she announced, "that they've sighted what they believe to be a Soulless, one we've never seen before, in the vicinity of Moore's Hall."

The way she looked across the room, from one head to another, put a grin on my face; it meant we were heading for a fight. Moore's Hall was a massive place, built a few kings before the last one. It endured into a money sink, all decked out in the pricey, pretentious stuff, and well looked-after. Sounded like an ideal battlefield to me.

We took all of the horses with us, so as to arrive with upmost haste, which always seemed to excite the animals. Funnily, they also seemed to delight in tormenting Fenrir, the Soulless appropriately stuck in a trailer, juddering behind General's white stallion. The racket didn't grind so bad on the ears until we got to Moore's Hall, which sat wide, eminent, and ghostly compared to the clattering of hooves and wheels.

Places like this, which tended to attract people like Medi's flower arrangements brought flies, were all closed during dicey periods, as a safeguarding measure. This happened more regularly than a person might think, when we talked about it like that, all official. Folks around here were used to the whole procedure.

But there was nothing here, no people for one, but no noise either, no earth shaking, no hellish creature threatening to tear off limbs. General gave the order to dismount, which Eris made clear she received gladly. It didn't make much sense trying to bring them into the Hall, the only thing here that stuck out.

"The Hall should be closed," Songbird hummed, "only, I don't believe it is. Did the watchmen say anything about it being unlocked for us?"

She pointed towards the face of the towering building. The doors were swung open, leaving a gaping mouth coated in white marble. General's eyes were already there, and she waved for us to follow her. Slowly climbing the front steps, I made out a figure inside, a stout man, with a head of silver hair, seemingly waiting for us in the middle of a series of pillars.

Eris laid a hand on my elbow, speaking in a lowered voice. "Is that Motte in there?"

"Think so, yeah."

She looked back through the door at the silhouette, her face squeezing in troubled thought. I recalled the day I had sent her out onto the Wall, to meet some of the watchmen, the old bloke probably among them. It seemed she felt the same instinct as me. Something about his stance, sloping shoulders, looking down his nose, even from this distance, wasn't quite right.

"Ah, you made it—took you all long enough." His casual tone echoed surreally about the open space. I squinted.

General marched ahead, making her first to see the yellow tint in his gaze. "Soulless; get down!"

As she roared back to us, Motte seemed to evaporate into the air as tiny particles of dust. Like a nasty trick of the light, he vanished. Not just me, though, the others had seen it too. General suddenly jerked to the side, as if she had been hit, barely remaining on her feet. And at the same time, she strode the opposite way, bolt upright. I blinked. And yet there remained two, General, and a perfect copy, except with those gleaming yellow irises and a strange twist to her face.

Fenrir barged by me, yelling, "Don't lose sight of them; their power allows them to take your bodies. You will be helpless."

"What the hell?" Leo managed, before he too was silenced by the Soulless, leaping into his shape.

It shifted again, from Leo to Lieutenant (letting out a vile cackle in his voice) then to Songbird, always lingering for a mere moment before moving on. For a few seconds, it got to me, and I went totally blind. Most freakish thing I ever felt, like a big limb booted me out of my own body. I came back quickly, though; for whatever reason, the thing clearly didn't fancy me much either. Then, as my vision refocused, a deep, grating laugh sounded up to the ceiling, cutting over the noise of stumbling feet. Looking up, I saw the kid, Hughes, walking away from his body, which squirmed for a while, attempting to take a step, before he crumbled into a heap, face-down on the marble. The imposter shot a smug look at the rest of us, showing off the pilfered sword in his grasp, and wriggling his fingers at his side.

He spoke in a voice that, while definitely belonging to Hughes, sounded distinctly off-key, as Motte's had before him.

"I knew I could find one. I suppose it is only polite to warn you all: there is no hope for you. Struggle as you will, you do insist so desperately, it means nothing to one so abjectly…undone. You are the ones coming for my master, correct? She wants me to kill you." He brandished the blade at our own pet Soulless. "Still, I think I will begin with the deserter."

Lieutenant leaped back, anticipating the resulting eruption as Fenrir and Kai's double lunged for each other. A mutual hatred of Fenrir might have been the one thing this fraud truly had in common with the real kid. Out of the flames emerged the huge, black mutt, unscathed. It landed on two feet, immediately shedding its skin, like melting tar, back to the man underneath. Lieutenant had given us the truth. I had witnessed the transformation with my own eyes for the first time—freakish as I had pictured it being, with flaps of cotton shirt poking pathetically out of a wiry, four-legged chrysalis, as if it could be peeled.

In the spare moment, General, Leo, Songbird and Lieutenant all started away in a scattered formation, endeavouring to get closer, absolutely, but more focused on avoiding the inferno, which the Soulless controlled with impossible efficacy. General briefly signalled me to stick to my position, or at least as well as I could manage. Medi stayed put, within arm's reach, her head flicking around, trying to keep track of all the bodies. She would have been more aware of one empty shell in particular, face down, twitching on the floor. I spun to my right, intending to direct Eris, only to find she had disappeared from my side. I could already guess where to.

"Sparks, wait!" I bellowed after her.

I caught a glimpse of her through the thickening smog, escaping to the boy's side. I tagged Medi's shoulder and made to sprint, never forgetting the imminent threat of the Soulless, which was having a field day with the full extent of Hughes's power. An explosion stalled me on my path, the heat biting at the metal tips of my shoes. The light seemed to bounce from every polished surface, straight into your watery eyes. I almost didn't dare glance up but, finding some scrap of faith, I looked to see the girl kneeling on the ground, her whole arm curled around herself, raised against the red flood.

She watched the Soulless dancing around but showed no inclination to move. By the time I finally caught up, I noticed another glow in the corner of my vision.

"Down!" I dived into her, one hand shoving her back, the other covering my head with a plate of metal. The boy wouldn't stir. I squeezed my eyes shut.

[Medi]

As soon as the clamour ceased, I raised my head from the floor. The grazes on my legs were already healed off, thankfully; I needed my Soul to be ready. I saw our Fenrir, standing like a cast figurine, amongst a slowly rising cloud of smoke. I could account for the others too, all milling around, dazed and coughing, apart from Tank, who had only now collected himself, and was lifting young Eris off of the dusty floor. The culprit had gone, permanently this time, and I found myself at last able dash over to them.

Kai still lay unconscious on his front. I turned him over carefully, helped by Tank's hands. His chest rose and fell as normal, and though his pulse yet seemed a little slow, I bore him in a far better state than I had feared.

"He's not twitchin' anymore, at least," my partner muttered, shuddering, before he turned to Eris. "How the hell did you get over here?"

"I've been told my footsteps are quiet," she said, still looking at the boy. "Thank you, I'm sorry."

"Now, brave girl, I'll have none of that. I just need to take a quick look at you, make sure we've got you all in one piece, okay?" Our voices crackled with the polluted air. I checked over her arms, before I took her chin, tilting her face toward me. "Okay, honey," I said plainly, still pinching her face in one hand, and bringing out my Soul in the other, "I'm going to need you to stay as still as you can. Look at Tank's nose, and nowhere else. It helps, trust me."

[Kai]
Everything ached. I tried to crack open my eyelids; they were heavy, and sticky, normally indicative of a bad night's sleep. White light poured in on my right side and warmed my cheek. My head swelled with it. Instinctively, I brought my hand up to brush at my face, triggering a dull pain where a bruise must have been. I thought I remembered hitting the ground.

That Soulless, I hardly had enough time to expect anything, as to the sensation of it leaping into my skin, but most noticeably, I had been about to vomit. The jabbing had spread upwards from the bottom of my stomach, before each of my senses shut down, blinked out one by one: first I couldn't hear, next I couldn't see, and then I fell.

Creepy bastard.

I assumed it had left me now, given that I was laid out, not on concrete, but a mattress, with a crisp white sheet tickling at my fingers and toes. And I could certainly feel again. Feeling was just unpleasant.

As my vision began to clear, my thoughts wanted to wander. I had no comprehension of what had happened. Did it get my Soul's power too?

What had I done?

At this stage, I noticed a figure shifting at my side. Straining my neck, I could see who had been watching over me, but I didn't much fancy a discussion. There hovered Eris, leaning over from a chair, knotting her hair between her fingers.

"You…" I started, though my voice came out more like a strangled croak.

"Hey, you're awake," she murmured.

"What are you doing here?"

"Waiting for you. Well, it hasn't only been me; we have all taken our turn, waiting here, in shifts. You apparently have terrible luck, that's all. You've been sleeping for at least a day. A few times already, we've thought you were stirring, but no, nothing."

She idly dropped her hand into her lap. I couldn't tell if she had meant to unveil the half of her face hidden behind it. Almost immediately, the walls spun around my head, either because I had sat forward, or because doing so let me see better—to clarify the glimpse I first caught. My head wanted me to screw my eyes shut, but another part of me could not stand to look away from the girl's left cheek.

Her skin bubbled up, like tightly crumpled paper, bloodshot pink in places, and speckled white in others. The damage spread from her temple, where hairs were left split and blackened, down to the corner of her mouth, just touching her top lip. The scarring had already healed to a miraculous degree, somehow. But still, I knew what a burn looked like.

She saw me wince and made a pained attempt at a smile.

"What happened?" I said.

"We call it Geist. The Soulless—it took your body. I mean, it tried the same with most of us, but you…I would have believed the thing literally stole your life out of you, the way you fell down. It wanted your Soul, I suppose. It could fling your fire around however it pleased, almost. Then it seemed to turn on you. Maybe you tried to fight back, no-one could be sure, and you probably can't remember. Maybe it wanted to prevent you ever waking up. Whatever you are, it would have turned you to ashes for it."

I noticed she had left out a crucial detail—perhaps the most important.

"Then why didn't it?"

She clenched her hands together and spoke slowly. "Fenrir went for Geist, while my Soul shielded you from the flames. Tank was there with you, too."

Suddenly, her wrecked face made complete sense. I could certainly picture it: this martyr running straight into a blaze, pushing her Soul until it snapped. The old soldier probably saved her from worse.

"Why would you do that?"

"What are you talking about?"

"What is wrong with you? Are you insane?" I said. I could hear my voice growing louder. "Look at yourself! What, were you fucking trying to get yourself killed?"

I came to an abrupt stop, just in time to see her countenance drop. Her eyes were wide enough that the dark stains around them almost disappeared. She wrapped her arms around herself, probably to stop herself shaking. Not knowing better, I would have assumed that I pulled a knife out from under the covers. She looked at me straight in the face, only fleetingly, after which she averted her gaze entirely.

Raising herself from her seat, she spoke in a monotonous voice: "I have to go and tell someone you're awake. Excuse me."

My throat constricted, trying to call out something, but the words refused to come.

[???]

I took a long look around. Sure enough, I rose only a short walk away from waltzing right into the military rat nest. I thought of Fenrir hiding, clueless inside there, and smiled. It felt odd, on this face.

Her limp body lay on the pavement, one hand touching my foot by the convulsing fingertips. Save for one arm twisted behind her back, she had fallen rather prettily. I was impressed. Foolish girl, standing out here like a placard, no purpose to her, just staring at a wall across the street. Even with her Soul, this body handled as miserably as the other boy's, if not more so. I could not get much done without one, but this whole business had begun to shed its appeal very quickly. I felt heavy, for a human of her diminutive size. I crouched down at her side, to grasp a better picture of her.

"Oh dear, Sunshine," I sighed, "whatever has this life done to you, hm?"

Before I made off, I caught sight of a metallic glint at her waist. Something shiny with a sharp edge, I guessed. Yes, out of a little leather casing, I pulled a humble dagger. She certainly did not get to keep it. I shoved it into the empty pouch at my side and headed for the stairway.

I would be the one to bring their end. If Fenrir and Wyvern combined could not manage something so basic, I would simply have to do it. And with one of their own serving as my weapon no less, this would be really quite poetic. This girl liked poems—though a good, long novel was better.

The stairway before filled me with a sense of glory; as I absorbed the sensation of those first steps, I became a lord, no, a hand, ascending out of the underworld. I had made it, me, myself. The handle of the door before me seemed to glow, a happy, innocent sphere. I felt an arm rising towards it, floating in giddy anticipation.

Before I could stretch out to touch their deaths, I heard, to my disillusionment and great chagrin, thunderous footsteps approaching from inside. I groaned. Whoever was coming had broken into a sprint. A slam, and the gates swung wide. The broad-shouldered man with thick armour and a bump in his nose appeared at the summit, the dark hole cowering behind him, teasing. With an inspiring fury plastered over his face, the soldier leaped down several steps at a time, driving a plated fist toward my face. I waited for it, arms hanging at my sides, waited for her Soul to strike him. Stunning white light fractured the space between us, the force of it impeding the collision, and causing him to ricochet. This girl's Soul manipulated lightning as armour. I stifled a laugh, as I understood then how she had been able to protect the boy from his own fire—by countering it with power from the sky.

Evidently, the soldier expected such a reaction, since not a grunt of pain escaped his lips. He knew her strength, and he saw no miracle in it. Instead he dealt his blow at such a trajectory that sent those foreign feet stumbling downward. He stalked after me, suddenly taking each step agonisingly slow, his thorny cheek twitching occasionally. This proved irksome, but of no concern. I simply had to surprise him. Drawing the dagger and charging at him with it, pointed end first, I aimed for the exposed skin at his neck. He blocked the pathetic little blade without trouble but, amusingly, lacked any sort of response, simply leading me in laps, deflecting every swing, but equally incapable of laying a hand on me. I thought I might instead capture him in my crackling white snare, grabbing his huge arm in my fingers, but this failed, again and again, no matter how many times I tried it. Fury lapped into my spongy limbs, every fibre tightening its grip. This Soul was faulty. He seemed to recognise the problem, giving an ungainly sneer, which served only to motivate me further, when I heard a sharp snap behind my ear.

The Soul had reacted to a second foe at my back. I wheeled around, correcting my gloved fingers around the handle of the dagger.

"Ah, I see."

[Emery]

"I recognise you, too," Geist continued, as it shrugged off both of my knives. "You were fascinating to live inside, if only for a moment. Maybe I should have tried to kill them with your learned hands instead. You are very good at it."

This replica of Eris looked wrong, adopting such a languorous stride, showing so many teeth, and with that spite on her tongue. Tank would have known her to be false, before he ever saw her eyes.

"You took your sweet time," he barked, as the Soulless made a stab at me. For all of its fearsome proficiency manipulating a Soul, its attempt with a blade left me almost disappointed. I used the opportunity to retrieve my weapons.

"I can always go and leave you to it, if you're enjoying yourself too much."

"Whatever. I can't touch her—I mean, it. It's too quick, and it bloody hurts to try. At least you've got those to chuck. What do you say we keep hounding it until it wears itself out of a Soul?" he added, while using his elbow to shove it back in my direction.

"That's all well, just as long as we don't flag first, right?"

"Good thing they're shittier at this than we are," he laughed.

I threw another knife, keeping one in my hand this time. It bounced away, like I had aimed for a brick, spinning through the air, and landing a few feet away with an irritating clatter. Though, no more so than the snigger that came from the Soulless's mouth with our every misstep.

We leaped around in circles, with our only goal being to stop them from advancing any further—all that we could possibly manage. Occasionally, Geist would alter its footing abruptly, making a break for an opening. I saw that, by their logic, there was no point in jumping into either Tank's body or mine; we were far too easy to put down. Right now, they were in the ideal position, and were not prepared to lose it. Eventually, they gave up on the stairs, instead seeking the left branch of the building. Anticipating this, Tank reached to trip them up.

"Wait!" I yelled.

Tank halted, letting Geist pass. Interestingly, the Soulless shambled to a stop as well, examining us in suspicion. I glanced to the fourth floor; something had moved up there. Geist noticed me, following my gaze. I immediately recognised the figure at the window.

"Get back, Tank!"

We both spun on our heels and dived the opposite way, my cheek almost smacking the pavement as a sheet of hot air poured over our backs. In the seconds before I could recover, I made out the distinct rustle and pop of burning, drowned out beneath a cackle that I barely recognised as Eris's voice. A sick smell drifted up my nose and I chose to cough, rather than gag.

I swung up onto my toes. Tank squatted next to me, and we both watched the thick smoke rolling away from us. Up at the window, the panes swung open, and Kai dangled out of it, both arms limply hanging down. I squinted, for through the mess of dark hair, his eyes appeared to glow, like white orbs shining out of his head.

"Made sure he got it good an' proper, didn't he?" Tank croaked, covering his nose and mouth.

I nodded, pointing him to where I looked.

"Ooh-err…" He squinted. "Is he alright, you think? I can't see."

"He's moving, at least," I said.

Tank lurched, whirling around on the spot. "Where's Sparks?"

He rose to his feet, spotting her sat up by a kerb. She looked about herself as frantically as her sapped energy would allow, feeling the sheath strapped at her side, and clearly relieved to see Tank jogging to offer up his arm. Taking a moment to seek out the spot where the Soulless had been incinerated, I uncovered Eris's simple dagger, looking sorry among the dust. I picked it up with my jacket sleeve. The blade was distorted out of shape, and the handle had all but melted away.

As they approached, Eris preferring to shuffle slowly onward by herself than to use Tank as a prop, I called out to them, waving the weapon in front of me: "She is going to need a new one of these."

She glanced, wide-eyed, from it, to me, to Tank. I had forgotten myself briefly, and the fact that Eris had been unaware throughout the whole ordeal. She did, however, observe the silhouette of General, emerging from the towering front doors, which I had found, tellingly, left rocking open earlier. Tank and I saluted her.

"The Soulless is eliminated?" she enquired, coolly.

“The best man to ask would be Hughes, ma’am,” I answered.

“I plan to get an answer from him as soon as Medi has properly seen to him. For now, I ask for your conclusion. Is it destroyed?”

I suddenly recalled the sounds I had heard, and the smell.

“Yes, it is.” I presented the mangled blade from behind my back.

“Pretty sure of it myself, ma’am,” Tank added, with a grimace.

“I would bet you are glad now that I put the two of you on a daytime shift. Relying entirely on the watchmen is not so expedient anymore, it seems. Either of you injured?”

“Nothin’ major that I’m aware of.” Tank shrugged and adjusted the armour plate on his arm. I simply shook my head.

She nodded once, and looked down to Eris, who silently swayed back and forth on the balls of her feet, looking past me, up at the window.

“I’d like a written report from both of you, by tonight. For now, Tank, make sure Miss Rayne gets to her room.”

He took Eris by the elbow, leading her up the stairs, steadily. General lagged behind, waiting for me.

“Can I take that?” she said, referring to the object pinched in my sleeve.

[Leo]

I was not mistaken; I could not possibly mishear that sound, one heard it so often in this place, with the heavy old wooden doors—just never on this, specific one.

I stopped walking, glancing over my shoulder at the broad oaken gates, flaking in places, but otherwise showing no signs of frailty. They stood out as the largest, most conspicuous entryway in the whole building, and asserted themselves as such by blocking out all nearby light, creating a section of dimness which sliced the corridor in half. No-one entered through this door.

I heard the sound again, clearer this time: the grating noise of tapping upon wood. The rhythm was odd, uneven, like when a kid tries making up a little song or secret code they can play with a stick and a tin can. But the lucidity of their musical ear did not concern me.

Rather, who the hell, in their right mind, waltzes up to a military headquarters to knock on the biggest door they can find?

I took the loop of the handle in one hand and wrenched it round. The door took an extra shove from my other hand to open it beyond a slither. Fierce brightness flooded in, racing to fill the void, and forcing me to squint.

"Aha, hello Leo!"

Whoever this was, he had an innately low voice, but tuned in an innocently mischievous tone. The blurred blotch soon sharpened into a young man, with dark eyes to match his mop of hair, and a grin across his face that appeared to mock the stupidity of this situation. He was tall enough for us to stand almost eye-to-eye, had he not been already leaning halfway over the threshold like an expectant puppy.

I had to ask.

"What is your business here?"

"You don't recognise me, then?" He took off his cap and threw his head back to look me up and down, as if to check he had not mistaken me for someone else. "My name is Benjamin Hughes, and I'm here to see my brother."

Ah, so the other engineer kid. That at least explained why his image had immediately tugged on the back of my mind—though it said little by way of his intention for appearing here, now.

"Right, my apologies. Still, I suppose you wouldn't mind telling me exactly how you were informed to bring yourself, and at this specific time. No-one has been advised to expect your arrival."

"Oh? General Elwin contacted me about recent events herself, albeit indirectly, perhaps. If you could point me to whereabouts I might find her that would be capital."

He had already crept past me into the corridor, peering around in all directions, suggesting he might find the way himself, if I refused to help him. This one could not easily be swayed either, I could tell. His comeback surprised me somewhat, to the point of serious scepticism, and I had to remind myself of the possibility that he was telling the truth.

"Fine," I started slowly, "but know that if you try anything, kid…"

"What?" he blurted out, with a wide stare.

"It doesn't matter. We'll head this way first; you've got a few stairs to climb."

He quickly fell into step at my left side, staying obediently silent for most of the walk.

"That *was* the front door, right?" he asked at one point, looking over his shoulder.

"I suppose so," I answered, with a sigh.

Another knock, on this occasion it was my own, on General's door. At the ring of her voice, I opened it, and had not yet stepped fully inside before she raised herself out of her chair. She wore an earnest smile, one I had not seen for a long time.

"Welcome to the mother ship, Master Hughes."

I noticed the boy's presence in the doorway, just his head, protruding from behind mine. General gestured for him to enter and, having now verified his story, I let him pass.

"You arrived even more promptly than I imagined you would. I trust your journey passed safely."

"I did as well as I could, ma'am. I had no qualms; I've acquired quite a taste for the city these past years, apparently, so I am enjoying the setting at least. Silver linings, I guess."

"I wish that I could have invited you here under better circumstances, such that searching for them was not necessary. I see Leo found you—I must apologise for not forewarning you in time,

Brigadier." She regarded me briefly, before turning back to Benjamin. "I imagine you're hoping to see your brother now."

"If that's possible, General, you imagine correctly." He nodded hastily, hands crossed behind his back and head dipped, even under her sympathetic gaze. His knotted brow left obvious creases across his face.

"Certainly—I'll show the way myself, and let my man back on his original path, if you'll excuse us, Leo."

We exchanged a quick gesture, and I went to offer an acknowledging nod to the kid, only to be met with an extended palm.

"Thank you kindly, sir. I'd give you a salute too, but I'm no military man, so…" He shrugged. I shook his hand, and let General take him where he needed to be.

[Kai]

Eris appeared in my prison of a room only a day after the attack. Having witnessed Tank pluck her off of the ground, I duly speculated how it could be possible. She crept in silently and leaned her back against a wall, facing away from me. My stomach seemed to shudder with a sudden onset of sickness.

"You're here?" I mumbled.

"I certainly didn't go anywhere. I'm here, and the most rested I have felt in a while." Her mouth jerked at the corner, in what might have been a smile, with a bit more effort. "I saw you there, in the window, when I came around. Tank told me that it was you, who got the Soulless in the end, said your eyes lit up and it looked creepy as shit—his words, not mine."

"Yeah, I did. It's just like the dog, to miss."

"This wasn't Fenrir's fault," she interjected. It irked me, how she felt compelled to defend our enemy.

"No, I guess not. That thing is gone now, anyway—I know, I saw. I watched it catch alight."

"Ouch," she said, with an amused ring. She tried to make light of the reality, but it still stung a little.

"It was strange. I might have been looking at you, but not quite, like I became the Soulless, all over again, only this time I remember what I did."

"It's not your fault either. Though it is ironic, isn't it? I'm sorry."

Feeling suddenly restless, I hung my feet over the side of the mattress, facing out of the window. "I have to say something to you, before you go running off, getting yourself possessed again."

She laughed under her breath which, I guessed, established her permission to continue.

"I shouldn't have yelled. I don't know what I said that made you so—I don't know. But it was wrong, and I didn't mean any of it. You're not insane, not even close."

"Well, I wandered straight into the path of a Soulless—I would say that makes me at least slightly nuts. But I didn't come here to die—only to do what I can. I knew you didn't mean to hurt me; I could see that in your face when I looked at you, which is just all the more reason why I shouldn't have acted the way I did."

"See, amongst all of your talk about whose fault this *isn't*, you don't ever leave any room for yourself."

She hummed, and folded her arms, but didn't say anything either way. I hated this feeling, this weight pressing down through my whole body, worse than ordinary pain. Guilt. Ah, that heavy realisation that there is always someone else, having just as horrific a time as you. In the silence, a sound at the door gave us both a jolt. The rigid tone of General Elwin's voice could be made out from the other side.

"Oh, maybe she wants to speak with you," Eris exclaimed, scuttling to open the door. I heard their muted exchange before she hurried down the stairs.

"Sorry, ma'am, I'm just leaving."

"That's quite alright, Miss Rayne. Perhaps you should head to get some rest?"

"Yes, of course. I'll be off now."

A conversation with General certainly sounded easier than the one I had attempted to start. But I did not see her enter, when I turned around. Instead, she followed behind a more familiar face. I scrambled to get up and across the room.

"Ben!" I cried, as I hobbled into his expectant arms. He smelled of home.

I felt him breathe out as he said, "It's good to see you, Kai."

"What are you doing here?"

"Dad and I heard from General Elwin. We know what happened."

I let him go, sinking onto the end of the bed. Ben took the wooden chair and slouched on it, fiddling with that stupid tuft of hair tied at the back of his head.

"You need to get that cut, before I do it myself."

"No way, I like it." He grinned. "You look better than I thought you would."

"How did you expect to find me, in two pieces?"

"Probably," General piped up, a reprimanding look about her face. "Come and see me again when you're ready, Benjamin, and I'll arrange a room for you." She left without waiting for a reply.

"I might have been out of here already," I added, "if the Soulless hadn't come back for another go."

"What?"

"The first time, when it took my body, it wasn't dead. Somehow, it made its way here, and it found Eris. It took her body, like it did mine. I was stuck up here when I saw it out of that window—a couple of the others were already trying to keep it out, but they couldn't do much between them. My Soul was pissed, is the best way I can put it. You sort of *feel* it." I placed a hand over my chest. "I just unlocked the window and opened fire, I suppose. My eyes glow, apparently; no idea what that means."

"You're pretty fierce, aren't you Kai? Who's Eris?"

"Eris Rayne, that girl you just saw leaving."

"Oh!" That perked him up a bit.

"She was there, during the attack. She's the other one, with a Soul, I mean. I'm surprised you don't know her; she's from the library."

"And what does she do? Levitate? Breathe underwater?"

"Hers makes shields. And I would keep her as far from underwater as you can get her. She is the one who protected me, while Geist—we call it—marched around having a fit with my Soul. That thing wanted me dead. She kept me alive. You…can tell, if you see her. She stopped here, waiting for me to wake up, and you know what I did? I shrieked at her. She looked horrible, like she was terrified of me."

Ben tilted his head, with that knowing smirk creeping onto his face. He blinked heavily and leaned an elbow on the back of the chair. "I'd reason that you shouted, because the one who's so scared of her wanting to protect you, is yourself. She sounds tough; think, she literally stood between the real Kai, and some ugly creature wearing your face. Somehow, I feel the last thing she's terrified of is you. Maybe, what you did was make her question her own judgement."

"You're starting to sound like Dad."

"I do try my best."

"How is he?"

"He's about as okay with this as he was the day you left."

"Shit…"

"Not what you want to hear, I know. Although, there is a sort of acceptance to him now, when we talk about you. He understands. He hates it, but he understands. That's what I think."

I looked to the window again, hands gripping at my knees until my fingers were white and aching.

"Any idea where I could find Eris?" he probed, fidgeting in his seat.

"Down one floor—try the third door on your left," I said, calculating the position of the room next to mine. I didn't badger him for his motivation. "If not, try the library, next floor down from that one."

"Sure, I suppose that makes sense. I'll be back soon." He swung the door behind him, but didn't bother closing it, perhaps to assure me of that last fact. I lay back on the bed, listening to his feet pattering down stone steps.

[Benjamin]
Kai guessed right, thankfully (I did not fancy navigating this minor labyrinth alone just yet). After a second tap on the old wooden door, it opened before a girl, who looked a tad too small for it. Sure enough, the young lady from earlier, only now I could see her from the front.

I noted first, as she peered up at me, her sleepy, grey eyes, which looked particularly stark next to the freckles which peppered her pale skin. I saw the scar afterwards. Medi had done an impressive job with her Soul in repairing the burn, doubtless, but the sight left my heart swollen anyway.

"You can tell," Kai had told me.

"You're Eris, right?"

"Yes, I am." Her voice emerged solid, if restrained. "You were in the corridor just now. Do I know you?"

I knocked the door out of her hands, when I bundled my arms around her shoulders, my chin resting on the top of her head. A shock needled my skin from almost every angle. "I'm Benjamin Hughes. Thank you for saving my brother's life."

As soon as I let her go, the pain ceased. She reminded me of that one time I had tried to touch a hedgehog, simply to see what would happen. Eris was perfectly still, her gloved hands folded over her chest. She clenched them into guilty fists when she saw the slight wince left on my face. I tried grinning instead.

"Got it—no hugs. Made you jump, didn't I?"

With a merciful sigh, she lifted her features a tiny bit, in the soothing sort of melancholy way that at once made me her ally. "You certainly did. It's alright, I don't mind. I am so sorry for hurting you. My Soul's an impolite arse." She gave a pointed frown, as though reprimanding her mindless protector.

"It's serving you well, that's all. Besides, it doesn't bother me. Measly flea bites, I tell you."

"Really?" she said, her brow raised. "Well, that won't do."

I took another step back.

"What are the gloves for, can I ask, anything in particular?" I had noticed them again as she adjusted them in front of me.

"These? I had them given to me, with my dagger." A certain, particularly glaring noun mingled in there. She realised it too, and so hurried along with her explanation. “They are lined with a sort of rubber, I think. It’s there to stop my Soul’s power, so I don’t go ahead unwittingly electrocuting everything I touch. I have shoes similar, for rainy days. They squeak a little, but I like them.”

“I get the drift—pretty good idea.”

“Souls like this one force some inventiveness, in people cleverer than myself.”

“Yeah, and they keep guys like my brother and I in a job. We enjoy the challenge.”

“Oh, I see.”

I offered her an open hand instead, which she took and grasped lightly.

“I should let you rest, like General Elwin said. Nice meeting you, Eris; I hope you’re well. He does too, you know.”

“I know,” she said, nodding at her feet. “Thank you, though. You are very kind.”

Considering it high time to leave her alone, I headed back for Kai. Eris saw me to the stairs, before I heard the door handle flick closed. I looked over my shoulder, to see nothing but the corridor, perfectly full of silence.

I liked to believe that they were friends. That way something good would have come from all of this.

[Leo]

I struggled to recall how exactly General had landed upon this topic. I had originally set out to report that my shift had concluded, and Benjamin was settled in his designated quarters. Now I leaned with my back against a stack of shelves, a sharp edge of wood nestled uneasily between my shoulder blades, far prolonged. I knew Aria had always danced at the edges of her mind, following her in her every decision. The difference lay in a further two, who now occupied that same space.

"I understand, General, but remember that they made their choice, and it remains so. You tried to discourage them. As it stands, jurisdiction dictates that there is nothing you can do to force them either way now. It comes down to the word of Governance."

"I know how it works. But they're children, Leo, who I'm leading into the bonfire. I never wanted to do this again. They're not soldiers. They're just *children.*" Her face sank into her hands and did not rise again.

[Eris]

Kai must have been discharged during my shift in the library. On my return, I immediately noticed his door hanging open, and then him inside, behind his desk, his face made clear by the lamp he leaned over. We kept to ourselves, in rooms separated by stone walls so substantial that we could well have been on opposite sides of the building. And yet I felt comforted for the return of the uncongenial company. I paused, and propped myself against the doorframe, but did not enter.

"Kai," I called. My voice came out feebler than intended, though I had failed to muster anything stronger all day. It happened, from time to time.

He flinched, with an irritated sound. "Could you not do that? You're like a ghost, creeping up all silent. Wear those squeaky rubber soles you've got. Cough, or something."

"Sorry. I'm guessing they let you out."

"They did, out of that room, anyway. Now I'm stuck in this one instead, until tomorrow," he said, straightening himself, arms folded.

"It is a change of scenery at least."

He scoffed, "Hardly."

"Fair point," I noted, with half a laugh, half a yawn. "It's better, to see you well."

He looked to me, with a dubious glance, and nodded. As I dragged my heels away from the doorway, he interrupted me.

"Hey. You okay?"

"Not really, no. I suppose my brain decided I should feel especially crap today." I shrugged and pinched the bridge of my nose between my fingers. "But I will be; I always am, given a bit of time."

His eyes, made darker by his scowl, flicked over my face several times. "Wait," he said, though I hadn't gone anywhere yet.

"What is it?"

He hesitated. "The way you talk… What's it like? I just mean—being inside your head every day. Especially here, with all of the Soulless shit, you brush *this* off now like it's perfectly normal," he said, gesturing vaguely at me.

I heard the wooden legs of his chair scrape across the floor as Kai lifted himself to his feet. He moved slowly, pensively. He seemed to take so long just to step around the desk and perch on the closer edge.

What was it like? It was still difficult to say. That, in itself, constituted a large part: that intangibility. Like being stuffed in a little room filling with smog that you want to grab in a fist and pin to the ground if only to stop it from choking you. But you cannot do that, because that's not how it works. It was like sinking into a pitch-black lake with rocks strapped to your legs. You can swim for it, maybe, flail and kick as much as you want, but where the hell are you going?

It was coloured grey—cold, empty, inconspicuous, most of the time. I thought that remained important, somehow. The way the frustration and the sadness and the strange bursts of ecstasy that made no sense at all conjoined into one numbing punch in the gut that felt just so—

"Tiring."

"Oh." He blinked tentatively, and quickly became very interested in the appearance of his own feet.

I felt like I had something else to say to him, something more sufficient than that. I paused, trying to grasp a sense of it out of the silent empty space in front of me, before continuing carefully, deliberately, almost like stepping over creaking floorboards in the dead of night.

"I'm fine." Kai's nose scrunched slightly. I noticed but carried on anyway. "I used to be much worse than I am now, standing here. I didn't even bother getting up some mornings, but I couldn't sleep either. I wouldn't eat unless someone told me to, and then I could mostly only stick rubbish. Maud was very good; she knew my conscience could not turn down a favour, so she cooked for me, or handed me the instructions. Even then, I only ever felt either dead, or terrified, or a gross mixture of both. And trying to get me to talk was tough work. I must have been insufferable; I can hardly begin to imagine." A dry chuckle rattled in the back of my throat. "But how do you fight against it, when you alone *are* the enemy? I spent too long wallowing within myself, I think. I couldn't see anything else beyond me, or maybe I saw too much; I'm not sure, actually. Then one day, I just sort of…came to. Realised that it was about time I stood up off my backside and starting walking on my own two feet, since only then could things ever get any easier. And then I fell over, arse over tit, one might say. So, I had to try again, until I could keep it up, the walking. At least, I hope that is what I'm doing. You get on. You persist, because really, there is no choice. I tell myself that a lot. It helps. After a while, I got used to it. You say 'normal'. Well, it is. It *is* normal, just part of the daily routine by now."

I stopped there, and hummed quietly to myself, satisfied with that. Kai still glowered intently at a spot on the floor, but his head tilted in my direction, brow stitched together in concentration. Only once the quiet had stagnated for a while, he glanced back at me. He took in a sharp breath, and immediately let it go in a ponderous sigh. I watched the line of his shoulders gently fall.

"Okay," he mouthed.

"I'm rambling out nonsense, aren't I? I always do this, I should just—"

"No!" He almost yelled, before I could finish which, it seemed, did not only surprise me. Kai's eyes burst open, and his closed fist tightened around the hem of his shirt sleeve, before it relaxed again. "I don't care. Why did you not even mention it before?"

"Have I not? You didn't ask. I am sorry; I never thought to. I'm so sorry."

"Don't."

He sighed for the second time; he begun to sound like me, which couldn't possibly be a good thing.

"Are you feeling alright?" I did not realise how ironic it sounded out of my mouth, until I had stumbled through the whole sentence. Guessing from the pointed look in his eyes, he noticed it too.

"Yeah, sure." His tone seemed sceptical. He rested his weight on his hands, and my eyes followed him as he spun himself back around the table. Suddenly, his voice lowered to a mumble that pulsed through my skull. "But, uh, cheers anyway; most people don't bother asking." A wry smile, but genuine.

"You don't want to spill melodrama at my face too, then? You know, just while we're here." My breath immediately caught in my throat. I should not have said that.

Expecting a bitter huff of breath and the usual icy glare to return to Kai's face, the laughter I heard instead sounded foreign in my ears. It did not last much, but it was a hearty sound, and it echoed from wall to wall like a drum. It spread a kind of warmth that reminded me of glowing coals, which seemed appropriate for him.

"Nah, I'll pass. Maybe another time," he said.

My chest deflated with relief, but the silence that followed did not quite settle comfortably; something still hung there that neither of us was willing to touch. I darted my view around the room, desperately searching for a change of subject, but found nothing. Thankfully, I saw Kai's attention divert to the doorway, at the sound of rapid footsteps in the corridor. He started fidgeting on the spot, anxious to find a way out of the room.

"That was Ben," he said hurriedly. "He is either lost or eavesdropping; either way, I should go after him."

Somehow, I doubted the latter of his older brother, but felt we were both simply glad for the break in the stalemate.

"Yes, of course, hurry, go."

[Kai]

As soon as I was finally deemed fit to return to my own devices, Ben wanted a personal tour of the entire military base. I had left him slightly disappointed, when I informed him I did not have permission to venture down to the underground floor. But this hardly deterred him, and he persevered nonetheless. Even when I asked him to give me a few minutes to organise myself, he then tried wandering off on his own, silently goading me to chase after him.

I found him milling around the stairway to the third floor. I figured he had seen enough of upstairs, since all of the rooms were close enough to identical, and discovered he had already stumbled upon the roof, apparently by accident. We therefore headed down, past the living quarters, an office or two, then the library, General Elwin's office, more bedrooms, the conference room, dining hall—all of which proved difficult, while he remained possessed by a desire to poke his head inside every single door, including the storage cupboards.

We reached as far as the front terrace before I ultimately gave up. I stepped out first and, seeing Fenrir posed in the corner, looking out at some undefined thing across the street and pretending not to notice us, I turned straight back around the way I came. However, Ben, who had skipped out behind me, now tapped on my shoulder, pointing.

"Who is that, Kai?" he bent his head and whispered. He scrutinised Fenrir's face, which I refused to look at, fearing eye contact.

"That's the Soulless, the one that attacked Flodside."

"What is he doing here, then? As in, *out* here."

"General brought it here after it batted off another Soulless right under her nose. I didn't see it happen."

"What? Where were you?"

"Out cold, by all accounts."

"Oh right, I see how it went, I think. So, he fights for us."

"Apparently so. I don't know. Can't say I'm terribly convinced."

"Huh…"

I raised my hand to wave him back inside, but he had already made off for the other side of the terrace. I groaned and, deciding that he had seen more than enough to make his own way around, let him do whatever he wanted.

[Fenrir]

I noticed Kai disappear back inside the door. That left me with his sibling to deal with. I did not look forward to interacting with a second like him, only taller, with a different nose. This immediate preconception served me poorly as, I realised, he embodied a different issue altogether. He scampered in front of me at speed, surveying me with an odd perkiness about his features. I could not tell if this was an improvement. I felt what I could only describe as peculiar, unfathomable reluctance.

"Can I help you?" I droned.

"You're a Soulless?" the young man said. His voice rang somewhat different to his sibling's as well, more pitchy, and the words easier to hear.

"Yes, though I believe your brother told you that already."

Thinking perhaps he could not believe it from my current appearance, I lifted one transfigured arm above my head for a moment. Bizarrely, this one did not flinch away like the others, instead gawping with wide-eyed intent as the armoured skin spread, then retreated as I brought it down to my side again.

"I heard you did a brave thing."

"I would not be so sure of that. After all, I could not tell you why I made such a choice. If I had an answer, believe me, I would have divulged it by now; I've been interrogated enough."

"Well, where did those come from?" he enquired, briskly, stooping to investigate the metal bands clasped around my wrists. I failed to appreciate why it mattered.

"I could not say," I said. "They have always been there. I assume they were put on me."

"Shackles," he said, almost silently. As I watched him mumbling to himself, something changed in his countenance. His face lowered momentarily, creating shadows that disappeared as instantly as they surfaced. I chose to disregard it.

He suddenly straightened himself out, thrust his upturned hand forward, and nodded purposefully at it until I offered up my own arm. With one set of fingers, he gripped my hand, holding it still, though utterly unconvincingly. I imagined he had already gathered that I was easily capable of escaping him, had I the proper motivation to do so. I heard I possessed "a certain air about me".

The other hand examined the shackle, turning it round, and round again, stopping a few times to trace over a hinge here, or a joint there. Then he jumped, like an excited child.

"I can take these off, if you would like," he chirped, leaning back lazily on the low wall, seemingly waiting for an enthusiastic response I did not have for him. I shrugged with indifference, which he evidently took as my agreement. "Kai," he yelled, "did you bring your—crivens, he's left me! Oh, never mind. Come along then, we shall simply escort ourselves. He will have the things I need."

He bustled inside, gesturing for me to follow. I played along, more because the strange man sparked some sense of curiosity in me, than out of any sort of duty to compliance. Whether or not the bracelets remained made no odds to me, although they must have meant something to him, since he was so eager to remove them.

The next minutes were a jarring and confusing contrast to the last. Once my shepherd reached his brother's quarters and promptly ejected Kai, sighing and muttering (to my private appreciation), he immediately sunk into his work.

As if only to make himself more unfathomable, his frantic persona from moments ago waned, replaced by a quiet and meticulous machine, whose focus exclusively addressed the puzzle to be disassembled, and the utensil currently pinched in his hand. His face was neither vivid, nor contorted with shade—but instead perfectly serene.

After spending some minutes looking at the identical wall opposite, and the floor, which also appeared largely the same, I realised this room benefitted from far more natural light than the one I would return to. I could watch him, see every tiny piece of metal deftly extracted from me. His chatter stopped too, the quiet instead occupied only by a slight tap or scratch.

The stillness lasted until the second creak of a hinge, and dull thump of metal hitting the desk. Then he switched again, declaring with a stretch of his arms: "There! My work is done. Now, I'd be willing to bet that feels lighter, if nothing else."

I regretted to admit he was not wrong. A relieved feeling spread, in some way, from my bare wrists right up to my shoulders, even within my chest. My only reply was to narrow my eyes and close my fingers around the spot where iron used to sit. Even so, he nodded, and retied the pointless little tail of black hair at the back of his head with a satisfied hum,

"You're welcome, uh—Hm, what is your name?" he asked, tilting his head to one side.

"They call me Fenrir here," I obliged him.

"Aha, hello Fenrir, it is a pleasure!"

"And who are you again?"

"I'm Benjamin Hughes." I struggled progressively to relate this Hughes to the other one. He held out his hand again, for me to take.

"Right, I suppose I should thank you for this."

Benjamin did not choose to speak a response, only to give a wonky smile and grip my hand slightly tighter as he shook it. I still maintained that he was utterly bizarre.

Afterward, he retrieved one of the shackles from the desk, and started to pick at it again with one of his tools. I initially took this to be a prompt to leave which, as soon as I made it a few steps, he vocally refuted.

"You are welcome, very welcome, to stay if you'd like some company."

The idea struck me as strange, and I turned towards him. I had been determined to keep out of others' company as much as physically possible, up to now. These people were, for the most part, comfortable to survey my movements from a relative distance, so the arrangement worked rather conveniently. I thought myself rightfully wary, and as I continued to look, unblinking, at Benjamin, his puerile grin gradually wavered. But, reasoning that I had nothing conceivably better to be doing, I returned to my perch to watch him work.

As before, that cool focus immediately swept over him, although on this occasion he could not stay silent, instead attempting constantly to make conversation. He apparently neglected to realise small-talk was not a skill I possessed.

I discovered he had quite the talent for it, however, able to redress my shortcomings in full. His brain seemed to hold an endless abundance of meaningless questions to ask, or personal musings to tell. It did not render the conversation much less exhausting, and yet I continued to dwell there, possibly because doing so seemed more productive than staring out over the city alone.

Either he forgot, or somewhere on his way Benjamin Hughes must have decided he did not approve of my given name, and took to calling me "Fen" instead, ignoring me whenever I tried to correct him. Other than to make the word a single syllable shorter, the change served no purpose whatsoever.

The sun had passed behind the rooftops, staining the room an odd shade of orange, by the time he had finally finished, both meddling with the bracelet and attempting to illustrate, at length, the merits of jam pastry turnovers. He had torn off on a tangent after I explained that I could not possibly have a "favourite flavour" (despite his insistence), if I had never eaten one.

"Here, you can keep that," he said, holding out a long loop of thick thread. From it dangled a tiny metal ring. "I took it from the lock mechanism. I know my brother keeps a padlock or something hanging round his neck. That and all the bits of metal he's jabbed through his ears."

"Me keep it? Why would I?" I preferred not to, simply because it would give me a factor apparently in common with the obnoxious child.

"Oh, I don't know, you don't have to, just as a reminder maybe."

Ah, of course. I took him as sentimental.

"What, to remember that?" I suggested, nodding to the deconstructed mess over the desk.

"Not to remember being stuck with those, why would you do that? No, no, I thought perhaps to remind you that you're free."

I could not think of a retort to that and, using the pause, he dropped the string into my hand. No way left for me to refuse it now. I noted to myself that I had been rash. I ought to be more watchful of this man in future, for it seemed I had underestimated him. He was, in fact, more powerful than I imagined.

[Leo]

General hardly saw me enter before she moved across the room. I closed the office door behind me.

"I received a message overnight," she said, mechanically, as she reached her desk, "in light of our reports on the two most recent hits."

"From Governance?"

She turned her gaze down to something laid on the table, with a look as though it might suddenly move. A suspicion twitched in the back of my mind; I stepped forward to see for myself.

"The Black Envelope."

"Yes."

The Envelope delivered a command, its message alarmingly clear, seeming to infect the wood grain of the desk. It was a sentence—the kill order.

"One imagines the assumption is, while these attacks are no accidents, whatever it is we are dealing with, it's not human."

"It is the same conclusion I reached. It makes sense."

"It does." She lingered on the unopened envelope. "Please notify Tank, Medi, Songbird and Lieutenant of this. And send word to all of the watchmen as well."

"And what of Hellhound and Garrison?"

"No, they don't need to be told yet. And try to keep it from Fenrir, too, if possible. That is, presuming he has not foreseen this already."

I brought my heels together. "Understood ma'am," I affirmed, and turned to leave.

"One more thing, Leo."

I halted. "General?"

"Fetch me Benjamin Hughes."

[Kai]
Ben and I ambled from the top of the stone fortress to the ground at wandering pace. Despite him having arrived nigh two days ago, this felt like the first opportunity we had been given, to simply exist in the other's company, not consumed in any way by the yawning mouth that this little war had become. We said very little merely looking about ourselves, watching the next right angle or sinking staircase crawl towards us. Occasionally Ben would make an offhand comment on some brickwork that looked barely different to the rest, or a small noise on the other side of a door. I made sure to censure his ridiculous ponytail again. On the second floor, we passed by Eris, at the sight of whom Ben nearly leaped out of his shoes in enthusiasm.

"Ah, she emerges from the shadows! Hi there, Eris," he chanted, so loud I thought I heard the sound echo around the corner behind us. I simply crossed my arms and bowed my head without a word to offset it. Oddly though, his outburst provoked a relatively uplifted, if slightly stunned, reaction. Her shoulders shook with silent laughter and she truly tried hard to smile. Ben had that effect on people.

"Good evening," she hummed, diving into the library.

We realised then that we eventually had to head someplace, ultimately deciding on the terrace. This would be the second attempt for me. I had not the faintest idea what Fenrir had been told by my brother; I only saw that the Soulless had hovered behind him as he brazenly paraded into my room. Having seemingly run out of safe hiding spots, I had headed to his own designated quarters, and made myself comfortable until he decided to return.

Though I seemed to be liberated form Fenrir for now, that did not exclude everyone else. Such was the danger of hanging around Ben for any length of time. We made it as far as the ground floor.

"Benjamin Hughes!" A shout cut down the corridor.

Ben stopped and wheeled around. His grin told me he definitely recognised the voice. "No way," he said. Emery strode towards us in no particular hurry, his hands in his pockets. "How long has it been, man? Ah wait, *sir*, is it now?"

"Can it!" Emery said, but with a laugh. "It's good to see you, friend."

It sounded a little foreign to my ear, the soldier laughing like he just did. They clapped their hands together and pulled each other into an embrace with the affection of old friends which, though unanticipated, did not surprise me.

"Yeah, likewise. How are you getting on?" Ben asked.

"Well, my face hasn't crashed into the side of any buildings yet, so you're safe."

"I should think so; I assembled it! But I don't mean the equipment—you'll take care of that. I am asking about you, Emery. How are you doing these days?"

"Better, now."

"Good, that's good."

"And yourself? You seem spirited as ever."

"But of course," Ben chuckled.

"I'm truly sorry about all of this."

"It'll be alright," he said, a typically fluffy response from him.

Emery nodded, and coughed, glancing first at his wristwatch, then down the corridor. "Oh, but I had better be going," he said. "I'll see you again at lunch, if you're staying?"

"Sure," Ben added, with a genial salute in his direction.

"Good to see you up, Kai," Emery called behind him.

I looked away from the wall at the mention of my name. Emery disappeared around a corner, and I heard an indistinguishable blend of voices already caught in another conversation. Then Ben got bored.

"So, Kai, the terrace, was it? Let's be off, then; you lead the way."

We barely took a few steps before we were stopped again. Leo's tone was not nearly so benign.

"Sir?" I began, searching his face.

"Not you—him." He faced Ben. "You had better come with me. General wants to see you."

"General Elwin? Certainly, sir." He moved to Leo's side and said to me: "You go ahead. I will be back, so wait for me."

He did not return for over an hour. And I found very little to do out on the terrace, in truth, except look. It definitely did not help to pass the time. Still, I could hardly consider abandoning that spot.

Something in the tone of his voice when he had asked that I stay kept me stuck there indefinitely.

I listed the potential reasons General could have for summoning him there. The further I went, the more urgently I hoped he had already been released and simply collided with someone else on his way back. That seemed more like him.

I knew, however, as soon as I laid eyes on him again, that the reality was much worse. He trod slowly, with care, his face knotted up, and he twined his fingers in front of him with pale, protruding knuckles.

"What happened? What did they say to you?"

He gave a dry snort of laughter. "It's fine. I'm just going to be hanging around with you lot for a bit longer."

"Why?" I made my suspicion clear.

"I have been asked, very politely, to help you catch a Soulless. You know, the huge one, big teeth and all that. Apparently, they are all after you—you and Eris—which means it will come back, and General Elwin has a plan for when it does, in which she appears to believe I can be of some use."

"You don't seem too happy about it."

"Well I suppose, in principle, I'm a lover, not a fighter. I can't say I *like* it." He shrugged.

"Then why the hell would you agree to this?"

"Because she asked," he replied, bluntly, strolling closer to peer over the wall. "You answered in the very same way, did you not?"

"I know what I have to do here, what I want to do. She offered me a prime opportunity."

"Opportunity…yes, that is one way to put it. But any noble, unsavoury business aside, how could I leave my brother behind?"

Part 4: Acrimony

[Eris]

It came to my attention that I had grown slightly too comfortable with thoughtlessly dashing down to the kitchen to boil myself a kettle. On one occasion, I arrived at the end of the ground-floor corridor, only to stumble upon Benjamin, fixated on the inside of the dining hall, leaning forward over his crossed arms, as if an invisible rope fastened the threshold and he could go no further. He did not speak at first, likely too occupied with watching the scene before him.

Heat seemed to radiate out of the room towards us, bitter and stifling. In all of the vast space, my gaze locked on the two lone figures standing uncomfortably close in the centre. Kai glared down his nose at Fenrir. Every muscle in the former's body tensed so terribly that he appeared to shake, while the latter seemed unabashed in every respect, apart from his eyes. A mere glance from him would be an attack all of its own.

This meeting had been inevitable—overdue, even. Still, I wondered how the two had managed to chase each other to this place. As I crept closer to Benjamin, I heard Fenrir start to speak.

"You will be pleased to know that I dislike you also, Hughes, vehemently. But what purpose do you have cornering me here?"

"I'm just trying to figure you out," Kai returned, "trying to suss how a Soulless that made to ravage my home, a Soulless that would have killed me if it could, is suddenly on my side. I can't say I have ever heard an explanation from you."

"And you think I'm going to give you one now?"

"You know, I think that selective memory of yours is awfully suspect as well, while we're at it. You know exactly how many of your kind there are, their creative little code names, yet for some reason you just cannot recall what sort of shit they're about to throw at us until they've already done it. What, you need to jog your brain or something?"

“Oh, so now you do want my help. Speaking of names, I heard they have one for you now. Hellhound, was it? How inspired,” Fenrir spat.

“General Elwin gave you titles?” Benjamin acknowledged me for the first time. I noticed a bizarre, relaxed veneer over his face. “I didn’t know that,” he added.

“Me neither, not for a while,” I whispered.

“What’s yours?”

“Garrison, apparently, but that doesn’t matter. Shouldn’t we be doing something about this?”

“I don’t think so, not yet. They’ve been building up to this for a while now. Fenrir should hear what Kai has to say. And my brother could probably do with being brought down a peg.” He nodded and gave a feathery sigh, before turning back to the confrontation of which we were spectators, right as Fenrir spoke again.

“And what exactly are you going to do to me, Hellhound?” he said.

Kai glanced over his shoulder before replying. His pupils darted between me and Benjamin. It turned my muscles frigid, to have my eavesdropping presence suddenly recognised. I looked away, leaving only Benjamin to stare right back.

“I’m not doing anything, for now. But if there weren’t good people stuck in this building with us, I would take great pleasure in burning you to a crisp. Keep that in mind, Soulless. General Elwin might trust you; I sure as hell don’t.”

He whirled around and marched towards us, without meeting either pair of eyes.

“Just try it,” Fenrir called, already headed unceremoniously in the opposite direction. “Once, twice—what’s a third time to me? It never has gone quite how you wanted so far, has it? I could tear your throat out.”

“Couldn’t manage to last time, could you?”

As Kai went to pass by us, Benjamin latched on to his shoulder. “What brought that on, Kai?” he murmured.

He looked around to ensure Fenrir was securely out of earshot. “You don’t—I don’t know,” he said, shaking off of his brother’s grip, and hurried outside, crushing his face in his hands.

[Benjamin]
I looked around the room. An uncomfortable, dream-like oppression rooted itself as I ran my eyes over the four walls. It came from the uniformity of it all. This space, mine for however long this ordeal went on, could literally have been any one of the tens of others lining the corridors, and it would have made no difference. Even in a hotel, the furniture might have been in a slightly different position, or a different cheap print would hang on the wall. On that odd occasion, one usually teetered around, too giddy with the evening's share of fizz to pay too much attention anyway. Here lay the opposite case. My restless senses insisted on picking up everything. I wondered if I could get away with a stealthy rearrangement of the place. Perhaps, I considered, I ought to invest in a house plant.

I could not imagine my brother lasting well like this; he had always been so attached to his own space. Still, he effectually buried himself in whatever work he had set himself to now. He was distracting himself from something, and I could not honestly deny the fact that at least part of that need rested with me; but with that in mind, it seemed my obligation now to leave him be to adjust on his own. I wanted to kill something. The reality was that I had landed here, powerless to up sticks until a corpse had fallen.

Pushing myself up off the mattress, which felt rigid with disuse under my palms, I wandered up to the window, my renewed resolve stirring up energy, which required an outlet. My hands clasped around the chilled handles, old and clearly jammed. I leaned my whole weight back against their resistance, until I could feel the latch beginning to become unstuck, only a little at first, then all at once. The panes lurched open with a labouring squeal, and a burst of air rushed into the hollow like it had been waiting out there for years.

Drawn to the slight, cool taste of the outdoors, I gripped the sill and peered out into the breeze. For its drawbacks, I had to admit this room allocation, beyond allowing me to be here in the first place, also had other merits. Foremost, the elevated post offered an astounding view over the cityscape that felt deceptively luxurious. Tall plumes of translucent smoke gradually dispersed into the off-white clouds peering down from above. A lone bird hopped along rooftop tiles, before plunging into the street hidden below. I smiled at the sight of the little fiend. It hinted at something equally admirable and enticing in that variety of freedom, no matter how aimless it had to be.

I rose onto my toes and bent a little further out of the window to see, out of curiosity, just how high off of the ground this floor lifted us. The rigorously-practised part of my brain had already estimated the concrete dimensions of the building. Still, despite what people say about not looking down, there was a thrilling, refreshing effect when you were up there, with all that empty space over and under you.

When I happened to direct my eyes downward though, my breath suddenly tangled up in my throat. The muscles around my face tightened, as if my eyelids could possibly squeeze any wider. I should not have been surprised to see Fenrir there; he stood in what I had gathered to be his usual spot, his territory, on the far corner of the terrace. He might have only happened to glance up, or maybe I had caused a bit of a ruckus in the process of opening the window. But, either way, he was looking up at me now. I faltered, for a second or two. The combination of gleaming eyes framed in his constantly statuesque face had a habit of almost putting someone on the spot. Almost. I waved my arm in a wide arc above me, prompting a curious tilt of his head. Only briefly, though, before he averted his gaze, crossed his arms and went back to observing the square out front.

I pondered how long he had been watching me before I noticed. Proceeding from that, I thought of how long he must have spent, simply standing there on the same terrace alone, and felt suddenly deflated. In fact, if I had not happened to see him in that moment—on the precipice, holding onto the bars of some invisible prison cell, and waiting for the daylight to pass by him—then I might never have acted as I did.

I backed out of the room, barely having turned around the right way before I reached the door, and narrowly avoiding butting my face into it. I left everything open on my way, unthinking—window, doors, whatever. My mind, so busy following several trains of thought at one time, buzzed relentlessly in my ears. I did not recall negotiating any stairways, but I ended up where I wanted in spite of that: the threshold between the ground floor and the terrace.

"That was fast," Fen barked. He turned his head an inch, his wispy hair concealing the corner of his eye surveying me up and down. "What do you want?"

"I am getting out of this stuffy old dungeon for a bit." I jumped forward and nudged his shoulder with my knuckles. "And you're coming with."

"But I am outside," he replied incredulously.

"Not out *here*, out there." I gestured first to his feet, then out in front of me, past the square. Fen followed the direction of my fingers without moving his face.

"I can't do that," he said, with a jarring lack of tone to his voice. "I am authorised to roam the grounds of the military base, and that's all. This is as far out of this place as I get."

"Oh, blimey, what are you going to do, prey on random city folk who impose zero impediments to you whatsoever, but only because you've stepped out of this little paved square? Give over—you'll shoot for me first anyhow. Let's go." I prodded him in the back and hopped down the few sloping steps to the pavement.

When I turned around, Fen had not yet followed behind; he stood on the edge of the patio, one toe outstretched, pointing toward the step below, as if about to put his foot down, but with a reverse force pushing against him.

"Are you coming?" I called, my arms swinging at my sides.

"Listen, you don't—can't possibly understand—"

"Fine then," I interjected, "I'll steer you clear of all the people. Guess I will check out the nightlife by myself."

His incredulous glare roamed around several times, snagging on my arms swinging impatiently at my sides, before he let his foot drop to the paving stone. The firm eye contact he maintained affirmed that he was, while willing, *reluctant*, and should anything go awry on this test run, it would be entirely my fault.

[Eris]

My neighbour had left his door open again. Today, he had stationed himself behind that wide desk of his, looking as though he had been there for some time. Perhaps Benjamin was lurking around this evening. I seemed to have found Kai at work. There were papers propped up with various tools, all lined up around him, in such a manner that I could not easily locate which thing he concentrated so intently on. I noticed he wore glasses, a pair with thick, oval rims that slid halfway down the slope of his nose. He had a tiny instrument, hardly visible, twisting between his thumb and first finger. There was a certain catharsis to be had in observing a craftsman like him, so enveloped in his element but, aware that I was gawking, I preferred to hurry into my own quarters. Kai must have caught me in spite of my good intentions, though, as I heard him suddenly speak through his coffee.

"Wait there; I've got something to give to you."

I stepped back, and saw he had risen out of his chair, reaching over his arrangement for a particular object. He carried it with two hands and offered it over the threshold.

"General passed it to me to do. I've never actually constructed one before; you might want to try it on."

He held toward me what I first thought to be a metal left arm, then realised was actually a gauntlet, plated all over in black armour. This was for me. Minding his instruction, I tugged my existing glove from the matching hand, shoving it into my shirt pocket.

The gauntlet felt akin to a gardening glove from the inside, only it fit perfectly. In my head, I suddenly grasped the reasoning for which Kai had rapped on my door the other day, brandishing a set square and demanding to see my hand—no, not that hand, the other one.

Initially, my eyes were drawn to the raised bump running from the bottom of my hand, up my wrist. I located a small, grooved handle jutting out from the top, which I tried removing, and saw I had hold of a knife. The blade looked similar to what I remembered of Dorian, the dagger I lost to Geist, though the handle was ornate by comparison. I returned it to its sheath, which made a satisfying whisper of a sound.

"It's still yours. Most of it is from the original, save for some of the grip, which I had to improvise. Why I couldn't use another one in better condition, I don't know," Kai said, looking only at the gauntlet itself, rather than at me admiring his handiwork.

The dark metal, with all its edges and angles, reflected the light rather attractively as I bent and straightened my knuckles. I also picked up on several thin lines of bronze-coloured detailing around the numerous joints, which all consisted of miniscule neat patterns.

"I got bored," he snapped, when I traced over one with my finger.

"I haven't seen real armour so pretty before. Thank you." I bowed my head graciously.

"Thank General Elwin. This thing was her idea. Just be wary of it; it isn't made of the same stuff as your gloves, so it won't block your Soul's power like they do. That's the point: this is armour to wear in a fight; don't want to be impeding your own weapon then, do you? I suppose you could go half and half, like that. You know, one charged hand, one safe hand." He spoke hurriedly, almost to the point that I could no longer follow him. Aware of my error, I gently twisted the gauntlet off of my arm, and wrestled to replace it with a glove.

"How do you know about—?" I started, but I trailed off upon realising that I had mentioned them to his brother, who could well have told him in turn. "Is Benjamin around? You don't usually leave your room wide open, that's all."

"No, he'll be on an escapade with the Soulless again."

"I guess you mean Fenrir. They're still doing that? Where do they keep disappearing to?"

"Who can be sure? This is Benjamin. He probably snuck out and is off robbing a bank or something, for all I know."

"But how could that even be? I mean, would anyone let them go?"

"Like I said, it's Benjamin. There's not much you could do to stop him if you tried."

"Oh, I see."

“Anyway…” He headed straight back into the room.

I understood that I was keeping him and placed a hand on the door. “Did you want this shut?”

He hesitated, tossed his hand in the air and said, “Sure, whatever.”

[Fenrir]

My kidnapper stopped in his tracks out of nowhere.

"Oh, would you look at that!" he said, patting my shoulder. "You don't see those too often around here. Look, see?"

"I am looking at it," I had to assure him, before he accidentally hopped into the river in his agitation. He was watching a white bird, floating on the surface of the water.

"Usually you would only see these fellows as they pass through, on their way to somewhere else. We have more over in the Western District. They don't like the city much."

He crouched down, precariously balanced on the water's edge, seemingly trying to get as close to it as he possibly could without actually swimming.

"Look at them though. The way their feathers all fold together pretty at the back, their little feet waving around." He demonstrated with his hands. "But then it's huge. It's so fat, with its tiny neck, it looks ridiculous, and yet that's the whole point. They are absolutely perfectly built for purpose. It's rather impressive, if you think about it. I never could have thought this thing up. These birds are special, you know—we protect them."

"I know of them, yes. That is a Cygnus Olor. They are the largest waterfowl native to this region. Back when there were monarchs in power, one of them held these creatures in particular favour. They were declared property of the crown. As such, to harm them became a punishable crime against one's ruler. These animals are not protected by law anymore, but the attitude appears to have lingered, and hunting them is still largely socially unacceptable," I recited.

Hughes twisted around, staring vaguely at me as though I had said something revolutionary. "Well," he practically whispered, "I just call them swans."

He looked to be paying no attention to his feet, so I moved closer, to placate him. I would not be responsible for fishing the man out of a river.

"Damn, you have a lot stored in that head of yours, huh? When did you learn that?"

"I don't think I did. I cannot recall ever not knowing those things."

"You certainly don't need to listen to me going on then," he laughed. The way he spoke puzzled me; he seemed to suddenly believe nothing in this place could possibly be new to me.

"I have never seen one, though. I haven't seen even half of the things that I am aware exist. And, clearly, knowing what a thing looks like is different to seeing it, is it not?"

"Yeah, I suppose so. Treason, eh…?"

I twitched at his mention of the word, as though I had been trying to remember it for some time and suddenly he reminded of it against my will. But I then realised he was merely contemplating the swan, making its way downstream.

"You're right," I added, "it is fat."

The light reflecting from the water shifted over his face slightly as he grinned, bringing, I noticed, a bright spot into both of his dark eyes.

[Emery]

I sat on the top step leading up to the terrace, waiting, and twirling my knife around between my fingers. It struck me as unfair, cruel even, to ambush him in this way, but I saw more than one man who needed forcing into a corner. I had to face this issue as much as him. This was the only way. I decided on an impulse, having considered intervening multiple times, but failing to act, that I no longer had any choice. I could not bear this weight anymore.

I thought, if I managed to clear my head a little first, watching light glance over the silver in my hands, then I could find some idea of what to say to him. A wise theory, in principle, but rendered pointless as soon as Benjamin reappeared across the square, much earlier than usual. He strolled closer, laughing at something he had already said. Fenrir followed at his side, slightly perturbed, and scanning his face; the Soulless no longer felt the need to trail a few strides behind. My stomach twisted around itself.

The sensation must have shown somewhere on my outer surface, too. It took Ben a painfully long time to notice me, but I could tell the second he did; his face instantly dropped.

"Emery, you're here…" he said, quietly.

I did not stand up. "I need to speak with you."

"Why him?" Fenrir interrupted. "This is about me, I presume."

"You head on inside, Fenrir," I told him. The knife's edge grazed my palm.

He climbed the steps towards the door, which I had closed behind me to save suspicion. However, he paused halfway, squeezing his hands into fists, before turning on his heels. He chose to stand stock still, peering down at me, with his chin raised in defiance.

"It's fine, Fen, you go ahead. This is on me," Ben added, attempting a wonky smile.

As thanks for his gesture, Ben now suffered the fury of those yellow eyes instead. I watched the grey skin creep from under Fenrir's rolled sleeves, spreading down his arms like blood trickling from sliced flesh. Neither appeared to notice this.

"Fine, then. I need to keep this quick. Stand where I can see you both."

Fenrir refused to shift, acutely aware that I was mumbling orders at him. Ben dragged his feet to meet him instead.

I sighed, but only felt I grew heavier for it. "You cannot keep pulling this shit, Benjamin. He is confined to this building right now. There are locks on that door to hold him in at night. You've been lucky; I'm the only one who has caught you, so far."

"I know," he said, his head bowed.

"What?"

"I got bloody lucky, the first time. It was stupid. I figured I'd be in for it there and then. But we got back, and everything seemed fine. I knew it had to be you on watch, so I've been keeping an eye out ever since. I have only ever stolen Fen during your shift." He crouched down on his knee, peering up at me from below. I felt suddenly exposed, burning under the last beats of sunlight, which glared over the Wall.

Rocking back and forth on the step, I confirmed, "I believed as much."

"Obviously you did. How else would the others miss me, right? Are you going to hand me over to General Elwin now?"

"I don't want to. I really don't want to."

"Ah, I know. It's okay. I did this." He meant it too.

"What if Wyvern had attacked us? We have a strict plan—"

"I am the plan. General discussed it with me, before any of you. I know where I need to be when the time comes."

"And what about him? He needs to be here. There is no way I could convince General to leave him to his own devices, no way. Someone has to know where he is at all times. That someone cannot be you, Benjamin. Shit, do you have any idea of the position this puts *me* in?"

"I sense that I am becoming more of a problem than I am worth," Fenrir interjected, a sardonic whine dripping into his voice.

In truth, I did not know what I was going to do. My brain seemed to want to rip itself in two, rather than help me. What Ben had done remained so blatantly illicit, but it also represented the very thing I had urged Fenrir to accept. This building was quarantine; it promised to give him nothing. I had wished after a companion for him so badly, and now one presented himself, although in an unexpected shape. That very thought had held me back all this time, while I watched from the rooftop, the pair of them escaping, again and again. I realised, in a sense, it did not matter what I chose; either way, I would have failed.

Ben took a breath and finally opened his mouth to speak, but he was drowned out by the bell's toll. The sound travelled strangely, twice as rapid than usual—a code meant for us.

"Now look what we've done." I almost laughed as if, in our collective frustration, we had inadvertently summoned it ourselves.

The three of us remained frozen and silent for a few seconds, bordering on disbelief, but as the bell seemed to strengthen, Ben moved backward away from the steps, wiping his sleeve over his face. He snatched a glance at Fenrir, and then returned to me, slowly shaking his head.

Over the mounting noise, he shouted: "I'm sorry."

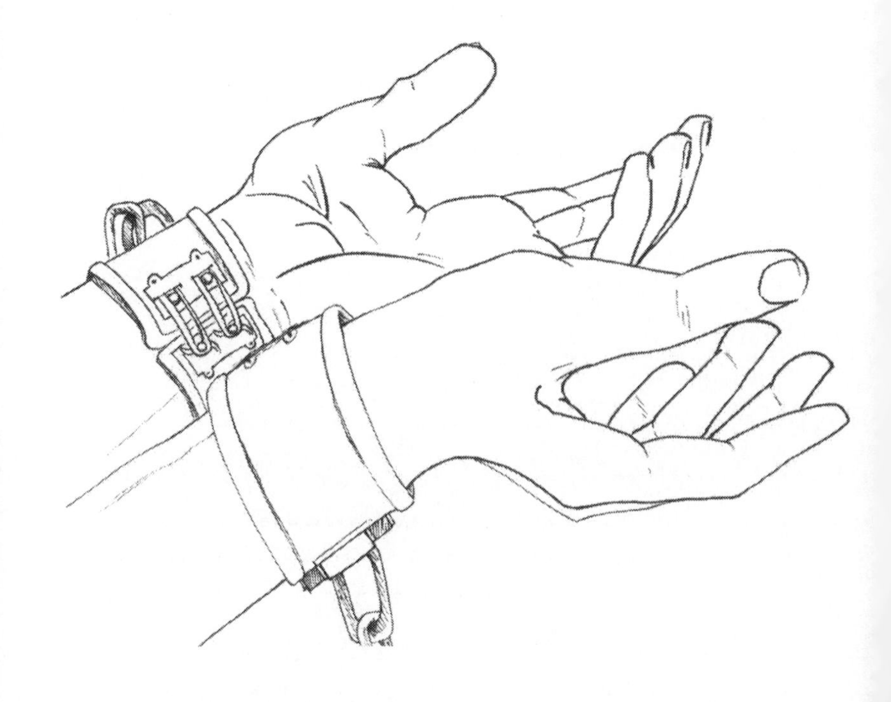

[Leo]

The sun, sinking well beyond the limits of the Wall, fired a blaze of colours into the circle of sky above us. The casual observer would probably consider it stunningly beautiful. But from now on, visibility would be poor, and only set to get worse. Soon it would be dark—no time for fighting the enemy.

General loaded her pistol again and, raising her arm vertical above her head, fired another red smoke signal. We had to wait, urgently leading our horses down the next wide, deserted road. Seconds later, a twin red pillar climbed up above the rooftops, still blocks away from its target. The message came from Lieutenant, accompanied by Songbird, Hellhound and Garrison, and it came punctuated by a quake from the colossus following us, so close we could feel its footsteps vibrating in the air around our heads.

General and I calculated the distance, knowing full well the other would be doing the same, meaning we both reached the same conclusion. We were too close.

She had decided to name the Soulless Wyvern, before she formulated a plan to kill it. Her instructions were drafted over days and multiple sleepless nights and succeeded, in my eyes, to account for the most eventualities possible. In our position, nothing was flawless, ever. But this touched as close as we could get.

Once the creature had been detected by the watchmen, she immediately deployed Lieutenant and Songbird, who were to escort the two young Soul-users, exactly as they had done before. It was the kids' lives, which appeared to be the quarry of our adversary. They followed the most obscure, narrow alleyways only Lieutenant could know so intimately, and which the beast would never struggle to navigate, cutting their way through to General's chosen arena: Interieur's botanical garden. Fenrir sustained a measured pursuit of them, close enough to be seen. General held him to this command with the promise that, should he fail, he could expect a blade in his gut.

In the meantime, she and I tracked Wyvern's progress, keeping it permanently within our sights, and attempting to lure it along the longest conceivable path. At the end of every street we traversed, she sent up a signal, to which Songbird was charged with replying in kind. Tank and Medi were carefully positioned in between, anticipating a need for the latter's Soul either with us, or worse, the larger group. As soon as the Soulless blindly hunted us into the garden, it would prove a one-way journey, with no exit. We would capture and destroy it.

Her stratagem, I believed, with a single miscalculation, had just blown a gaping puncture through its side. I tried to convince myself that the kids could not run any faster; they were doing the best they could. Taunted by the reality of failure, it seemed we might have been prepared for any uncertainty, except this. Yet, by her unchanging face, General refuted me, told me I had been deluded. I had missed the trick. Somehow—only this once—her composure failed to ease my nerves.

She stopped. In the centre of the road, she halted, and turned to face behind us. The creature was coming, at any moment now. Its great shadow grew ever larger, consuming the space between us. Its hunger seeped into the air. I was so tired.

"Leo?" she said.

"Ma'am."

"You are going to forget the Soulless; instead, you will head directly to Tank and Medi, and tell them to go straight to the rendezvous area with all the haste you can possibly muster."

"I won't leave you alone with that thing, General."

"That was an order, Leonardo. Twenty years, don't you dare do this to me now."

Before I could protest again, Wyvern rounded the corner. Its ambivalent glare found General and her poor, frantic stallion with ease. She managed to steady him, but then dismounted, striding towards the Soulless's front on her own, studier feet. She drew out her rapier, directing the tip at its drooping jaw, regarding the monster with a fierce poise that rightfully suited the regal nature of her blade. I watched her begin to speak.

"I know what's about to happen. You sense it too, don't you? It's there, in those beady pairs of eyes you have."

The massive head plunged until its chin touched the ground. A tectonic wail erupted from it, sending the horse into a frenzy, circling around me, desperate to escape impending doom, but not without his master. My mare began to flick her snout and pat at the pavement in anticipation. The end of Naomi's sword would not so much as quiver; she would not let it. The Soulless saw as much, from the way it retreated its scaly neck a few metres, muscles quivering in rage.

She tossed her head back to look right into the face of the hulking, trembling creature with those steely eyes, and a barbed smirk. “I know. But that’s fine,” she said. “I’m prepared for this. I’m done. Do you know who I am? Do you recognise this face? You tried to take my children. Oh, you try your damnedest, bitch: we *have* you.”

I could not stay, would not disobey her any longer. I refused to bear the thought of her, turning to avoid one of Wyvern’s talons, only to spot me, still dumbly watching her struggle. I forced my mount around, towards an alley, which would convey me to Tank and Medi, and hurtled into the darkness.

Behind me, I heard the mingled screams of a Soulless, and a lone, abandoned horse. Nothing of my General though. My eyelids grew hot and prickling, as with every harried clack on the cobbles, I came to realise I would never hear her again. She was right: twenty years. All of that time, and I had never understood her.

[Benjamin]

As we had planned, a group of four entered the garden first, on foot. I recognised Kai at the front, his shape almost completely hiding Eris's. My thumb twitched as they stepped over the mark I had chosen—the exact point at which I would release this trigger in my hand and watch the Soulless drop like a shot kite. Emery hurried them into a swaying bed of white flowers, sheltered by the branches of several old, sad-looking willows, still managing to sprout some green even at this time of year. Those trees and I would keep them safe now.

They were followed, seconds later, by Fen. He used the same track to their hiding place, under the bank of petals. I could not stretch far enough around the shrubs to search for him, not without giving myself away. Next were Tank and Medi, both on the back of a single steed, which stormed along the path, Medi leaning around her partner's shoulders, searching. They were forced to make for cover, however, at the quaking sound of my prey approaching. General and Leo were nowhere to be seen, seemingly having redirected themselves, the Soulless snatching at their heels. I could not afford to dwell on their reasoning. She was here. I shuffled my feet and shook a few tiny blossoms out of my hair. They fluttered down into the long grass like snowflakes. This was such a pretty place; I thought it a dreadful shame, to taint it with something so ugly.

And ugly she certainly was. Massive too, about as tall as those giant trade ships, that we would catch the train all the way west just to see show up at port, and almost as big as the gossipers made her out to be. For now, anyway. Both my heart and lungs stopped, waiting for me to pull the switch. My body grew cold. Focus.

I let the bolts fly.

Galvanised ropes steered by hooks: two lodged into her right side, another in her left, one trapped her raised right foot, and the last stuck in her front. I watched, she stumbled, but she did not fall. She seemed to recognise that fact as well as I did, and she began to struggle against the restraints. I cursed under my breath but gave myself no time. My extent reached far beyond this.

I took up my crossbow and sprinted for the giant. The garden had never been huge, but as I drew closer, into the space dimmed by her shadow, hearing only the incessant thumping of my own feet, I felt the power of a thing so immense, it rendered everything else impossibly small.

Staggering to a standstill beneath her, I fired the first hook into the ground behind me, driving it down, deep into the moist dirt. I had to twist my arms around the device and yank it over my shoulder against the cord's resistance. The black blotches in her eyes slid downward, knowingly. It was me. Not the one she hankered after, but I was very much in her way. Still trying to shift her limbs, she produced a deep, rumbling noise, enough to send vibrations through my skull.

"Nice try, gorgeous," I replied, closing one eye. "You can't escape from me."

With a toothy smile widening between my lips, I made the second shot. Its metallic tail whipped through the space between us, the spinning reel inside my weapon hissing in my ear and turning it hot against my cheek. I buried the arrow squarely under the creature's chin. Taut silence ensued, until I released my hands from the trigger, and violent snap rang out. The wheel knocked into the reverse motion, drawing both ends of the cord back together. Down she came. The beast the size of a ship would sink like one.

A faint whiff of burning itched my nose. I found myself almost disappointed that I wouldn't get to exhibit Plan Number Three as well.

[Kai]

Wyvern's head was pulled to the ground, like a chunk of the moon plummeting from the sky. Having tossed his crossbow, Ben just stood there, watching it fall. Even with ropes protruding from its flesh, it could stretch open its brutal jaws. He saw it coming. He knew, like me, and he tried to run eventually, but he could never move fast enough.

It crushed into the ground, taking my brother's tiny silhouette with it. The impact jostled my hideous view. As I stumbled frantically forward, I felt a rush of air, and caught the four-legged Fenrir clattering towards the wreck—too late.

"Ben!"

That voice, it stung in my throat. It sounded like my own voice, screaming from above the water.

[Fenrir]
My vision filled with eyes and teeth and red. Wyvern's shrieking seared inside my ears until my hearing ceased. Admittedly, it could have been my own deathly howls doing the damage; I could not truly tell the difference. I felt the ground about my feet grow sodden, with the blood of a dying man.

It hurt.

I would never have heard the soldiers coming. The scene played out in ringing silence as the large man known as Tank hooked a blade around Wyvern's jaw, heaving her bloodied, screeching face away.

In the meantime, the shell covering my skin could only be described as collapsing in upon itself. The illusion of strength washed from my body, a swift reminder of its more erratic nature as of late. At some point, I must have fallen onto the ground, as the vague picture I could make out suddenly flipped on its side.

I saw a shape, which I perceived to be the younger Hughes brother, bowling towards the maw of my captured kin with enraged resolution, blade pointed straight at the back of her throat. That was all, before my sight suddenly failed under a blistering veil of crimson.

"*There is no hope left for you now,*" I thought. "*Burn.*"

I knew it: she was gone.

[Eris]

How many seconds had passed? I had stayed under the protective arms of the weeping willows the entire time. I saw the Soulless upturn the garden as it entered, saw Benjamin fire five great hooks under the creature's serrated skin, and saw him crushed under its downfall. I saw, but hardly perceived it for what it was. Fenrir and Kai vanished from my side, followed by both Emery and Aria. They left me there alone. There was so much noise. Medi—I forgot when she arrived—seemed disturbingly composed, with Tank at her back, considering she knelt in the bloody dirt underneath Benjamin's torn body. Strange, in my awe, I believed I saw her eyes glow.

She retained her impossible serenity even when she turned her head behind her, spotting the smoke signal billowing from between the irregular, sloping roofs some several streets back. The cloud climbed in swells and folds, staining the amber sky with a slowly dissipating black haze.

We all watched the message paint itself above our heads in unbroken silence, each of us isolated within ourselves and our own understanding of what that curling black smoke meant.

Death. The word repeated itself, over and over, curling its talons around my dumb, fractured mind.

Out of the stone maze, Leo soon emerged atop a feeble-looking mount, which bobbed its long face in despair and fatigue. In tandem, he pulled along a white stallion, struggling against its restraints. He brought no comfort with him, and he knew it.

They danced hypnotically into the centre of the picture, and into the sight of the others. I shook. My hands shook terribly. My eyes would not move; my whole body refused to move, and my mind was useless in commanding it otherwise. Through the slag, I was dragged back to the ruined scene by a woman's unbounded scream.

Once I finally reached around to look, Aria had already torn towards the man and his wretched horses. She would have surely tripped over her own misplaced feet if Emery had not scooped her up from behind. His arms locked themselves around her shoulders, and she instinctually clung to him like a cliff edge, crumbling beneath her fingers. He spoke into her hair incessantly, even as both of them crumbled to their knees. Faintly, though it may have been my wavering consciousness conceiving it, I thought I watched Emery slowly rock her from side to side as she sobbed.

[Medi]

The notepad gaped up from my bedside, blank. But not until the next morning, waiting in the unconscious boy's chair, on a scrap leaf of paper, could I finally bring myself to begin writing:

"Medic's Report

Name: Merida Grieve

Date: XX/XX/XX Time: 0700

This report has been written on the morning following the mission, allowing for time to gather my thoughts.

My primary focus at the scene was the casualty, Benjamin Hughes. The impact of the struggling Soulless caused the loss of the left leg below the knee, and the entire left arm. I reached him in time to close the wounds and restrict blood loss, but my Soul (Empathy) lacked the capacity to recover either limb. As of now, he is placed in a bed under surveillance, and though he will require extensive further treatment, his condition appears to have stabilised as much as is likely in the circumstances. It may be beside the matter, but I believe our Soulless ally, called Fenrir, should be noted for his assistance.

Hellhound, in exterminating the target, suffered harsh burns on his hands. He has, as yet, rejected treatment by my Soul, so I have opted to simply dress the burns as well as I am able.

Leo and Tank sustained wounds, which were eventually remedied, and warrant no further action.

I am not certain the same can be said for Garrison. She suddenly became non-communicative, and her responses to all stimuli were severely delayed. It is best explained that she was unconscious, despite being physically awake. Even as I write, while she seems to be catering for herself, she is slow and ragged. The night must have been difficult for her; I left a mixture of remedial flowers in her dorm—lavender, chamomile, eucalyptus et cetera—in the hope that they might grant her some repose. I will continue to observe her, although if I were to assume, she understands more of these episodes than I.

The events of yesterday caused a number of fatalities: these include a group of civilians on the outer edge, who declined the order to evacuate within the Wall, and the fine, valiant leader of this force—General Naomi Elwin."

[Kai]

Even in the wake of blood and death, an army came every morning for breakfast. The grieving man still had to eat. In the worst upheaval, routine prevails.

In hindsight, perhaps it was this quality Eris found so necessary. I had arrived in the hall late, and so discovered her already seated, segregated slightly from the group of Leo, Tank, Emery and Aria, all talking in hushed tones to Medi (who made notes on a sheet of paper), and from Fenrir, who also sat alone, staring disinterestedly at a wall. I went to set myself down across from her. Leo had noticed me enter and regarded me with an affirming tip of his head.

My arms smarted if I laid them on the table. Instead of eating, I watched steam rise from the toast stacked on my plate. The sickly smell of jam made me nauseous.

"You really are the 'do as I say, not as I do' type, then."

My head snapped up at Eris's voice. It was hoarse with neglect but behind it, with the flash in her weary grey eyes, I felt a scrutinising jab. She might never have intended to express it out loud.

"Really?" I contested anyway. "This is the first word you've uttered in, what, twelve hours? And the first thing you do is call me a hypocrite."

"I wasn't calling you a hypocrite."

"Yes, I think you were."

"No, I just looked at you, and..." She breathed deeply, with some difficulty, and held her face in her hands. "...I felt it. Then it reminded me of what you said to me. I know I am no better."

"That's not what I meant. You still remember—no, of course you would." I rambled on, looking away from her face to my bound hands. "But this was different. I *had* to save my brother."

She seemed to consider this for a second, then asked, "How is Benjamin?"

"Alive," I muttered.

Eris nodded, barely. The piece of buttered bread in her fingers had since returned to her plate. Her mind had drifted elsewhere again: to General Elwin, certainly; maybe to Ben, or those Soulless that still remain, of things I had yelled out in panic that of course she would remember. Perhaps she saw fire, catching her cheek or swallowing my hands.

I watched her seize up, her whole countenance tense with discomfort. My stomach turned. I scratched at the backs of my hands. Wherever she kept going away to, I could not, in good conscience, leave her there, not now. But I was not Aria, or Medi, or Ben. I did not fix this.

"Come back," I demanded. This time it fell on me, to vocalise a thought I would have preferred to keep contained. We were too exhausted, the both of us.

Her palms smacked suddenly against the table, and she gave a dreary hum. "Right," she said, turning fixedly back to her breakfast, which in turn reminded me of my own, getting cold in front of me. "Sorry; I shouldn't keep doing that, it gives people a tidy fright, I know. Eighteen people…they just could not stand running for nothing anymore. It's not even like we have the creature's skull to hold up and show for it. Did you know, I had not thought about them at all, until this morning? This is just so wrong. I feel my chest is empty. What is happening to us?"

"I don't know."

My voice stammered dry. I took a gulp of coffee and grimaced—it was disgusting.

[Eris]

I could hardly say what brought me to the roof. The wind blew the door shut behind me with a groan, almost trapping my fingers in the hinge. Emery had already claimed his usual spot there, at the edge. He fixed his gaze on the clouds, refusing to acknowledge my presence. My legs were trembling at the knees, and I could not stop it, so I sat myself down on the damp concrete. Emery's sigh rattled into the breeze.

"Eris, it's raining," he advised.

"I know."

I figured I had angered him into leaving, from the tense scrape of his boot's steel toe. Instead, he sank to the floor beside me. He let out another breath, rubbing his temples with his thumbs. We simply remained as we were, still, whilst I tried to convert the sick, heavy feeling in my gut into actual coherent speech I could offer him. Drops of water patted impatiently at my face and hands.

"Aria's gone—Aria has gone to be with her father," he said.

"Why did you not go with her?"

He screwed his eyes shut, shaking his head. "I couldn't."

"I want to tell you that it's going to be alright," I started, tentatively, "that this will all turn out okay in the end. But I can't, because that would be a lie. It's not. This is not okay. This is never going to be okay, and I am so, so sorry." My hand clapped over my mouth, stopping whatever sound clawed up my throat from tumbling out. It was not my time for that.

I began to doubt that I had even said anything outside of my head, since Emery had not reacted at all, but then I felt his frigid hand close around my wrist and give a weak squeeze. A single, broken sob burst out, the awful sound echoing, before he muffled it in his sleeve.

[Fenrir]

It had been six days, if my count was correct. I had spent them in the quarters designated to me, sometimes asleep, sometimes lying awake in the dark. Occasionally I would light the lamp in order to read the clock. I could not tell if any of the soldiers bothered to lock me in at night.

This would be the first I had seen of Benjamin Hughes since I had lost all my senses and reawakened in a car on its way back to the military base. No-one thought to inform me of the precise procedure before but, apparently, for the first time, those other than the medic and Kai were permitted to enter the room. Emery came to tell me so, once he had returned from the Elwin household. He had chosen to busy himself playing messenger.

I could not decide where else to go, what else to do with myself. I had forgotten that the younger Hughes would inevitably be at his bedside already. I marched into there, after a period of deliberation further down the corridor, and their muted conversation ground to nothing at the sight of me. Kai acknowledged my presence by surveying me from head to foot, and he placed a hand on his brother's shoulder. Without a sound, he then raised himself off his chair and slid by me, swiftly and silently making himself scarce.

The door clicked shut behind; I heard his quick footsteps fading down the corridor.

I hesitated before I took up the empty chair he left behind. Dark eyes followed me, blinking slowly, but deliberately avoiding my face. Their usual bright lustre was missing. Even when I faced him, he remained muted and still, save for his fingertips, which tapped relentlessly on his empty left sleeve. So, the task of filling the void fell to me. Not having many options to choose from, I had to progress with the first thing that came to mind.

"Hello, Benjamin."

He gave me a certain resigned glance that, from nowhere, prompted all my instincts to desperately demand I look away. However, never one for blindly giving in to orders, I refused to concede—a decision that both filled me with more regret, and that I simultaneously lost the right to take back, with every passing second that we lingered there, waiting for what, exactly, I had not the slightest idea.

Benjamin had to be the one to break the impasse. It was always going to be him. He dove suddenly toward me, his brow furrowed. I braced myself, expecting a vicious crack of his forehead against my skull, perhaps an attempt to break my nose, but instead met with the more perplexing sensation of his mouth on my own.

It was really very simple in a literal sense. He had merely kissed me. No, it was everything else odd that arrived with that: the sudden feeling of frailty that bloated my head, left it swimming, as though I were falling, so sudden and invasive that I might have been convinced, if I had not forced open my eyes. And the sharp terror that rose through my insides, not that required me to escape, but that wanted to stay and fall, to allow this upheaval to continue, to go with it. And the fact that, even above all of that, I could myself focus only on his softness, the remnants of some sugary thing he had eaten, on the way the pores of my skin prickled under the hand he briefly brought to my face, before he flinched away with a harsh breath.

Benjamin's eyes darted frantically about my face, as he shuffled back until he hit the wall. "Shit," he said, "I misread that. I'm so sorry, I shouldn't have just—"

"Wait," I tried to interrupt.

"No, it's not fair. I could feel it. You should've just shoved me away. I can't carry on jumping to conclusions and thinking that—"

"Stop."

He finally halted to glance at me, once I grabbed his loosely clenched hand, still hovering out in front of him, so tightly I could trace the skeleton within. I seemed powered by some impulse, probably the same terror that had not quite left me yet.

Suppose I did not care. What then, Benjamin? I wanted to remove that pained look from his face, which had no place being there, of that I was most certain. But I did not know how to communicate any of that to him. My meagre attempt merely culminated in narrowing my eyes and bending my head in various directions after which, having observed, he spoke in a lowered voice, though the two of us were the only ones around to hear him.

"Fen, are you trying to…?" He raised an eyebrow at me, which I took with slight offense.

"I want—Yes, I am, I suppose! I don't know what to—I don't understand any of *this*," I replied, more shrilly than I initially intended.

He released a sigh, and laughed, finally, a tinkling sound that seemed to lift up the air it touched. "Crivens, man! Who does? Don't panic so much."

"You can hardly talk," I said.

"Don't give me that. Look, here."

He reached forward to place his hand over my eyelids, plunging me into darkness, and frowned when I tried to open them again. The same hand came to rest around my shoulder, thumb drumming lazily on the side of my face, until I realised I was supposed to follow suit. This proved startlingly difficult to achieve when one could not see anything. I should have reminded Benjamin of that detail, but before I had the chance, he pulled me closer and kissed me again. He moved slower, more deliberately, as though giving me time to make sense of it all. I did not, but now that seemed, to me, like a waste. Instead, I tried leaning into his warmth, and in return I felt the corners of his lips quirk upward. Whatever he had skipping around in his odd, buoyant thoughts must have passed into me, as I found myself dozily smiling against him as well.

Recognition struck me. I jerked away, shaken, although the dumb expression was already creeping back over my face, in spite of any, more perturbed look I tried to summon in its place. I could not recall ever smiling in this ridiculous way. What few memories I did have were useless. I glanced to Benjamin for any indication; he scanned my face, that bright little glint returned to his eyes, but they were clouded, awash. At the same moment, I saw a tear escape from the corner of one, which he hurried to blot away as soon as he noticed it too.

[Kai]
Aria managed to intercept me in the corridor. I was not aware she had returned, and tried determinedly to avoid acknowledging her, keeping up a steady stride, until she practically jumped sideways into my path. Her lips pursed, almost disappearing into her face as she examined me. She leaned forward, her hand on my arm, possibly expecting me to speak up first.

"Have you come from Benjamin's room?" she eventually questioned.

"Fenrir's with him now. I wouldn't try going in there."

I did not make an effort to imagine what they were discussing. Ben had wanted to see him; I knew that much. He had attempted to rein back his relief when the Soulless barged through the door, but he always broadcast everything so blatantly on his face. I could not simply discard the hatred of Fenrir I kept barricaded in. But this went beyond me. I had to try to give them privacy from me, both in that room and in my scrambling mind, even if all I could do was to leave him my chair.

I slipped out of Aria's grip and slid down the wall until I was sitting on the cold floor. She bent forward to check me over, perhaps for injuries, or that I was still conscious, her hands resting on her knees. As soon as I reacted by fixing my bent collar, she took to the other side of the long stretch of stone wall, planting herself opposite me. She absently unravelled her hair and went to tie it into the same braid again. I realised she would not leave until she had answers. She had devised an unusual, yet ruthlessly effective tactic of interrogation.

"My name," I started, "isn't Kai."

"No?"

"No. My actual name is Gaius Hughes. Stupid isn't it? Makes me sound like I'm a thousand years old, but my mother liked it for some reason, so it's what I've got."

"Are you close?"

"We were, as much as we could be, I suppose. I don't recall that much of her."

"Oh, I am sorry, I should have realised. I will not press anymore; I simply could not help asking."

"It doesn't upset me. It was a long time ago."

"It changes then? It gets lighter?" Her voice suddenly grew just a little louder.

"I suppose so. I am hardly the best person to ask, you know. I was only small; I didn't even understand what had happened at that point, when Dad told us she was gone. If I remember right, I asked him when she would be coming back."

"How horrible."

"Don't do that, comparing yourself to me. This is basically all I have ever known. Our situations are completely different."

"Are they though, completely?" She stopped, and curled up against the wall, with her eyes gently closed for a few seconds, before she seemed to recollect why she had come in the first place. "You had a point."

I had to think back first. "Right…Mum. One thing did stick in my mind about her—besides her outlandish taste in baby names—something she constantly said to the two of us. She taught us to be protective. She wanted us boys to make sure, something like, no matter what else happened, what else we lost, we would always have the other when we needed him. But now Fenrir is in there, and I don't think—I don't know."

"You cannot shield him from this."

"I shouldn't. I tried, but he doesn't want anyone doing that, not this time."

"I understand."

"You do?" I felt a migraine coming, right behind my eyes.

"You look like you are struggling with the thought, though."

"I don't know. I feel like the best—the only thing I can do, is leave this alone, do nothing at all."

"I think you are right. But that still bothers you. It that because it is Fenrir?"

"Maybe so. I hate him. I hate him so much. Don't you?"

She held her head up with her hands. "Not anymore, certainly not like I did before."

That irked me. She made little effort to conceal how she detested the other Soulless. What changed for this one? I realised how lonely I might be by now. But surely someone had to be left, to at least hold him accountable for what he had done.

“But,” I continued, “Ben’s different. He is so taken with Fenrir, you know. Out on the terrace, he saw him first. He gets this whole air about him. And I’ll probably never figure out what Ben did, but the Soulless would’ve given his life for him, just as I would have.”

She shook her head, gazing up at her thoughts. “You cannot take that away,” she said.

“No, I can’t.”

Aria seemed to be making herself comfortable on the floor. I would not let her fall asleep, only for someone to trip over her later, and wonder how she ended up down there. As I lifted myself to my feet I, too, felt onerous to move. I tugged at her shoulders, until she wrapped her hands around my wrists to be craned up.

“Please, do not worry,” she said, the strain showing in her voice. She patted my chest. “I will make sure he is okay.”

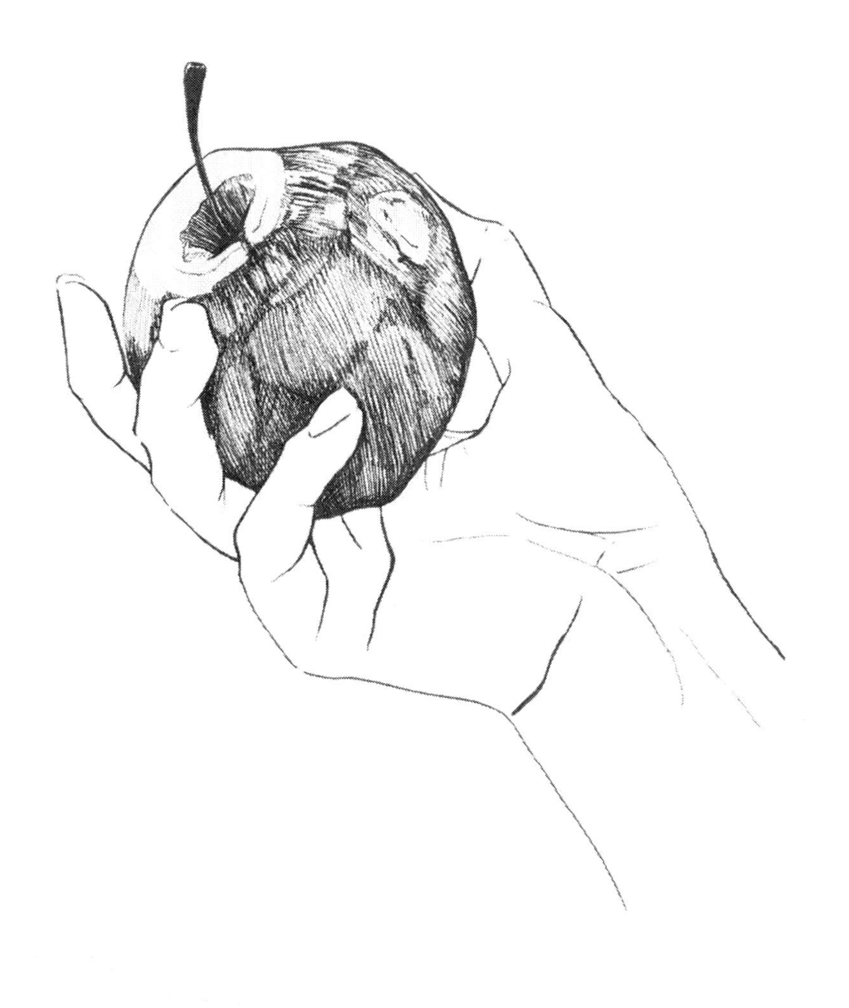

[Benjamin]

I wanted to go outside for a while. Not even into the streets, just anywhere but this room. Frustration bubbled up in my chest whenever I went to shift that arm or wiggle that foot and still felt nothing. Not pain—just nothing. And that only made the feeling eat away at me some more, because the proper, gracious part of me knew I was lucky to be here at all.

The door's hinges croaked again, announcing my fourth visitor today. This was nice. People made me restless, but company sat so much better in my head than total solitude that I appreciated it at the time. I popped my eyes open.

Peering, very delicately, at a spot on my face, she pulled the door closed, as though I looked asleep, and she was deathly afraid of waking me. She had something wrapped tightly in her other arm. As she turned around, I saw her scarred cheek and remembered. I gave Eris Rayne my best smile.

"Good evening, stranger!"

"Hey Benjamin," she said flatly, but with a twitch of a smile.

"The seats in here don't exactly look the cushiest but feel free, if you want. To what do I owe the lady's presence?"

Her mouth fell open while she formulated what to say next, blinking a few times with round, sleepy eyes.

"Uh—Well, I have wanted to come and see you all day, since we were told you are allowed visitors, but I struggled to think what I could even do to help. I mean, it is just me, and I'm pathetic at this sort of thing. And Kai was not very helpful either so…" She looked down to the book she cradled. "I had an idea; maybe I could read. I always liked hearing people read. Still do, it helps me to sleep sometimes. I can't profess that my croaky voice will have the same effect, but it is all I could think of. Sorry."

"Bah, absolute nonsense! I like the idea. I think it sounds quite cosy. Better than flowers or anything like that. Hold on a tick; let me get comfy before you start." I shuffled around, burying myself into my various pillows and covers, while Eris dragged over one of the atrocious straight chairs. "So," I asked, "what're you reading me?"

"Oh, it—I couldn't decide what you would like, so I picked out an old fairy tale, the proper version too, mind you. Not some crap adaptation of it."

I had been about to laugh, but she looked so mortally serious in that moment that I decided against it.

"Is that okay?"

"Pardon? Oh, of course, whatever you like," I replied, waving my hand nonchalantly.

"Are you sure?"

I turned my head away and shut my eyes again, in the hope that, perhaps, she would be more comfortable if she did not assume she was being watched. Otherwise, I would only feel guilty.

[Eris]
"That's it."

The tale was a relatively short one, and suitably easy reading. Even my own eyes were heavy and mind beginning to swim a little, by the time I finished.

I glanced up to Benjamin's shape, smothered in crinkled white linen. He still faced away, but the smirk barely visible on his face revealed that he remained very much awake.

"My apologies, what a total waste of time that turned out to be, right? Gosh, I feel right awful now," I said, and meant it sincerely, yet for some reason I could not help but smile with him.

"Quite the opposite actually, I can't remember the last time I felt so well-rested. Your book is capital; haven't the foggiest idea what happened in it, but it worked, whatever it was."

"Honestly, I cannot truly recall either. I cocked up a few words somewhere in the middle and must have stopped paying attention after that," I admitted, those botched sentences still knocking around in my head.

"You did? I never noticed. I kept drifting off elsewhere. You listening, Eris? Thank you. I'm grateful. Got that?"

"Wh—Of course, you're welcome anytime. It is no trouble to me."

"I may take you up on that," he hummed, looking very weary all of a sudden. "Speaking of people who need some rest, you look utterly spent yourself. Go on, you make me feel a villain."

I complied, with due haste.

Over the following three days, I would return to Benjamin's bedside four times. I read aloud each evening, after which he would thank me insistently and immediately shoo me away to my own room. To begin with, our little routine seemed to work impeccably. The old solace of holding a book in my hands, combined with Benjamin's consistent delight at it, gave me a small sense of comfort.

It would be short-lived. By the third day, I became far too restless, not because too much happened around me, but because so very little did. The loss of our General—the reality of her death at a Soulless's hand—left the building suspended in limbo. Everyone retreated to their own unspoken territory, haunted, yet unprovoked by the phantom still left dangling over our heads.

"One more," Fenrir had said little else since he woke. *"She has one more left to send for us."*

So, we had two more, in truth, according to his word: the one who called themselves Morrigan, plus their last remaining servant—two more. But how were we supposed to survive this? General Elwin had not. With every passing hour, the walls closed in a little more. My breath glanced hot off the stone, back into my eyes, left them weeping.

My fourth visit to Benjamin came with a rushed note from his brother. Kai had abruptly requested I deliver it to him, voice terse, and gaze preoccupied. I quietly set down the steaming mug I had prepared for him, took the fold of paper, and assumed he was to be left alone. Benjamin nodded, clearly with greater understanding than I, as he opened it in his hand.

The next day, visitors were prohibited from his little room.

[Aria]

"Have I changed, Emery?" The room was still, but my voice slipped out so small it rumbled inside my head. I could not look at his face, so I opted instead to look vacantly past him with a pathetic glaze over my expression. "Before," I murmured, "when I acted so horridly strange towards the apprentices, you scolded me for not being true to myself. And you were right, of course you were. My trouble passed, and everything felt okay, for a while. But now, it just seems too different. I want to go back. I wish I were your Aria still. But I look at myself now, and I just cannot find her. What should I do? Have I really changed so much?"

As I spoke, my chapped fingers worried the creases of my shirt, tracing the raw blemish still left hidden underneath, gingerly, as a sort of distraction, perhaps. I must have looked dreadful, as Emery caught the offending hand and pressed his gentle fingertips into my palm.

"You have. But given the valley you have been—are being dragged through, I would be more disturbed if you hadn't," he told me, in a tone soothing and familiar, reminiscent of being bundled in a warm quilt. He tapped my forehead with one finger. "So much of this is changed. You have seen, and heard, and been made to know far too much to avoid that. But your heart is all the same. Believe me, it's strong enough. War hasn't taken our Aria from us yet." He reached up and brushed the wilted hairs from my cheeks. The slight coarseness of his fingertips brought some of the lost warmth back to my face with each little touch. "You carry on, just as you are," he said, and waited for my reply.

I desperately wanted to thank him, as I knew I should. To tell him, however many times I must, that he was more wonderful than he would ever believe—I knew that much—and that I refused to lose him too. But I failed to find the proper words, should they exist (perhaps clever Eris could have told me), so instead I offered him the loveliest smile I could possibly muster, and grabbed hold of his hand before he could take it away. I kissed his palm. It was such a small gesture, really. But looking into my face, he took my other hand and brought it to his own lips, with steel in his shining hazel eyes.

"It's alright," they said, without need for words, "I understand."

All at once, a heavy burden of doubt and loneliness lifted its tight grip from me. And in that brief moment of clarity and unwavering trust, I felt I might not be abandoned here after all; whatever mama had seen, she knew it meant enough, and I would prevail, even without her. Not yet, not for quite some time—my mother was gone, taken from me by an animal that probably had no comprehension of what that meant. I was missing a whole piece of myself, but others surrounded that blank space, still in need of me, right now. Therefore, I would continue, resume. My heart would not fail me.

Without thinking, I fell forward, hiding my nose in Emery's collar. The crisp fabric gradually turned wet under my face, and I realised I was crying. He chose not to speak yet, simply stroking my back with one hand, and resting the other over my knuckles, where they had collided with his chest. I hardly noticed him, as he carefully coaxed my fingers out of the tight fists I had made. I waited for my breathing to slow and with it my thoughts to straighten out a little. I knew there was a good in tears, or at least, in their ability to clear out the mind.

I could not decide how long it must have been; the puddle on Emery's shoulder had dried into a wrinkled patch rather like a used tissue. Even then, I found I preferred to stay very still for a while, lulled by the steady drum his heart made against my fingers, and the slight rise and fall of his lungs.

Finally, I said in a low, scratchy voice, "This is going to happen a lot, isn't it?"

"It should," he replied, simply.

A pause. "We need to gather everyone together first thing in the morning. I would like to speak with all of them."

"Really?" he said, though his tone was not altogether discouraging.

"Yes." I sat up properly to assert my point. "Yes. But before I do that, I need Leo."

With that last remark, I rose to my feet and flew out into the corridor. Hearing the door swing closed, a shiver of guilt coursed through me, as I realised I had left Emery behind, and quite clueless, after having been so patient with me. But I needed to find Leo before I lost what I had to say, this entire revelation had come so far out of the blue.

Thankfully, rather than purposefully wandering the building as I had so often known him to do, he had retreated to his own quarters for the time being. He appeared from behind the door with a withered expression, which he tried to fix upon noticing me knocking on the other side.

"Leo, are you feeling well enough to talk for a bit?"

He made a baffled noise first, before he said, "Of course I am Songbird. I'm fine, be assured."

"Do not be silly."

His face moved into a tilted half-smirk, and he nodded in a small, private reply. Leo could admit his facade, though noble in principle, did not work on everyone, all of the time.

"Could you come to General's office?" I added.

"As you wish."

He stepped out and followed me all the way there, even insisting on closing the door behind us, while I waited on the faded rug not quite covering the office's floor. Part of me expected him to start calling me "ma'am", which led neatly on to the subject at hand.

"I have a—actually I have two favours to ask of you, Leo, if you will hear me out."

"Go ahead," he said, and bowed his head, a sign that he was, really, paying courteous attention.

I turned on the spot, getting a picture of the room around me. It seemed so big and gaping all of a sudden. "I believe, word roved around that after my mother retired from her position here, I would take up her place. I know I talked an awful lot about it, at least."

"You certainly did. General Elwin often described your fearsome determination in that regard. A crafty little glint appeared in your eye, supposedly, whenever you looked at that chair." I watched Leo's gaze shift briefly to the empty armchair lined up at the opposite side of the desk.

"I suppose I did not know that. But, did she account for this?"

He stood, moving to face away from the chair. Maybe he took my question as one not to be answered.

"I am here to ask you to take up her title, to be the new General. You can do it. I am not stupid enough to think that I could just get up and lead these people. It just makes more sense to me. If you are willing, the name—the chair, per se—is yours. Please, Leo." I exhaled, and felt my body sag, like only the air inside held it upright.

"Raise your head up, Elwin." He patted my shoulder as he snuck past me. I stared as he slowly dragged that very chair out from under the table and lowered himself into it with a deep sigh. He rubbed the back of his hand over his eyes.

"It's not as cosy as it appeared from over there, for one thing. Hell, I haven't stepped foot in this room since she last left it. Suppose I shall have to dig through all this stuff; I never much liked the look of those shelves. Maybe I'll start with those."

"Then…"

"You mentioned a second favour you had in mind, which was what?"

"Oh, the other thing." I stumbled over my words at first. "I meant to ask, if by chance you did decide on taking up my mother's command, for you to summon the watchmen for tomorrow morning, on my behalf."

"What for?"

"I would like a word. With everyone I can."

"I see." He started leafing through the papers currently littering the desk, as if I had disappeared. After a quiet minute or two, he glanced up from under his brow. "Did you leave Emery stranded somewhere?"

I took a little step back, taken off guard by his apparent gift for rummaging inside my brain at will. "I am not sewn to *Lieutenant* by the hip!" I contested, seemingly implicating myself more than I helped, given the raucous laughter he let out. "Yes."

"Go on then, away. You've got a whole building of soldiers—who I can guarantee aren't in the mood for a lecture—all to round up. Go on." He slouched back in his seat, wiping a hand over his eyes. "I've got this."

"You're right. Thank you, General."

[Emery]

Aria straightened herself. On another day, at this point, the low mumbles would gradually die out. But now, only the slight scuff of her shoe filled the gap.

"Look up now soldiers, I have to tell you something," she started. Even with a razor's edge, the sound was birdsong. "There will be an end to this. General Naomi Elwin is gone. She did not abandon us; she did not pass on. She is dead. She died, and she died on her feet. She saved us, knowing we would be okay. I know that I am not right now, but I shall be. I will not allow her sacrifice to amount to nothing. There is still one fight left before the path for our enemy is clear. One more, and it is coming for us. I say let it come, so that we may finally have our triumph. Let us bring this war to rest. Wake up soldiers; it is time."

The resolve radiating from her voice, from her words, did not betray the tremor in her hand. Somewhere in between verses hers had, concealed behind our backs, searched out my own, already hovering there in case she had a need for it. I watched her, careful not to turn my head too much, focusing on that tiny dark spot in her right eye.

"And such a fine morning it is," I whispered, the unruly smirk still creeping into my voice, but low enough that only Aria would hear it, or no-one would. Carefully unknotting our fingers, I dropped silently onto my knee.

A breath was all it took, before they fell together—Leo, Tank, Medi, the watchmen—into perfect formation before her. But she twitched when the two young apprentices followed them. They offered up the same salute, which, by reasonable account, neither would have known before this. It was not theirs to give. I glanced up at her eyes, which were now fretfully scanning from one bowed face to another, as though she wished to affirm the identity of each one in her mind.

"I can't exactly join in with the gesture but," an uncannily blasé voice sang from the threshold, "I'm here too, if that'll be enough."

Benjamin Hughes hunched over like he was drunk, a hand pressed against both edges of the doorway. As he blundered a little further into the room, one clumsy steel foot scraped against the floor. He took a moment to grin, jubilant and exhausted, at his younger brother, who reclined on the ground, evidently having lost his balance in shock.

After which he turned to look into Aria's face and said, darkly, "Sure, I'm ready. Let's give them hell."

Until then, I had not seen him, could not face him. I did not deserve it. Fragments of an illusion lodged in the underside of my mind, shrapnel of him, grinning gloriously as he tore out my throat with his teeth.

[Eris]

I hesitated, standing dumbly at the door, hand half-outstretched towards the handle, before I chose to knock first.

Assuming the muffled grunt I received, in fact, constituted an invitation, I entered to find Kai sat behind his wide desk, still flipping purposefully though a stack of papers. His arsenal of tools had now, for the most part, disappeared. I could not quite see his eyes from behind the rims of his glasses, although he must have spotted me.

"What is it?"

His voice still had an edge to it, which tempted me to simply turn around and leave him to his work. I realised that I perhaps should have figured out why, precisely, I chose to disturb him before I did so.

"Thank you for, um, for elbowing me back there. I'm glad you knew how to react to that, unlike me," I said, with a trembling laugh, clasping my fingers together.

"It's fine. She was pretty overwhelming."

"She was incredible; and the way she sang for us afterward, so stunning. I cannot comprehend her; in a good way, obviously," I rambled.

Kai stopped and rested his chin on one fist. "Yeah."

"I—I didn't expect to see Benjamin. He seemed rather pleased. With his shiny new arm and leg, I mean. I don't know how he managed to make his way to that room all on his own."

"Sheer audacity, if I had to guess."

"Mm, I'm guessing that it was your work. It's amazing. That is what you've been up all this time, right?"

"That's right." He squeezed the bridge of his nose between his fingers.

"Is there anything I can do?" I asked sluggishly, kneading at my face with the heel of my hand. "Probably not, I know; there never is, usually, but I just feel like—"

I glanced over, and barely caught the glint of two silent tears creeping down the slope of his chin. I gasped with no sense for courtesy. Kai stared unblinking at the open door, his face slowly melting into a bewildered expression.

"I just had to build new parts…for Ben. My brother, he's trying to walk around with this metal leg and shitty contraption for an arm stuck on him." He locked on to my gaze briefly, the agony on his face too awful and strange to bear. With a blink, more tears fell, before he curled into his arms, glasses clattering into the table underneath.

Without contemplating over it, I approached him, dragging my feet to make sure he heard me coming. I took up a little wooden stool to his left and collapsed onto the desk next to him—Kai did not shift. I lifted one hand, and placed it on the back of his head, thumb patting the short hair at the nape of his neck.

"I don't know what to tell you." I murmured.

I could not be certain how many minutes passed before he spoke, only that my elbows had begun to ache from resting on the rough wood.

"You know," he said, lifting his head just enough to peer over his glasses, "a coffee would be great. The one you left for me before went cold. Sorry about that."

I had to grab the stool to avoid it toppling to the floor behind me; such was the enthusiasm with which I leaped up at this welcome opportunity.

My excursion to the kettle gave me chance to mull over what had been our first real conversation in days. It had involved so few words for what had been said, and the ones I had managed seemed to hold little weight. And during this compulsive period of reflection I happened to remember that, even in that whole, agonising wait, I had still failed to ask if he was okay.

Yet, when I crept back through the door, he almost looked restored, save for the telling red swell about his eyes, more obvious now without the lenses. He seemed bemused at my return, from the look on his face, which only increased when I held out one of the mugs in his direction. I wondered if he had even noticed me retreat in the first place.

"Oh, you actually got one… I was half-kidding when I said that to you."

"Only half," I contested, "and I thought it couldn't hurt. You don't have to drink it if you didn't want it."

"Of course I'll have it," he said, snappily. "You're pretty much the only person in this place who can make a proper one anyway. Here, I'm just not used to it, that's all."

He took the mug, and I noticed him blink his glassy eyes a few times. I considered carefully whether or not to question it, given the previous result of me doing so. My face must have spoken for me. He looked down, pressing his lips together, something turning over in his thoughts. I waited a while. He stayed silent. Then, all of a sudden, Kai spilled out over his edges. Some component in that coffee-infused steam melted away the mask for a few remarkable minutes to let him breathe a while.

"I wasn't always like this, I don't think. Such a miserable bastard, I mean. Actually, from what I remember, I was pretty meek and quiet as a kid. Still, I never as smart as Ben, never mixed well with other kids. I couldn't figure it out like he did. But everyone had to have friends then, didn't they? Had to have people to play ball with after school or whatever, right? So, I went along with whoever would take me. There was what, three of them? Plenty of others came and went, but it was always them, always those few in the middle. They never liked me, really. I'm sure of that now. Not even in a punching, kicking, head down the privy way. I would have known what to do with that, no doubt. Can't say I'm even offended by it—there probably wasn't much of me to like. But I was useful to have around, I suppose. I didn't speak a word, no matter what they did. Yeah, I made a bloody brilliant doormat. I reckon that's why they let me hang around like a clingy little lost dog for so long, kept eyes off, trouble away, right until I outstayed my appeal. Then they just wanted rid. They tried all sorts to shoo me off. I stuck there, mind you. I don't know how many kids it worked on before, but not me. I could be fucking persistent, if nothing else. Perhaps they did too good of a job convincing me I had nowhere else to go. Ha, played themselves, didn't they?"

He spoke of a past life, something distant, disconnected from himself, in his mind—just a memory that he thought had lost all its magnitude, either through neglect, or overindulgence. I struggled to keep up. Kai's train of speech, usually so regular and complete, became momentarily scattered. I could mostly salvage a creeping sense of a bright little boy growing ever more alone, and more bitter, as others had their play, and tried to dispose of him. He never named any of those peers; who they were individually held no importance. They had become a single entity, a legion, to him.

"As soon as I could get to work, and away from the lot of them, I did. That shit would never happen to me again. I'm not sure when I decided that, but I did. I stopped troubling myself with people. I gave up. You would have been spitting if you had seen me then, I reckon."

"Why? I don't believe so. Just think: you're choosing to sit here having coffee with me, probably the most difficult person to deal with here. And I'm not angry. Actually, that's not true. I am angry, but not with you—with people who find it agreeable to treat others like ragdolls. If anything, I feel sad."

"Why didn't you say so? I would have shut my trap."

"It's no problem. I would want to talk about it."

The longer I sat there, watching a spot on the wall just past his nose, the more grateful I became for Benjamin being here, still with him.

"I'm not trying to suggest I'm excused for the things I said to you. It doesn't work that way, I know."

"You already made your apology, Kai. I forgave you a long time ago."

"You know what?" he said, taking a gulp from his mug. "I'm not sure I even noticed that I'd changed, before Ben said something to me. I didn't understand it at the time. We'd probably been making dinner or whatever, when he looked at me and said: 'You used to laugh so much.' Dad didn't come back with anything; he just glanced up, with this look on his face. I remember being pissed off at it but, underneath all that, sorry for something. He looked a lot like you—sad."

[Benjamin]

A riled alarm blared in my ear. I really needed to move that thing across the room before I made myself deaf. I smacked it with my book in retribution, and sat up, ready for my incoming guest.

Right on schedule, exactly between breakfast and lunch, Medi strode into the room, an impressive black bag slung over her arm.

"Morning, morning," I chimed.

"Good morning, young Benjamin," she replied, pulling over a chair, and depositing her luggage beside it. "Ready for this?"

"As ever, I suppose."

"Any lingering pain? Feeling nauseous at all? Dizzy spells?" she listed meticulously, examining both my shoulder and knee with unblinking eyes.

"That would be no to all three," I said, though I had to check afterward anyway. Questions like those always instilled a certain nagging sense of doubt in oneself.

"Then I think we can assume this is working and get on, wouldn't you agree?"

"It seems to be getting better to me, although I can only speak from a technical standpoint, really. Have you had to administer this whole procedure before?"

"Similar, but this is my most unique case. Even with my experience, I am still coming across new developments in the field, it seems. It's kind of a reassuring thought, actually."

I grasped how the mechanisms themselves would function fairly quickly, from the hinges, switches, especially with the steel frame finally fitted to my right arm and across my back, linking it to my artificial left. Lying down was cumbersome and uncomfortable at first, though some well-placed padding would help later. I was at the advantage of having already toyed with ideas like these with my brother before now. I made an effort to understand the more organic side of the process, the melding of metal to bone, tendons and skin. Though, frustratingly, on several occasions the pain had been enough for me to pass out in the middle of it.

"So, you've always been with the military?" I said.

"It's all I've ever done. Why, do you think I would be better off someplace else?" she probed, with a goading twitch of her brow.

"Obviously not!" I gestured at my current state. "What do you take me for?"

"Alright, you pass." She smirked, thankfully, and continued rummaging through the bag. She untucked a pair of cloth gloves, the ones with the peculiar pads on the palms, and pulled them on. This ritual, I could tell, had been carried out many, many times in the past.

"You never considered a different path, then? I mean, my course was always fairly much laid out for me, so I didn't have to choose. I don't mind it, but I do find other people quite an interest."

"You're a bit of a curiosity yourself, mechanical man. Although, if I'm being honest, you're not really wrong. The military wasn't my first choice. It certainly didn't seem ideal at the time. Heads up."

She poked the centre of her palms with her fingertips and laid both hands over the joint between steel and ruined flesh. I hissed impulsively through my teeth.

"How's it feeling?"

"Excruciating as a hot poker," I managed.

"Good man—that means it's working."

"So…"

"So, when my Soul surfaced, I was pretty young, maybe Songbird's age. At first, I thought it only affected me, so when I discovered I could heal other people too, it was, well, I got so excited. I could become a doctor, the best in the Southern District, one who could help everyone with a touch of my hand. The little bit of pain it caused me seemed negligible." She paused, lifting her fingers from my arm. I felt the nerves in my entire body settle. "I hadn't yet refined my ability anywhere close to my current ability, but I knew I would, in time. I was absolutely determined. That didn't work out how I had thought, though. As it turns out, my Soul can only repair wounds inflicted on the body. It essentially works by accelerating the body's natural healing process. It can't replace what's been lost; you know better than anyone. And in terms of disease, infections, anything genetic: completely useless. On your back, please."

"Who was it?" I interjected, before she moved to start on my leg, and the sting silenced me again.

“She was a family friend. I loved her—I mean we all did—but… She had known her life was being cut short for years, by the time my Soul’s power became known to us. So, you can imagine, when we thought that I could save her, we had never been so delighted. My family, they were so proud. She thought she’d woken into a fantasy herself. Perhaps things would have worked out better, if it had been…I don’t know. She forgave me in her heart, of course; she was so lovely like that. After I found out the truth, I felt pretty lost for a while. It was hard. But I also think it made me more determined to make the most of myself, which is how I ended up here. I couldn’t save everyone, but I could save some; I could save some very brave soldiers who’d given themselves up to protect our home. And the occasional person in the city who I get called out to treat.” At that, she let go of me, and fell back in her seat, tossing her gloves back into her bag. “That’s how I see it,” she said, her face unwavering, “and if I look at it that way, I think I chose as well as I could.”

I rose up off of my back, disregarding the smart in my leg. My voice still came out a little hoarse. “Well—and I don’t mean to speak out of turn here, I guess—but I think your folks should be proud. And I think you deserve to make yourself happy. You make it. Just look at this shit.” I bent my elbows and furiously wiggled my fingers, all mechanisms perfectly mirroring their flesh-and-bone twins, to emphasise my point. “That’s mad.”

She smirked, searching through her belongings again, and said: “Careful with those, mister—that there’s something *I* can’t fix. Here, have some sugar.”

I caught, with both hands, a bright object hurtling towards my face, perhaps a reward of sorts.

“Lollipop?” I shrieked at it.

This was the first I had seen of Medi having these. Usually she prescribed a strong, sweet coffee, which worked fine, but here she presented a treat that did not fall into my hands often. It was even a red one. I immediately popped it into my mouth.

“Oh, and by the way,” she added, hesitating at the door, “I tried again with Kai, but he is still refusing to let me try healing him anymore. He seems absolutely adamant.”

"That sounds about right. Knowing him, I imagine he's concerned about accidentally setting you on fire. The risk isn't as terrible as he thinks it is, but he wouldn't like those odds anyway. It's not your fault."

"Yes, he said as much. I suppose it is up to him. I've wrapped up his hands and arms as best I could, but I'm afraid there's not really anything else I can do for him."

"It's alright. Thanks, Medi."

[Kai]

The pocket watch reflected up from the desk at me, lined up in front of my crossed hands. I turned it over; Eris's stint in the library would normally have ended several minutes ago. I listened vaguely for her faint pads down the corridor. She had ought to turn up soon, lest I surrendered and shut up my room for the night.

She had taken to wearing the squeaking shoes now, at least, though I still lurched at the sound of her weary voice. It struck as if a part of me did not expect her to actually appear at the door like she had before. She floated around, neither in the room nor out, waiting for me to recognise her. I looked her way and hummed.

"Good night," she said, blinking heavily.

"You're going to sleep now?"

"Oh, I doubt it, but I'm not much good for anything else."

"I'll just hand this over then," I said, jumping up from my chair.

She hurriedly straightened herself, glancing about her in panic. She was obviously unprepared and thinking she might have noticed some warning of this ambush. I had next to no explanation to offer her, so I opted to simply dangle the watch in front of her face until she realised I wanted her to take it. The silvery chain hung between her fingers as her gaze drifted from the skipping second hand, up to my face (I noticed at that point, how much I towered over her head), then she curiously held the little trinket up to her ear. She seemed satisfied with it, so I turned my shoulder, but this time she did not scarper, perhaps because I had not mistakenly tried to lecture her on this occasion.

"Hey, Kai?" She was stilted; I imagined cogs turning in her head. "I don't know if this is the best way to put it, it's a strange thing to say, but so it goes: I see you." I think she added something after that as well; maybe she caught herself with a quick "I think".

A noise that sounded too coarse escaped through my nose. "Uh, shit, okay." The numb sensation behind my eyelids had to remind me to blink.

She sidestepped towards the door but lingered tentatively. Her reddish hair bobbed against her shoulders as she nodded. A tiny laugh, but it still did not sound quite right.

"Thank you, for this." She motioned with her hands, referring to the watch nestled like glass between them. "I almost forgot to say."

I had forgotten the watch entirely for a moment.

"It's nothing, seriously. Like I said, I mess around with that sort of thing all the time. Always have—keeps me busy." My hand waved dispassionately off to the side. I had only thought that it suited her. "And, you're alright. I get it."

I doubted she knew what I was mumbling about, at first, but then the little tense creases around her eyes dissolved, and I felt secure. As if someone had thrown open a window in the room, the air seemed to get lighter and the silence gentler.

Eris moved like a ghost; I barely caught the sound of her footsteps when she wobbled out of the room, and carefully closed the door behind her. I hoped that she really would get some rest, despite what she said—the sun looked to be swallowed up by the horizon very soon—but that might have made me a hypocrite. Besides, Eris had a constant stubborn aura to her that I did not feel like fighting that day.

My head shook, and I laughed to myself.

[Benjamin]

"How are you doing?" Fen said, fiddling with the cuff of his sleeve.

"Better. At least, I think I'm improving. It is still pretty surreal, to think that a Soul like Medi's could manage this. Making this sort of progress at such an improbable pace, being alive at all even. I'm not quite used to it yet. Put everything together and it is all like a dream to me."

"I see, I think."

"I think so. Ah, I'll get there. I just thought about having another practice, actually. Lend me an arm?"

He approached me, one arm outstretched. His gaze restlessly shifted between it and me, unsure of himself.

"Perfect!" I reassured him.

Using Fen as my crutch, I rose to my feet, swaying a little still, but that was fine, for now. Burnished eyes carefully watched my feet and hands.

"Now what?" he said.

"Just over to the window, then backwards again. You should be able to simply..." I unwrapped my fingers from around his wrists and let my hands hover over his. "...Follow."

"Right."

"Right, and: one...two—"

Fen seemed fixated on my left foot, as we walked up and down, up, then down again. Moving forward was easy; going backwards proved somewhat trickier. At one point, I caught on to the picture the pair of us coincidentally made, quietly stepping up and down in time, as it happened, with the hypnotic tick of the clock mechanism. Up, down, one, two, tick, tick.

We were dancing.

It felt like a breeze rushed through my head at the idea, though of course, whimsy would strike in the middle of a backward stride. My metal ankle dropped at the wrong angle, and I already knew the whole thing would collapse underneath me. It seemed such an awful shame. This would not be the first time, and I readily braced myself to hit the ground.

I heard a sharp intake of breath and noticed, after a second, that I had not fallen down like normal. I became aware of a pair of sturdy arms wrapped under my shoulders, holding me, which I recognised as Fen's, partially transformed—armoured, grey and cold. It was not comfortable at all, but I could hardly help feeling suddenly protected.

"You okay?" asked a low, tentative voice in my ear.

And I laughed. Not so much because I found this funny, but out of some irresistible burst of elation, a gut reaction of sorts. I could not even discern what brought it about; I got to my feet, we walked, then I caught myself in a reverie and fell over, but Fenrir caught me. And I laughed into his shirt, grasping his braces in my fists like it was hilarious.

"Are you okay?" I heard again, in the same tone, once I had eventually recovered and grown silent.

It dawned on me that Fenrir still persisted in a partially transformed state. I probably leeched away at his strength as he spoke. "It happens sometimes," I said, hurriedly. "I'll be okay, absolutely fine. I'm sorry, Fen; look, I'll just go sit down for—"

I went to shift myself, but before I got to finish talking I had already been hauled off the ground, over to my bed, and slumped against a cushion again.

"You know what Fenrir? I think I sometimes forget how much stronger you are than me."

I tried catching my breath. He stood like a sentinel for me, staring straight down at his crossed hands, without a word. It was one of many times, wherein I wished I could just *know* what turned around in that mind of his, right then. But, I supposed, that would be far too easy. No matter what I wanted; these things took time, did they not? They were to be won.

"Why, I am in a strange sort of mood today." I threw my head back with a frustrated, petulant grumble and slouched onto my right side. A cramp slowly began to spread down my trapped arm.

"You are strange. Really, you are a confusing man, Benjamin."

Hearing any my own name in his voice sent up a flush across my face. I could hear him skirting around his words, trying to figure out his own point.

"Confusing, huh? That's new. It sounds a little prestigious, actually. I like it."

"I don't understand you. Worse, I cease to understand myself whenever I stay around you. It's infuriating."

He suddenly ducked down, reappearing in my field of vision to glower at my eyes. I blinked slowly at him and let him continue.

"But, I like to hear you laugh, I think." His speech had slowed right down from its nervous ramble. "It puts me at ease." Then he sighed, something I had never heard from him before.

"That's good. Is that a good thing?" I questioned.

"Of course it's a good thing," he scoffed. "You—"

He cut himself short mid-thought, eyes wide. In fact, he came dangerously close to pouting. I reckoned he had either caught himself, realising he was about to say something dreadfully embarrassing, or he had gotten himself stuck.

Fen proceeded to make one of the most melodramatic grunts I had ever witnessed, let alone from his mouth, and dumped himself on the floor next to me. Clearly, it tickled me somehow; I could not help snorting. I managed to seize a glimpse of his little tentative smile, before being forced to roll onto my back. I could not feel either of my arms anymore, and the sun stung relentlessly in my eyes.

"Can you have a favourite sound? Is that the sort of thing people have a preference for, generally?" he asked.

"Oh, yes, I should think so."

"Alright then."

"Mine would have to be water, I think: rain, rivers, the sea, or whatever."

"Hm. I expected you to say raspberry jam turnovers, for a moment."

"Oh, come on, just because they are objectively the best kind."

"Who said…? Wait—sarcasm."

"You got it. What would a sandwich even sound like?"

"How should I know? What would laughter taste of?"

"I can't tell whether you even mean that or not, but either way, last time I checked, I couldn't tell you."

"Ah, shame. And now I feel hungry."

"Knowing this world though, I imagine there's someone who does know. Still, begs the question."

We fell silent for a few minutes, probably both wondering how exactly we had arrived at this juncture. I did not mind; I relished Fen's small, wistful tangents.

I yawned, before saying: "You should come with us to the beach sometime. We take the train; it doesn't take too long from my town, a couple hours at most. Maybe it would be better to leave Kai behind. He detests the sea. I can hear the waves already—oh, I'm not asleep, right?" I shook my head, rousing myself from my trance.

"Not yet anyway. Just go to sleep if you're tired."

"Nah, I don't want to."

I waited for him to argue back, but he hesitated too much for that. Instead, he took a breath, then spoke in a careful murmur.

"You make me feel safe, you know."

I watched him tracing circles on his palm with his other thumb. "You finally found that word you were searching for, didn't you?" I said.

"I had a sense of this one being particularly important. Don't ask me why."

"What is it you're worried about, Fen?"

"I don't fear I am in danger at all. I'm not. It is a different sort of feeling than that, I think."

"Ah, I see. Then I'm glad. But then, hey, have you ever really been afraid before?"

"Just once." He did not elaborate; I only saw his eyes flick momentarily in my direction.

"I'm guessing you don't want to talk to me about it."

"I don't believe it would be of any benefit. Like I said, that was different."

"You think so? Still, I hope you'll share it someday."

"Why?"

"So I can help!"

"You can't. It is long finished now."

"Not in your head, it isn't."

"That shouldn't concern you. I can handle it just fine on my own."

"I have every confidence that you could. But you don't have to. Hell, if I may be frank, I don't want you to."

"This is nothing. I hardly see why it matters so much to you. You just like people. I get that—no, I mean, I don't get it. I can see it, though. But why are you so intent on me?"

His odd, strained tone troubled me, and I propped myself up onto my elbows to look at him properly. One of his hands reached under his collar, closing around something small. Seeing it again, I recognised the thread tied at the back of his neck.

"Why did you protect me from the Soulless?" I asked him. "Why did you let me drag you out into the streets of Interieur?"

He suddenly raised himself onto his knees, glaring at me square in the face again. His expression held firm, even if his white knuckles betrayed him.

"Sorry," I admitted, "I suppose that wasn't fair of me."

"You owe me nothing," he said, ignoring me.

"You don't owe me anything. And yet, here we still are." I paused momentarily, considering whether or not I should continue. I thought I might be sick. "I have to ask you, Fenrir. You remember what happened, when you first came to see me in this room?" I sounded horribly tired.

"Obviously. As far as I have been made aware, it's the sort of thing that should prove difficult to simply forget."

"Yeah, you're right. That wasn't really my question. I need to know; did you honestly mean it? I'm pretty sure I remember it right, how you reacted. But hearing you talk like you are, I can't stick not being certain anymore."

His face softened a little. "In truth, my experience of all this is so limited, I would be tempted to trust your judgement of the situation. But I will say this: you took me by surprise which, I suppose to your credit, is not easy. You are also exceedingly intelligent—more so than your brother. So, you should realise from my past actions that I do whatever I wish." He crossed his arms and tossed his head to reiterate, which drew out half a smile from me. "I told you that you are utterly confusing, and that is true. But you can stop being so anxious. How I felt that day, it was…pleasant, so good, and sweet, and gentle. I don't know; you could put it more poetically than me."

I sat up and laid my head in my hands. "Don't be daft," I almost shouted, in the midst of a loud breath. "Bloody hell!"

"Feeling better?"

"Much." I stretched forward, to squeeze his shoulders gently. "Thank you, Fen, for that."

Fanning theatrically at my face, I fell back and sung, “So many compliments, though! You must be in particularly good spirits today.”

“What?” He looked genuinely puzzled. I gave it a few seconds for our words to process. His face turned out quite the picture.

[Emery]

I lined the end of my toes up with the edge of the rooftop. This short wall enclosed the whole space, presumably to stop clumsy soldiers dropping off the side of the building or similar embarrassments, but I could scale it effortlessly on one foot. A couple of lonely figures trailed through the square below, like beetles. Not Benjamin and Fenrir this time. I waited for these ones to disappear, until only a pair of crows remained, tilting their heads at each other, as if they had not noticed me while they clung to the same wall as I did. No human eyes watched, no-one distinctly obvious, anyway, and yet I was entrapped by an invisible presence. I felt too heavy, again. I had to get out.

I hopped off of the ledge, dropping my jacket onto the floor; I would need some momentum to reach far enough. I took a run, feeling for my heels against the stone, cleared the wall, and launched myself over the edge.

The birds also fled, menaced by the sudden burst of movement. They feared for someone's life: either theirs, or mine. As my body sliced the air it whipped my hair against my face and screamed inside my ears. Be it blinding sun blistering my skin, rain trying to drown me in a gutter, or wind like this, in every confrontation, nature went to punish me. I would be killed, defying nature, one day. I aimed and adjusted my wire to the tiled slope opposite. The harness pulled on my chest as it yanked me away from the ground and back towards the sky.

I bent my knees upon landing, and simply let myself roll onto my back, wherever the slant of the roof carried me. The surface seeped dampness through my shirt and into my skin. My arms lay outstretched on either side of me, like true angel wings. I allowed my eyelids to close. Cold air seemed to rush into my lungs, if I dared open my mouth.

The atmosphere around appeared to barely fall still, before a bell rang over the chimneys. I counted the strikes; the time was around three o'clock. The bell reached three. And then it continued on. Five. Six. Seven. I looked up again and ran a hand over my face. Eight. Nine. The number ceased to matter.

"Wake up. It's time."

Turning my head, I opened my eyes again. Aria looked down from the taller rooftop, leaning over the wall and clutching my jacket to her chest. I would have to clamber my way down the windowsills. One more left.

Part 5: Ambiguity

[Kai]

Leo held out his arm to stop the group, and then slowly waved us on. He had spotted the target, lurking metres from the shimmering surface of the lake: the last Soulless. Next to my memory of Wyvern, this thing looked miniscule. Though, impressively maybe, when I presumed nothing could be more grotesque than her, I had been mistaken. From a distance, it looked like an emaciated goat, but on closer inspection, rather than round hooves at the bottom of its feet, a set of fat, clawed toes padded at the floor. For some time, it didn't appear to notice us coming, at least until it happened to twist its face in my direction. I felt my nose wrinkle at it. Past its shoulders, the creature's skin weathered away, exposing the whitish frame beneath, including its skull, empty and deceased. Only its eyes, of course, hung limp in their oversized sockets. The Soulless crept towards us, in no hurry. Each movement of its limbs looked puppet like to me, thanks in part to its skeletal build, and otherwise to the sheer mindlessness with which it advanced.

I squinted at it, because it appeared to wind open its jaw, at a bizarre, impossible angle. There was a distinct snap, as its face wrenched itself apart. Its hollowed yellow eyes didn't shift even while, out of its throat, another demon crawled with the same decayed face, clawed feet, and horns wrapped around its head. Scratch that, an exact clone had birthed itself in front of me. I reminded myself that we had come seeking a Soulless, but still had to scrub my eyes incredulously.

"This is Pan," Fenrir confirmed. Clearly his flawed memory had inexplicably held this information from him until now. "And its main purpose is duplicating itself." I pictured him in a circus master's garb, flourishing his hands. As he spoke, the freakish things doubled in number at least twice over. And again, whilst he added, "I imagine you are beginning to realise that for yourself."

"No shit," I muttered. Tired of my stomach churning at the sight, I stepped forward, ahead of the others, held my breath, and drew out my sword in one wide swing. The mob erupted in a blazing arc. I straightened up when I saw ashes in the air, victorious, but glanced behind at the faint sound of more footsteps.

"Not so fast, Hellhound," Emery called, already facing them. There were a dozen approaching him, and more appearing all around us, dislocating their bones and clacking their teeth. As they drew closer, and ever more numerous, I thought I heard hissing. It echoed, like multiple voices all whispering over each other. The sound escalated, louder and louder, until two words could be discerned, repeating over and over ceaselessly.

"Still alive."

"Still alive."

"Still alive."

I gripped the hilt of my weapon tighter.

"Watch your backs." Leo's voice rose over the rabble, sorely reassuring. It meant he heard them too.

Medi laughed, enthused. "Nice, that sounds like I get a look in; it's about bloody time!" She yanked round the halberd hanging over her back.

"Shitting hell, clear a path," Tank griped, but joining at her back. The pair of them marched into the fray, stifling their expressions, looking rather like zealous grins.

Emery and Aria headed in the opposite direction together, while Fenrir charged away alone, with a splitting roar. I covered the portion of our misshapen circle closest to the riverbank. Whatever their outlook was, I could not shake the suspicion that we were being rapidly surrounded and massively outnumbered. However many creatures I slaughtered was meaningless, since a double would always stagger out of the dust.

"Still alive."

"Still alive."

"Sti—"

A bright flash fired a little way to my right, which a nervous flick of my head revealed to be Eris. She raised her left hand—the one with the carbon-plated gauntlet—in front of her face. The remains of a Soulless fell onto her shoes. She whirled around before too long, painfully aware of several more gradually creeping behind her. I noticed her trying to find Leo's eyes, up on his horse, and she started speaking, right before I had to fend off a set of teeth aiming for my chest.

"Sir?"

"That's a strange look in your eye, Garrison. What is it?"

"I have an idea. Or, rather, the thought came to me some time ago, and I sense that now is the appropriate time to make use of it."

"And what do you need?"

"Do you not want me to propose the strategy to you first, sir?"

"Just tell me what you need, girl, and keep it quick." He concluded that sentence with an abrupt stab somewhere I had not been looking.

"Alright: I need you to hold all of these back for as long as you can, whilst I go that way on my own. I need Kai—I mean Hellhound, of course—to run, around the edge until he reaches the other side. That way, when they do get through, they will all be heading in the right direction, I hope. And whatever anyone does, if I am still on my feet, no-one touches the water. That would be all, sir."

"What about a signal?"

"Oh, I didn't think, so sorry sir. Forget I said anything."

"No, I mean do you want a signal? Would it help, yes or no?"

"I suppose so." Another loud crack.

"Lieutenant!" Leo immediately roared. "Soon as one of these little demons gets out of your sight, give us red smoke, got it?" He did not wait for Emery's reply; instead he pulled up beside me and grasped hold of my wrist. "Quit gawking and put that away, kid. You heard the girl."

"What?" I spat out, as he lifted me halfway onto the saddle, and left me to rearrange myself. The hulking mare stamped through the skull of another Soulless. My shin collided with the metal armour coating her leg, the biting sting stealing away my voice. My Soul burned a few more in spite.

"You think I'm about to let you try and scramble over there on your own? Not likely."

As Leo dragged us away, I saw Eris, growing rapidly more distant, step one foot into the lake.

[Eris]

It was quieter out there. Not quite serene, not like libraries, rain, or four o'clock in the morning. But the shuffling of close footsteps had dwindled, and the sounds of yelling and murmuring and scraping metal on bone all melded together to a drone in my ears, nothing against the gentle swill of the water about my waist. Through the persistent images of what could be happening behind me, I was to keep moving onward, onward.

The centre of the lake beckoned me with its calm, with the plan, a promise to myself. I did not find it strictly necessary to reach there, but goals meant ends, which had brought me this far.

To my right, the flimsy landscape seared orange now and then, like the sun, roaring at any opportunity from behind a marching bank of cloud. I looked over to them once: a mistake, arguably, but I deserved it. Its head set firmly forward, the dark, shining horse pressed on, impervious to any and all that erupted around it. How I ached with esteem for the beast. Not unlike its pair of aides. One man twisted around uncomfortably to face to the rear, a white hand reached out, as if to retrieve the explosion he himself wrought. The other seemed to watch me, although his guise was impossible to decipher from here. I told myself that it would be steadfast, knowing, and typically unreadable—but the sneaking resurgence of guilt in me would never believe it.

Still, in such treacherous straits, it should not go amiss to try.

I heard a boom, muffled by distance, but still clear as a bullet. I stopped, to feel the water pulse, lukewarm now, against my skin. I had to unglue my toes from the wet mud, so I could turn myself around. I may have lost a shoe in there—I could not tell. If I craned my neck, I could watch the tower of red cloud swell in the sky. The first clone had made it past the soldiers. Or perhaps it was the original Soulless, the root. Would that matter? Should this work out, I would never get to know.

Emery tracked the escapee into the lake, then suddenly backed away to swing at another, realising several more replicas had already slipped past him. Aria made a quick, sweeping movement with her lance, cutting at least three of them through the middle, before a straggler lunged at her back. Emery threw a knife between its eyes.

The strange, feral creatures squirmed, and reared their horned heads as they crashed down into the water, as though they understood the danger, but were compelled forth by an overriding sense of purpose.

I made one last, hurried glance over my shoulder; Kai looked back, still with Leo, safely on the opposite bank. The fastest path to him was now through me, and inevitably, every member of the horde followed, in a single manic stampede.

I reached both arms out to my sides, trying to breathe. I watched the first one, only metres away now, watch it come closer, pale bony jaw stretched wide. Nearly there: I did not know if I was ready.

The light that came first, then the noise. A vicious white bloom welded my eyelids shut, and stretched over the lake, from edge to edge, followed by the same familiar snap, just longer and crueller. My body contorted upward, pathetic and compliant. And my Soul, too, seemed to be forcibly wrenched from me, as though the water surrounding us could drink up its power endlessly. Merciless screams of countless Soulless raised a hysterical uproar that vibrated over the burning cauldron's surface, and then stopped.

Nothing.

Havoc rose and fell like a sigh. My toes sank down, through the thick water back to the bottom. Feeling gradually returned to my body in the form of an anxious needling under the skin, perhaps my poor tired Soul chastising me. Although the ringing persisted, other sounds leaked underneath—a splash some distance behind me, and a word or two cried, high and piercing from much further away.

Water wrinkled against my back. A shadow rose up over my head. My fingers traced over my wrist, over the grooved handle of my knife, sheathed.

In a single step, I turned, grabbed hold of the Soulless's jaw with my metallic hand, and drove the blade through the creature's throat.

It was gone. The air swelled and squeezed around my head, the scene blurring, focusing, and again, incessant. My heart throbbed inside my skull. I looked out. Through the fog, I caught glimpses of dust, like soot, drifting between my fingers. I staggered somewhere horrid between reality and vacant sleep but, somewhat significantly, still living. Still alive.

The last of my resilience escaped into the water, as I realised once I began to fall further down, under the rippling velvet. I failed to notice the clamour of multiple feet approaching, until two hands hooked under my arms, hauling me high onto the back of a gallant beast.

Hopelessly, I tried to speak, most likely an apology—since whatever inconvenience could only be my own fault—maybe scavenging for the promise of safety, something more than a brittle assumption. But nothing intelligible made it out of my opened mouth.

Merely, Leo gripped my shoulder a little tighter, and said in his soothingly flat tone, "You did good, kid. You did okay."

I heard dry ground under the horse's shoes and, faced with it, I wondered how on earth I might heave myself off its saddle and back to my feet, which pounded at the very thought. Leo instead grabbed me round the middle, transferring me down like a parcel, into a different pair of arms. I blinked my aching eyelids open enough to recognise the dark wool from Kai's pullover, itching against my skin. Heat seemed to radiate from him, enough to dry out my clothes and banish the chill snaking through my bones. He smelled of used matches, and his entire body rattled with his odd, irregular breathing.

"Shit," he uttered, "you're such a tiny thing."

Listening to his cracked voice, I realised Kai had likely been the one shouting across the lake. His words suggested I was not too heavy a burden and yet, almost immediately, he dropped to his knees. His arms did not break their careful circle around me, however. I found I could not keep myself awake, my vision beginning to fail. In the fade to darkness, I saw Kai grating his teeth as he looked down into the lake.

[Leo]

I woke to the clatter of someone with a heavy fist at my door. Through the curtains, I saw the moon still dangled well above the roof, and the streets below burnt yellow just below the windowsill. I could not tell how long they had already waited, but they quickly gave up, and shoved the door open themselves. Tank's face appeared in the gap, despite him previously volunteering to take this shift.

"What?" I groaned, massaged away a headache.

"Garrison came and asked me to wake you, sir. I spoke to her, and I agree; this is really somethin' that needs your ear."

At that, he swung the door into the room to reveal the girl stood beside him, searching for me inside. Her face looked somehow grey, even with my bedside lamp giving it some light. The muscles around her eyelids seemed to struggle to prise them open and her wrist shook, as her hands held a small pile of papers close to her chest. And yet she managed to look more awake than either Tank or myself. This was the same glare she had given me at the lake.

"What have you found, Garrison?"

"The one who created the Soulless, the last one as such," she started immediately, "we were told by General Elwin that her name is Morrigan. Do I have that right?"

Fenrir had given her that label, the same one adopted by the rest of us, albeit with considerable reluctance. I recalled the morning after her interrogation of him. She had called for our attention at breakfast, to provide us with the name of our enemy, and a telling sneer. Often, I would enter her office, to find her holding her written report in front of her, fixed on the only word at the very bottom: Morrigan. Sometimes I expected her to tear the paper in half. Sometimes I figured I would do it.

"Yes," I confirmed for Eris.

Taking a small step, she held out the documents towards me. "I might know where she is."

I noticed I felt oddly calm, faced with her revelation. It may have been that, in all the times I had declared that we "still don't know", or "haven't tracked her down yet," I had truly been waiting for the answer to eventually, miraculously appear out of someone's mouth (though perhaps not in the middle of the night). That, or fatigue was simply blunting my senses.

"Let's go to the office first," I said, slipping a pair of shoes on my feet.

We went there, if for no other reason, then so I could offer her a chair. As I entered, the Black Envelope lay in the middle of the otherwise empty desk. I swept it into a drawer. Eris swiftly filled the space with a map, an ancient-looking broadsheet, presumably from the archives, a volume of "*The Origin of Souls*" by Larsen, on top of which she placed a page of writing in old cursive hand. Off of the floor she recovered a scrap of paper, depicting the words "*still alive*". This, in particular, caught my attention.

"These words," I addressed, "this is what the Soulless was shrieking today." My head rang with the memory, so many echoes of an identical cry.

"Pan, yes. I haven't been able to get them out of my mind since. Something about it felt so off, to me. I believed, at first, it was mocking us, that it presumed, mistakenly, to have the upper hand. Then, I wondered if it might have been merely incensed, because most of us *are* still alive, including Kai and me. And only after that did I consider *her*." She pointed to the name on the book. "What if Pan never alluded to of any of us at all?"

"We all thought the name was some sick gibe," Tank mused, "but, hell, what if it isn't? She had a Soul, didn't she? I'd believe it, even without this."

"What is that?" I asked, glancing over the steeple of my hands at the map Tank referred to, which showed the streets of a county in the Western District.

"Morrigan Larsen conducted the majority of her work in the West—here." Eris pointed. She directed my eye to an isolated dot drawn on the outskirts. "Much of this land around Flodside here belonged to her, which is why it is such an empty space now, just a through road, if anything. No-one made claim to it. But the building is still there to look at, or the pieces of it are. It was ruined in the first attack, the one in which Fenrir caused my Soul to surface. Nothing else nearby was levelled like that; he tore up roads and stripped rooftops on his way through, for the most part, at least until he happened upon us. Somehow, Larsen's place looked more like

Fenrir had hammered into it headfirst. Also, it doesn't add much, but…" She unfolded the newspaper with shaky fingers, finding a small passage and turning it towards me. "…That place was also the last one they ever tracked Larsen to."

I read the paragraph she showed, and again, a third time for good measure, straining to decipher what all of this said and what it implied when threaded together. Each item set out before me lectured in its own, slightly different voice, and they all spoke at once, not unlike the Soulless itself.

"Tank," I said, "do me favour and wake the Hughes boys. Bring them both here."

"Got it, he said, with a yawn.

[Eris]

I suddenly felt so very weary. Clearly, my brain had decided that, having finally expelled those invasive, unthinkable thoughts, it could totter off to sleep now. Only I could not yet; the crack I had made stretched too big. It exposed the chance that I had actually guessed right. I felt my back slide down the back of the chair until I curled into an undignified slouch.

"Here, take this one," Leo murmured, making the effort to lift his big, cushioned throne over to my side of the table, so that I would not be left with a choice.

The siblings entered together, in similar, confusing states of half-disarray. The younger, for instance, wore his glasses, but no socks. Kai shot me a quizzical glance. Tank wandered in behind, leaning back on the same corner of the desk he had briefly vacated. I could not tell how much he had already told them both. Leo observed them, hesitating when he saw Benjamin try to rub under his right eye, only to forgetfully poke himself in the left with his metal hand.

"We thought it sounded important, sir," he said, when he noticed the gaze upon him, peering down at himself and shrugging.

"I need your opinions on a question," Leo replied.

He moved the map to the centre of the desk, drawing them to approach, and begin to see what lay sprawled in front of them. To the array, I noticed, Leo had added another sheet—a more recent document in appearance, in clear, typed letters. Their eyes explored the whole picture, several times between the two of them; I noted that the two shared the same, slightly puckered look about their faces when immersed like this. Leo quickly realised the map had lost the attention of both, and knocked on the wood, snapping them out of their distraction.

"Look at this, and see if you can tell me something: based on what you know about the Soulless, is it possible that they all originated here?" He indicated the little black spot I had marked towards the top-left.

"That is Larsen's research grounds, isn't it?" Kai said.

"Is it possible?" Leo repeated, and stepped back.

"Wyvern," Kai began, after a pause, referring to Benjamin, "you remember how fast it moved?"

"Do you have a pair of compasses to hand, sir?" he simply replied.

After that, the two sank into a mechanical process, punctuated by a constant flow of words, numbers and hand gestures. Kai hastily assigned his brother the arithmetic to deal with, to which the latter groaned and rolled his eyes.

"I hope you don't mind us drawing on your map, Eris." I jolted at the sudden inclusion of my name. Benjamin politely turned it around, so I could see the result, as though I had worked terribly hard on my contribution. "Because we have."

"Oh no, of course," I mumbled.

The page had been overrun by black marks, lines, and numbers indicating speeds, distances, time frames. Crammed into the margins were miniscule calculations I could barely read. I had no hope of understanding all of it but, in particular, a pattern of long, straight lines seized me, all linked to different figures, all shooting off to different points on the right of the map, but all leading from my little dot. I took in a slow, cold breath and sighed.

"You need to go and ask Fenrir if he remembers anything like this," Kai spoke to Benjamin in a low voice.

"He hasn't got any memory of there. He had no idea where he was; how would he know?"

"I get that. Just ask if he remembers going up a slope or seeing the backs of some houses or something."

"Fine."

In the silence left by Benjamin's absence, Leo mindfully gathered up the pieces scattered over his desk, placing them in a square stack in one corner, save for the map, turned intricate diagram, which I still mulled over. Tank paced in a leisurely stride in front of the door, at first grinning to himself over something, then peering out into the corridor, looking more austere as more time passed. I sat, trying to imagine the conversation Benjamin would wake Fenrir with, while tracing the tiny margin numbers in front of me. Every now and then, I forced myself out of a dangerously long blink. Kai took off his glasses, folding and unfolding the arms, over and over, until Tank stopped pacing.

"Here we go," the latter whispered.

"Fen says he thinks he remembers running up a hill about that steep," Benjamin spouted at his usual volume, momentarily forgetting the late hour of the night. "He might have seen houses too, but we're not certain on the relief."

"That's fine," Leo said.

"That all you wanted, sir?" Tank added.

I did not realise until my eyes wandered back in that direction but, in the doorway, Fenrir had silently materialised, arms folded behind his back. The dim light falling over his face made even the Soulless look weary. Benjamin seemed aware of his presence, at least; his head now tilted down, and turned slightly over his shoulder, keeping an eye on him.

Leo towered over me. "You're proposing that Morrigan Larsen is the root cause of the Soulless, and that she is here?"

"You can ignore this if you think that's best," I said. "In fact, I would rather you did. Something just did not feel right, but that's an everyday conundrum of mine, often unfounded. I am merely making a suggestion, given we have nothing else, of a possible risk I chased, doubtful as it is."

"I think she's right, sir. We can't just do nothing; sitting here and waiting for the answers to come running to us is not an option anymore," Kai rambled.

"Calm down, Hughes. I'm not arguing with her."

"What?" I said, choking a little.

"I am going to call a meeting tomorrow afternoon—by then I believe I can formulate a semblance of a plan moving forward. I suppose you should all expect a laid-back train ride." He smiled for a moment. "I will rely on you to ensure the message makes its proper way around, Colonel. The Watchmen might be alone here for a while."

"The question now is how soon we can get over there," Benjamin added, lightly, looking up at us for an instant. But, when I peered again over his shoulder, Fenrir was gone.

[Fenrir]

"I think I should like to take a nap in my own bed first. I like new places as much as anyone, but there is something delicious about welcoming home back after this much time. Then…shit, I think I left half a commission behind—that thing for the stationmaster. Ah well, it's already late as is; that'll please Dad."

Benjamin leaned placidly on the sill under his open window. Attending the conference between the soldiers had bolstered him, releasing the spring of levity anew. Returning here with him had almost become a habit anyway, but in these moods, I drew towards him to be heartened. I pressed a hand against the clot, felt I could seep out, like a wound prised open.

"You will be home soon," I hummed, from opposite him.

"What will you do, Fen, when this whole mess is past us? You've got a lot ahead of you."

"I haven't considered it. The idea never occurred to me."

"Maybe you should, it seems as though it's about to be particularly important for you."

"No, there's no point."

"Why?"

The voice had changed, all of his determined enthusiasm gone with that one word. I took a breath. At this point, I could not think of any way to evade the truth I had already realised, some time ago.

"Talk to me, Fen."

"There is no future. After Morrigan Larsen falls, I will cease to exist as well."

"What? I don't understand. I mean, from the way that sounds, it's like you're going to—"

"Die? Yes, I suppose, in effect." I cut him off as bluntly as possible; I could not bear this conversation, with Benjamin sounding so confused and vulnerable—so human. "Given what I am, it's logical. Reason dictates that, once the source of the Soulless is exterminated they, or rather I, will also follow. I know this."

"That's crazy, Fen. You can't talk like that. Quick, come with me, there's still some time to deal with this," he blundered, already making a lunge towards the corridor.

I held out a hand to stop him. "Don't bother. Don't act like the fool I know you are not. Your superiors cannot realise the things I do, but they are right. We will storm the den where she hides and end her, end this. It is why your brother is here; in fact, it is why you are here. You came to destroy the Soulless—and in that you most certainly succeeded. Your enemies are mere motes of dust in your wake. Now there are only two left: Morrigan, and me. She has to die. I will die. There is no alternative, and no fix. It's fine."

His face slowly twisted, as he grasped what my words divulged. The shadow that crept over his eyes seemed to haunt me, like I had seen it before, too long ago to truly recall. Both of his hands leaped up to cover his mouth and he turned away from me, muttering words I could not decipher. I thought he hated me then.

"I'm sorry."

It was not an untruth. I was painfully sorry, for even existing in the first place, I figured. Benjamin whirled around, like he could listen to my thoughts. His whole face under his eyes glistened white, drenched, and those wild orbs themselves looked swollen and bloodshot.

"Why didn't you say anything—anything?" he bellowed.

I did not move from that spot. I found myself consumed by his face. He looked like a tempest; even his clothes were wonky, and his hair seemed to stand up in odd places. Everything flared red, as he filled the room, tried to shatter its stifling walls by will of his pain alone. I was swept up by him, as always, but I would not yield.

Why?

"Because I know how it felt! I was there, do you remember? I stood right next to you—or most of you, anyway—while you lay in a puddle of your own blood. You were dying then, Benjamin. I knew it. And I could do nothing!"

"What do you mean no—?"

"There is nothing to be done for me! I am doomed to my fate."

"Then it's a good thing I don't believe in higher powers and their damned fates, isn't it?" His voice plunged suddenly deep and deliberate, almost a snarl.

"You should just leave me be," I retorted, probably uselessly—but at least I held the last word.

I soon regretted it. Benjamin refused to look at me as he leaned over to the head of his bed, to snatch a cushion, and then stormed into the bathroom, throwing the door closed behind him. He held out his arms the whole time, I realised to maintain a distance between the two of us. Only then, as I had to watch him there, did I notice his metal leg finally functioned almost seamlessly.

Deathly silence prevailed at first. And then I heard him scream. The sound was guttural, weirdly muffled. He had tried, poorly, to smuggle it away, but that sound served greater purpose than words could. It struck me in my core, such that I wished I could cough up the repulsive feeling it left, if only that meant it would stop.

It took him a while to resurface, and when he did, he twisted the handle slowly, dragging his heels slightly. The rage in his eyes had abandoned him, leaving him only tremendously exhausted. I could not decide which cut worse.

Without saying anything, he made his way towards me and, mostly ignoring my half-outstretched hands, both of his arms, one warm and shuddering, the other rigid and cold, wrapped around my back, clutching me tight to him. I shuddered, as though specks of me had already begun to float away. My lungs were heavy, my face ached, and the air was too hot. My hands snaked past his middle, gripping the back of his shirt. I had to keep him close.

The weight of his head lolled onto my shoulder.

[Eris]

I tried distracting my busy thoughts by escaping to the library, though it seemed of little help in that regard, as hardly any work lingered that I could think to do. It seemed fitting, at least, to finish my pet project now, so close to the far uglier conclusion that I had yet to fulfil. I would have preferred to keep the latter out of my mind, at least whilst it still lurked behind a long train journey, and whatever waited in the rubble on the other side of it.

Tank wandered in, after how long I was not entirely sure. He paused for a moment, to size me up from head to toe. I sat on a table, feet dangling where they did not quite reach the floor—doing nothing.

"Here Sparks, you look like you need it," he said, handing me a decorative little glass, which fit snugly in the curve of my palms. It felt slightly cold. I held it up and sniffed its contents—definitely alcoholic. My face recoiled back from it. I would sound as polite as I could, though the low, rumbling sound that had already escaped me did not help.

"No, thanks."

"Just try it, seriously, and then I'll take it back. I can have two, I don't mind."

I smelled it again, swirling it around. Tank snickered. I took the smallest sip I could manage, went without thinking to hand the glass back, but then looked back at it; this certainly did not resemble any of the vile things I had tasted before.

"What is this?" I asked.

"That'd be rum," Tank said, bemused.

"I see."

I lowered the glass back into my lap. As I peered into it, a thought sprung to mind. It seemed strange to me that it had not been brought up already, in all this time. It felt like so long. In fact, it struck me as somewhat stupid, to ask the question now, but I had to know.

"Tank," I mumbled, "what is your name? Your true name, I mean."

"My real one…? Oh, I get it. Sorry, guess I never told you. My name's William—Will Burkhart. But don't call me that, s'weird when anyone does these days."

"Alright, if you say so." I watched him take up a chair and start rocking it on two legs. He tipped his glass up, throwing a swig into his mouth and swilling it between his cheeks with a satisfied grumble. "I don't know how you do this, Tank," I added.

"Eh, you mean this?" He stared down his nose into his drink. "Well, it's real easy once you—"

"No, I'm talking about how you keep fighting like this, all the time, for so long. You seem so content with it. Maybe you're right: rum is the answer."

"C'mon, not all the time. My city ain't that bad, you cheeky shit," he said, with a small break for thought. "That's life though, ain't it—struggling to survive 'til you die? The content folks just found a way to make a bloody good time of it, I guess. Not you then, Sparks?"

"Me? I am at peace, but content? I'm not sure I'll ever get there. Sorry."

"There's a difference? Huh, let me think about that one, then. Content, am I? I guess I do relish a good fistfight. Lets out a lot of pent up shit, it does," he pondered, nodding, rather pleased with himself.

"That kind of reminds me of what Maud told me once. She said I sap up too much energy in some bloody war with myself, and that's why I'm so tired. Perhaps I'd be better spent beating up the other brutes."

"I like this Maud woman you keep harpin' on about; sounds like a right decent lady."

"The pair of you would get along rather well, I imagine," I said, a tiny smile sneaking onto my face.

[Aria]

I climbed up to the rooftop two steps at a time, propelled by my abundance of energy, although not necessarily of the positive kind. I could not find Eris either in the library or her quarters, so I assumed she must have retreated here. I had to remind her that time was approaching, fast.

When the iron door struggled its way open, revealing her silhouette as she stood looking out over the city, I lurched back for a moment, taking in her appearance. It really was her. Her hair looked much better once I convinced her to let me trim off the split ends. One side hung significantly longer than the other, but she carried it without care, as though it were the latest style sported by all the nightclub ladies. Her clothes were something I had never seen before, though, and her posture appeared so different with them. She wore all black, disregarding the rather incongruous brown leather pumps on her feet, and the most extraordinary little coat. With big brass buttons and a gathered trim, in it, she appeared like a more menacing version of the grand, century-old countesses. The reason behind my disbelief might have been that, of all the soldiers in this place, I had least expected this metamorphosis in her. Fear, rage, and despair did this to people; the wretched Soulless alone could not aspire to achieve it. I almost feared to speak up, with her face so dreadfully stoic as it confronted me.

"Are you ready to go, Eris?"

She crossed her hands behind her back. "Yes."

"And your weapons?"

"Of course." She regarded me with a smile. It was not so gentle anymore. I had seen this expression spill over Emery's face before. Perhaps, if I looked into a mirror, I would observe the same in myself, now.

I accepted what had to be done, to restore her, like an acquaintance, a formality. I could only hope in my heart it was not oo late for Eris, taking some consolation in the fact that, to my admittedly clouded) belief, she seemed to be one of few in this ight who could not possibly be destroyed any more. She had only one direction left to go: onward with all the power she could alvage.

"Alright then sweetie, I will see you out front."

Part 6: Corruption

[Leo]

I slammed the cabin door behind me. The train expected to depart for the Western District in around five minutes. Walking down the length of the gangway, I found the soldiers in their chosen cabins. Tank and Medi had taken one, seated opposite each other. Pulling the door aside revealed Medi, handing Tank a mug of whatever she had brought with her in her metal flask. Seeing me, she offered another, which I tried to turn down.

"It's only tea, Leo; just take some," she said.

I rolled my eyes, but at least took the warm cup with me.

A little further along, Songbird and Lieutenant reserved another compartment to themselves. Theirs was immediately much quieter when I cracked open the door, the two of them sitting on the same seat, arms and fingers woven together. She looked up from his shoulder briefly, to offer a small hint of a smile. I nodded, so as to acknowledge her, before I left them with a trace of peace.

Eris accompanied the Hughes boys, and she simply peered up at me with a heavy, slightly puzzled expression. Kai spoke instead, naturally, not so subtle.

"Leo," he snapped, as soon as I appeared, "Remember, we are going around the outskirts of the town; it will be a faster journey."

It would prove slightly more efficient, indeed. It would also avoid the risk of wandering a step too close to home. I decided to keep this observation to myself.

Benjamin waited a while longer to greet me, facing out of the window, tense wrinkles forming around his eyes and, when he eventually did, the same enmity accompanied it to the surface. He squeezed his hands together so tightly in his lap, he risked cutting the circulation to his fingers—or snapping one in half.

"Try to relax, Hughes. I can't have you hurting yourself."

He coughed and let go for a second or two, only to grip his knees instead. We were able to leave Benjamin at the base when Pan arrived, but he was the first prepared to take off this morning, and he refused to stay. His orders, for now, were to remain behind the main group, out of danger, even if this meant waiting outside the building entirely. I could understand his distaste for the idea, having to turn his back, being unable to act, or even to be present as a witness. What happened from this point on ascended out of his control. But this was the path he chose.

"Keep an eye for me, Garrison," I added, flippantly, on my way out.

Fenrir continued to wander in front of me, waiting, I assumed, for me to guide him to his designated seat. He peered about himself constantly, tapping the floor with his toe as he walked. I guessed he had never been on a train like this before. He certainly did not trust it.

I opened the door to another empty cabin, closer to the front of the train and, sure enough, he clambered inside, perching bolt upright on the middle of a seat. I slouched in the corner, by the window, and took a sip from my drink. Medi had not lied, and there was no doubt that she made outstanding tea. She infused this one with something herbal. The door stayed hanging open.

I turned to Fenrir. "I'm not going to keep you stuck here," I said. "You can go sit with Hughes if you want, or Lieutenant; it's up to you. I know for sure I wouldn't be your first choice."

He did not move, nor did he reply. Merely, he shook his head, facing out of the window and pulling at his shirt collar. To my amusement, he did lean slightly forward, when the wheels beneath us screeched, smoke clouded his view and the train rolled into motion. His nose almost touched the glass.

I could not pretend to know what had happened, but I decided I would have to grow used to my unusual company. Though I resisted calling it fate, something did not want me free to bathe in my sorrows just yet.

[Medi]

The train bobbed around now and again, as it jostled down the track, bumping my head against the side of the seat. All other lines had been halted to facilitate our upmost timeliness, and I gained the sense that we were taking a detour, since we had passed the last field I recognised about half an hour back. This only added to the sneaking sentiment of foreboding I appeared to have unconsciously associated with this place we were headed to. Even before leaving, I could not say I had envisaged this to be a pleasant journey. Realising that, I felt rather embarrassed; undoubtedly, Garrison and Hellhound's home was really quite lovely. What, or rather who, might have been hidden there for more than a century had nothing to do with them. In the brutal task of unearthing her, though, they seemed all too instrumental.

I did not bother to wonder why those two in particular. Having had my Soul for this much of my life, I had grown quite used to being swept along with the Source's tendency for randomness. It did not have reasons, or targets. My thoughts meandered towards different enquiries instead. Like, for example, what—if anything—had occurred in the interim, all those years after Larsen vanished, that meant all this needed to play out now, where we happened to be. Maybe the chaos had been building, very slowly, the whole time. Or, something had been holding it back, until it just failed to do so. Maybe we would find the answers at our destination, or maybe not.

"Well, we're on the bloody train now," Tank had said, once I tried airing my thoughts to him. I detected an uncontrived, even absurd wisdom in some of the things he came out with. After his input, he sat drumming his knees and whistling for a while, until he sighed, mumbled a word or two about stretching his legs, and went strolling into another carriage.

On his way out, he almost bowled over Songbird, who narrowly avoided some embarrassment by ducking under Tank's arm. She spotted me through the door and slid it back open.

"Medi," she said, breathlessly, as if she had come running down he length of the train, "how are you—alright?"

"Sure, I'm good," I answered, though apparently unconvincingly, since she perched on the pew directly opposite, and gave a pensive hum.

“What is on your mind?” she said.
“Just Larsen, I suppose.”
“Are you afraid?”
I shrugged. “Who, me? Nah, I don’t think so.”
“Not even nervous about what she might do, what she might be capable of?”
“What’s the use in being scared, you know? If the old grizzly bear has taught me anything—” I flicked my eyes towards the gangway Tank was likely still stumbling around in. “—it would be that. And I believe him. Easier said than done, I know, but it’s gotten him this far.”
“So then, what is it?”
“I’ve just been thinking about…the right thing. When we get there, if we really do find Larsen, we all know what we’re going to do.” Seeing Songbird lean forward, her mouth open, I marched on before she could speak. “Don’t worry, I know why we have to, and I won’t try anything else. But as I think more about her, I realise she might have found the means to immortality. She might actually have done that. I can’t even begin to wrap my head around that sort of power, or what we would be able to do in this world with it. And we are going to destroy her. Can we come home, after today, saying we did the one and only right thing? I don’t know.”
Listening to me ramble, she had started absently plucking at a loose thread in the seat lining. “Me neither,” she said. “I only know that this has to end—whatever Morrigan has become, now, has to end. Perhaps we will find something at the house, once we finally get there. Something no-one is seeing at the moment.”
“Maybe, though if she is even there, like Leo thinks, then I doubt anything we find would change much. Governance’s word, the Black Envelope, it’s all absolute.” I considered for a moment, before I reached over to rest a hand on her knee. “I’ll help you. Whatever happens, I’ll help you.”
Songbird smiled, and in a blink, I found her arms flung over me, squeezing me tight around my shoulders. I returned her embrace for a second, but I leaned back at the clatter of the cabin opening once again.
“Lookin’ dire, ain’t she, Songbird?” Tank had returned from his impatient jaunt.

She laughed, a light, chirping sound, before she realised she was rocking back and forth in Tank's spot. She suddenly leaped to her feet with a gasp, seeming to float out into the gangway. Her ballerina footsteps soon disappeared under the rhythmic beat of the track beneath us.

[Kai]

"I reckon I can get in this way, sir."

Tank positioned himself on one side of the door, pressing his hand against the frame, with Eris on the other. His observation was directed at Leo, who nodded in assurance. He readied his bladed arm in front of him and beat his way through the wreckage. After ensuring her superior had entered securely, Eris also stalked into the gloom, fist held before her face in an uncannily similar fashion.

Seeing this, I rushed after them, pausing to haul Ben over a tricky beam I had skipped over on my way. I faced a single room, strangely lit by the scattered beams creeping in from fissures in the roof. It might have once been partitioned up by rustic brick walls, but I had difficulty discerning where all of the rubble came from, it was strewn so indiscriminately. The way the building appeared to have fallen struck me as bizarre, as though someone had gutted it from the inside out. Dwelling on that observation, however, proved bloody challenging over the toxic smell leaking out from the corner opposite me. Under a stack of collapsed shelves, splinters of glass littered the floor. A couple of planks were still fastened to the wall on which a number of sealed, labelled jars were lined up. Moving closer, the light glazed over their surfaces, causing whatever sagged inside them to gleam in a yellow hue. Encased within each I could pick out a dark, organic shape. The liquid was alcohol, for preserving carcasses. I scowled.

Something cool caught on my sleeve. Initially, I assumed it would be Benjamin, but looking over, I saw the top of Eris's head. She also glanced at the jars, covered her nose and chose somewhere else to search.

"See anything yet?" Leo did not need to raise his voice in here—somehow that which remained of the building still succeeded to isolate us from the outside world.

"Nothing yet."

"No, sir," Medi called.

"Nah," Tank added. "Well, other than a whole load of weird crap, which I can only pray is a scientist thing, else I won't know what to think."

Behind my view of Eris, under a shadowy patch, I picked out a tall cabinet bureau, softened at the edges. I supposed nature would have eaten away at the antique wood significantly after all this time. It held dirt-smeared models and instruments I had never seen before, and stacks of peeling books that, in another circumstance, I imagined her gathering up to carry back and rescue. I clambered over there, kicked aside a crate that had been pushed against a wall, only to discover nothing, and hastily return to where I could be properly seen.

My head swam as my mind tried to methodically process every aspect of the scene. At my side, Eris took short, fitful gasps, never quite recovering her breath. Her eyes darted around her head, like she needed to be watching every tiny, dim cranny in the room at once. The scratch of cautious heels on the floor trailed beneath us, the only sound. The place was a perfect ruin, exactly as I had imagined it to be. No matter how long I stood, waiting, there was nothing wrong here.

Say the wall swelled and bowed, plaster flaking away, infested with damp and mould, and Morrigan had dropped out from the void, wailing and headless—that might have weighed down upon me less.

"Hey," I heard Emery call. His voice struggled against the weight of the section of roof he strained to shift. Aria scrambled to help him, she too jumping at what he had found. I hurried over, slightly ahead of the others, and saw it. A door interred in the brick, a small and rickety thing, already with a couple of narrow holes where it rotted away. Through those, a passage could unmistakably be seen, hollowed out where a chimney should have been built. Emery reached out carefully, to try turning the handle.

"It's locked," he said simply.

"But there's no mechanism on the outside," I pointed out.

"That mean we're checkin' it out, Leo?" Tank kicked a small clearing in the debris around his feet as he mumbled. Leo hummed to himself, stroking at his chin, but we all continued to stand in a silent circle, watching the door, as if we were all restrained by the same foretold idea of what, or who, could be buried beyond it. Benjamin sensed it, and suddenly jostled his way from behind Leo, staring daggers past all of us.

Pausing before the door, he pivoted on his one good leg, driving the metal version through the wood with a grating snap. And having destroyed the lower half of it, he grasped what remained in his hands, and tore it from the frame, all without a single word or glance behind him. I waited, until he took his first steps down into the void, then I could not watch him any longer. I scrambled down the stairs after him, before anyone could try to stop me. On the edge of my vision I saw, as I turned a corner, Fenrir vault a wooden beam and dive through the wrecked doorway close behind me.

The three of us emerged from the narrow passageway into a basement, directly under the building. The darkness smothered me tighter than any other I had felt. It seemed impossibly thick, like mercury, such that my eyes ached while I struggled to adjust. From the way both Ben and Fenrir ground to a halt, after merely stepping into the room, I trusted they experienced the same. Perhaps this was the natural view to be had, being buried alive. For a while, all I could make out were the rough stone walls expanding out on either side of me, apparently without end. Then the corners finally materialised. I observed a slightly lighter shade of grey soak across the uneven surface, slowly finding its cracks and joints. It had not only been the loss of light that had instilled me with such a sensation; the damp, frigid lid shut so tight upon us, anyone could have reached up and touched it.

Almost as soon as I had staggered into the basement, the rumble of footsteps rolled down the stairway, growing increasingly loud and numerous. At this point, I could have pretended the noise drowned out Ben's sharp, almost pained intake of breath. I wanted badly to simply ignore him. I could have continued to watch the cramped space around us melt into view, maybe calculated its dimensions for no obvious reason. Instead, I had to look across the opposite side of the room, to see the figure he saw, cloaked in the frills of some archaic dress, and a veil of red hair. This was Morrigan Larsen. She was here—still alive.

Her eyes were not blue, like in that picture. They swam with the same putrid colour as the glass specimen jars, like all of her brood. She stood still, and lopsided, far less perfectly poised than she might have been in the past, seemingly afflicted by the thick, flaking chain knotted round and round her right arm, which welded her to the floor.

She watched in silence as Ben strode up to her. In one, almost fluid movement, he joined his hands in front of him, took one last driving step and, bending his knee, swung both round to the left. The metal club of his fist made a dull thump as it collided with her jaw. Her face flew to one side, though when I looked to inspect the mark on her cheek, the ice in my body burned.

Ben struggled to straighten himself, and once he managed it, he met with the same sight of her teeth bared. The woman thrust out the arm hidden behind her back. Out from her elbow, pasty skin transfigured into darkness that seemed to devour the lesser shadows inside the basement. It stretched out, further, far beyond the length of any real, human limb—like a spider's leg—and at the end, moulded itself into a five-fingered claw. The shape made a faint tearing sound as it moved through the space between Morrigan and Ben, clutched him by the throat, and threw his body against a wall. A shower of dust fell down from above his head. A hysterical scream strangled itself inside my chest, stifled by smouldering air. Witnesses always said, it wasn't the fire that killed you. As my eyes gaped wide in a distraught reflection of my brother, I noticed his arms were crossed in front of his neck. The phantom hand wrapped its talons around the metal one, and it looked to be slowly burrowing its way through the steel, like sodden clay. Ben choked against the force crushing against him. A stone seemed to push on the bottom of my stomach, weighing me down. I attempted to move, but Fenrir answered faster. His silhouette cracked and warped from a scraggy man to a dog in one furious, pitchy howl. He traversed from one side of the compact room to another in a manner of a juggernaut, teeth clamping over Morrigan's living shadow, cleaving the appendage in half. It swiftly evaporated, revealing her actual, tiny hand underneath.

Ben, released from the noose, dropped to the floor with a small cry. That scream finally escaped my mouth, but in the form of a low, animal bark. I had a complete view of his mechanical arm, slumped inert in his lap. The apparatus reaching over his body, connecting the two sides, had snapped when his back slammed into the wall. A wide tear split open the forearm section, exposing its lifeless innards in shreds.

"Do you see?" Morrigan finally spoke. "My Soul will rip its fingers through any matter that threatens me: steel, flesh, the very air you breathe. It is all powerless." I found her voice troubling, no higher or lower, louder or softer than I anticipated, but different. It was tainted by something inside her, like how a person changes when they should be shedding tears but finds they cannot.

As the words fell from her mouth, she extended her reach, seemingly without effort, back towards Fenrir. He had almost melted back into his human shape, except for his hands, which snatched hold of her supposed Soul, inches from his chest. It evaporated in his grip, and she twisted around in an abrupt change of tack. Now the hand drove at the group condensed in front of the stairs. I saw all six of them trying to scatter into the tight space in a jumbled mass. I braced myself for a sound—a crash, or an agonised yell—and flashed through various images, each of a different body skewered on the end of that jet pike. I made myself sick. But Morrigan was stopped, in spite of me. The hand burst into white flashing specks, before reeling back into its master in a series of jagged convulsions. She looked across it, beady-eyed and sniggering. Her attack had been intercepted by its mirror image; another hand, cloaked in black, reached out in front of the crowd, its fingers tensed, as though squeezing against Morrigan's sheer force.

Eris stepped a little further out of the light. Her outline blurred, while the sharp angles of the gauntlet continued to flicker like shards of painted glass. Her face suddenly lit up, tranquil, as her Soul reacted to another, creeping assault. Morrigan bent over and gasped, her fingers laid across her chest, like an impetuous child.

"Ah, there you are," she said.

Eris looked at her, unmoving, before she replied, "You should have died."

"Died? Gracious me, no—don't be so hyperbolic, dear."

In the pause, Fenrir's consciousness had shot back into his body, and he tried to lunge at her side, only to be swatted away with ease, by the appearance of a second set of talons. I traced it backwards to its origin. It seemed to burst out of the floor, after sinking down from Morrigan's other shoulder, the one chained to the concrete. She had her Soul, she said: it could destroy anything. But what with the way she manipulated it, that was no Soul, not to my eyes. Fenrir had to transfigure his limbs once again, most likely to avoid breaking them in the fall.

"Does it satisfy you, to destroy things, to consume them?" Eris continued, as though she had seen none of it. "The taste of our flesh, the sinews chewed up between your teeth, do you enjoy it? I think you have misunderstood me. You should be dead. But never mind your head about it; you will be soon."

"That's what you dragged yourself all the way here for, to kill me? Oh, how sad. You seem to be a valiant little creature, in spite of your flapping tongue. I'd hate to tear you to pieces."

"That is why you hid yourself in this filthy pit, no? You would hate having to go to all the trouble. You sent your demons to wipe us out for you, but they failed. They all failed. And they brought us here, back to you."

Morrigan's twisted demeanour switched at Eris's response. She had failed. At once, some last scrap in her broken persona snapped. The grin on her face dropped, and she threw herself forth, as much as she could, swiping and stabbing at the air, striking Eris over and over again. The noise was a nail against my eardrums. While the small, steadfast girl held herself straight enough, I saw her knees begin to shake and her chin droop. Morrigan would never get past her, not while she still stood, the realisation of which left me numb with dread.

I looked to Leo for permission, or at least guidance, finding him already waiting to catch my eye.

[Eris]

I could barely make out a low, rattling voice approaching from behind me.

"Hey."

She would not stop. Therefore, my Soul could not either. A sheet of white-hot light shielded me, but my flesh still imagined the sensation of claws tearing into it. Perhaps it would not even feel like that. Perhaps I would feel nothing at all. The voice came closer.

"Hey, Sparks." Kai's rough, warm fingers wrapped around one of my raised wrists. The bandage wound around his arm grazed against my aching skin. "You can rest now."

"No, I *can't*," I managed to hiss through clenched teeth.

"You need to stop."

No.

"Let go now."

My eyes wrenched shut.

"Eris, let go!"

The grip on my wrist tightened and I buckled, falling to the floor. In that second, the pain stopped, what had survived of my light blinked out and there was silence. I caught a brief glimpse across the room of Morrigan's face, painted with a toothy grimace. I thought she might have yelled, only to be instantly consumed by the roar as the basement erupted into flame.

Two arms grabbed me around the middle and hoisted me back to my feet. Now Tank's words rumbled in my ear, under the crackle and hiss of the fire, which disappeared almost as quickly as Kai had summoned it. Noxious smoke seeped out from damp wooden beams embedded in the basement walls.

I caught the end of his command. "…On his signal, you stay." He released my arms and pointed at my feet, clenching his brow to further emphasise the point.

Another boom. I flinched against the light. My eyes struggled to focus in a room constantly switching from dull gloom to searing red, then back to darkness in seconds. My skin prickled, and a wave of my own blood suddenly seemed to breach into the outermost edge. My Soul had died and returned to me.

"You're awake?" I said to my hand, glancing down. My voice hardly complied. The dry taste of smoke crawling down my throat grew more potent with every breath. "Good, I should think so too. Don't abandon me now." An explosion cut me off.

"Just look at you. What a perfect little executioner you've become." Morrigan's slick tone reached just barely within earshot. It was not meant for me anymore; she spoke to Kai.

I did not want to look up at him. I could not be sure what I would see.

He stooped slightly, although still on his feet. His arms hovered stiffly in front of him, keeping himself steady, I imagined. His sword lay abandoned in the dust a few feet behind him. I had never seen a tightrope walker myself, but I imagined it would feel like this—watching a person so willingly teeter on some edge that is entirely unknown to you. Not able to look away out of fear of missing something crucial, yet at the same time feeling so unbearably nauseous you do not dare open your mouth to breathe.

Just seconds ago, that had been me. Me, trying to stay upright while Morrigan's shadowy claws split through the space between us, only my Soul to stop the hand ripping through me. Better me alone than them, I had thought. The thought still persisted in my mind, only now it escorted a heavy tremor of guilt.

Finally, after several dry coughs and a frantic gasp to unclog his lungs, he called out to the others, "Go!"

For a horrified moment, I believed he intended for them to go, up through the door, and leave him behind. And hearing thumping feet, I believed they had obeyed him. The pain of betrayal sank lower, until they all flew by me at once, weapons facing firmly forwards.

[Kai]

She went for Leo first, with one groping claw, and Tank with the other, bringing both to a halt. But both survived it, and carried onwards, her inky talons driving instead into the floor. They sunk into the dust, emerged again to grab at Medi's heels, and then to reassert their presence upon Fenrir. He locked his long fingers with those of Morrigan, his impenetrable armour holding back her unstoppable violence. I could see the strength draining from the Soulless, his grip quivering but, unlike the soldiers, he refused to step aside or divert her aim, for behind him I knew Ben was still sprawled on the floor, peering up through his matted hair. Tank was the one to rescue them, slicing his blade through her wrist.

Morrigan's eyes flickered among us all, tracking each body in the charge like clay pigeons. No-one seemed to get close—or rather, whenever they managed it, their efforts were immediately forced undone. She soon spotted me, uselessly clutching my knees, a mere bystander. I was an open target. And as her oversized claws closed in on my neck, I remembered that my Soul had succumbed, exhausted; I barely kept on my feet. Even my weapon had skidded far enough out of my reach. I had nothing left. For that second of realisation, I felt suddenly angry—angry that I could have let myself make it this far, only to perish here. My eyes fell to the floor, forcibly resigning me to my fate.

Only the sensation did not arrive. Certainly, I imagined it all over my body, what it must feel like to be torn to pieces, but when I looked up again at a familiar popping sound, among the white flecks floating in front of my face, Eris appeared. She held out something in her hand: my sword. She turned her back to me once I took it from her. As she did so, I thought I glimpsed her eyes, shining like bulbs, as Medi's had done when she strained her Soul trying to fix Ben.

"Why is it that you keep saving me like this?" I said, though she might not have heard my hoarse voice.

Instead she replied, "I still have my Soul. Do you?"

"No, but I have this." I twirled the blade in my hands.

"Can you walk, though?"

"Far enough to swing it at that bitch, I can."

"Fine."

She marched forward, yanking the dagger from her wrist. I followed at her back. While the others threw themselves left and right, evading Morrigan's grasp, she moved on, constantly, following some foreseen track, not unlike an automaton. She trod so steadily, and so quietly—always so damn quiet—that, until she stood but metres away, Morrigan appeared not to see her coming. She frightened me sometimes though, in this case, not enough to rouse my Soul.

What should I have done then, when at last Morrigan struck back, from not just one, but both sides? I saw that on our left, and reached my arm over Eris's small shoulder, slicing it straight through the middle. The right though, it was just too fast. I had not even a chance to give a choked wail of agony and fear. It plunged into her stomach. I saw her stumble back and waited to watch her body crumble. Only she did not; Morrigan held her there, propped up like a puppet on a stick.

The room tripped to a halt. If none of the soldiers would move, then I would be the one to do it. I limped for Morrigan, holding on to the idea of my blade cutting right into the witch's heart. Although, when I took a proper look at her countenance, it gave me pause. Her eyes were wide, and she turned as still as a stone effigy. I turned back sheepishly to Eris, and immediately recognised what was wrong with her.

I could not find a scratch on the girl, not a blotch of blood, save for the grazes I gave her earlier. Her face stirred, perfectly alive. The corner of her mouth twitched into a subtle smirk, which impressed me in how highly it suited her in that fleeting moment. Barely observable past the fountain of white light pouring from her, her armoured fingers bound Morrigan's crackling, decaying hand. I heard her voice, an apathetic sound.

"It should have been a pleasure, Madam Larsen," she said. "Now kindly get the fuck out of my sight."

Movement from behind caught my attention, and I whirled around, sword readied across my chest. Yet, the shift in the air was not Morrigan's doing; her arms flagged to her sides. As she inhaled slowly through her nose, the figures of Aria and Emery revealed themselves just out of her sight, their faces veiled in deep shade. Two birds, they moved in a seamless arc almost too swiftly to truly see. Emery ran slightly ahead, suddenly grasping Aria's wrist. Without a sound, and he hoisted her off her feet, her steel-tipped toes aimed impeccably. I felt myself flinch in my shoulders, as the young woman's shoe cuffed the back of Morrigan's head. Their prey lurched onto her knees, with an awful noise bursting out, in what I had to assume was her own voice.

The pair stumbled past us in a mess of darkness and air. They moved with such momentum that they were helpless to stop themselves. Both scraped against the dirt, raw, blackened grazes covering their hands.

[Eris]

"That's enough, lovely. It's over."

Morrigan's tone had changed since that startled, choking sound. It fluttered into my ears, an ambient hum, although less soothing than it should have been. I found it viscerally frightening, and impossible to forget that, mere seconds ago, she was a devil putting us to the slaughter. She looked forth towards Aria, both women collecting themselves off of the floor, though their roles here had instantly reversed. Morrigan moved her steady hand away from the back of her neck; a cloud of black powder fell out from behind it. On her feet, she patted at the skirt of her torn, burnt and tarnished dress, brushing away the loose grime.

"Allow me to explain, please. Above all other reasons, you should know that I did this because I was afraid. Fear is at the very core of all of this, as it lives beneath an endless variety of cruelties. You understand—I can see it in your face." She lifted and pointed her finger in my direction, long enough for me to notice, before clenching her fist and drawing it close to her chest. Her brow knitted together, yet her chin remained perfectly level. "But I was alone. I was alone, and afraid of death, to put it plainly, of becoming lost, of the idea that one day, everything may have been for nothing. I was afraid of this. And look where it brought me." Morrigan's gaze flickered about the ceiling as she said that. She seemed to pause so that she could watch the dust parachuting down from there. "I am not criticising, of course. If it were not for the reality of it looming over us, forcing us to act, well, where then would we all be? It is one of those impulses that keep us moving, thinking, doing; it proves that we are alive. It is hard, and yet it is necessary. For when one tries to throw their shadow away, tries to cover it up, escape it, even to forget it: that is when it consumes you. Then you have lost. I realise this now—too late for me, though."

She gave a breathy chuckle then. Her words began to blend together in my mind; I could no longer tell if she articulated an observation, or an instruction. I heard someone else speak a way behind me.

"You…What did you do?" It was Aria, though I hardly recognised her voice. She sounded vicious, as though her tongue were laced with some foreign poison.

"It does not matter who you are, or what you have done: past life, death awaits all things. That is inevitable—an unshakable rule. I considered myself the anomaly. I took something that did not belong to me; it does not belong to anyone. I knew that, of course, but I did not think of it. I had ceased to care. I was to become immortal. People called me so many wonderful things during my life. I have been a genius, decisive, determined, brave even. I could have chosen to live on in those memories instead. But I know that I ceased to embody bravery the moment I used my Soul to take a piece of the Source in my own hand. The Source, that miracle that gave me everything I had, it became a weapon again, and it has taken so much already. That is what I did." Morrigan's hand hovered in front of her mouth, making her voice muffled. "I knew something was wrong as soon as it took hold of me. I am a scientist, you see, of the incorporeal. I tried to stop it. For so long, I tried to contain that thing. I tried." She dropped her shoulders, in a limp gesture towards herself. "My mind begun to decay into something abhorrent. I locked myself up down here and destroyed the keys, for all the good it did, praying my lonely Soul would be powerless to help me."

"Everyone thought you were dead. You disappeared, and no-one could ever find you. You haunted us, hung off our shoulders, for all this time!" Leo grew louder and louder, before he cut himself off, suddenly. I made out the rattle of Tank's armour, and shuffling feet.

"I know. I designed it that way," she added bluntly. "As it turned out, I got exactly what I wanted. I was never going to die; I was the anomaly. Then after all of that, I came to the conclusion that the choice had never been mine. As soon as I realised I would run out of time, and energy, I used the last of what I had to create Fenrir—a Soul given physical form, the first of his kind. The opposite way around to how it is supposed to go, but I could only manage so much, and it seems they all made do. Fenrir, perhaps, resembled my own make-up most accurately. Thus, I imagine he inherited a sizeable portion of my memory, aside from the small details I had to withhold from him. A new-born, with the power of a Soul, and a scholar's knowledge of the world: that was Fenrir. I fuelled his mind with my best intentions. And yet, something has happened. On the one hand, he is my twin, an extension of myself, and on the other…You seem confused. I should elaborate. Fenrir's purpose involved breaking outside of this place and causing the two Souls I released to surface, in the closest pair of potential humans who happened to cross his path."

I grew suddenly conscious of numerous eyes, all raking over me at once. I wondered if Kai experienced the same. Morrigan carried on in spite of this. The edges of her silhouette had already evaporated away, and the rest of her would be soon to follow.

"After that, he would turn against me. I would be unable to command him anymore. Although I had assumed that, by said juncture, I would be gone anyway."

"You mean to say you used your last moments of sanity to contrive your own death," Benjamin interrupted her. His breath raped, still unsteady, and he wobbled slightly on his feet, gingerly shifting his weight from his left leg to his right one and back again.

"At our expense," Kai added afterward, head resting in his hands.

"Half-sanity at best, lad. And yes, I did, to an extent. Though I never could predict how much of my design she—that is, me—would already know, and could tamper with. Or what kinds of outside variables would come into play." She gave a pointed look toward the elder brother. "The only thing I can think to tell you now is that I am sorry, but that would be self-indulgent of me. To be truthful, I cannot remember anything since I surrendered control. It is as if I fell asleep, and now I am waking up in the morning. Perhaps the only difference being that I am about to die." The whimsical voice, and slight tilt of her head with which she added that little afterthought made my stomach turn. "Tell me now, honestly, what happened? Exactly how many have suffered because of me?"

Morrigan referred to Aria as she asked this, but she did not answer. Instead she merely stood there, looking first at Morrigan, then into empty space. She tried opening her mouth a few times, but it only clamped shut again.

She looked so lost.

Not even Emery could find anything to say for her. In fact, he looked very much the same as her. It scared me, in an odd way.

Eventually, Leo spoke up in their place. "I'll tell you. Nineteen people were killed because of you. Of those, eighteen were ordinary folk, who had nought to do with you or any of us. The ninth was our

General, Naomi Elwin. There were thirty-three other casualties. Four of them are young children. And among the rest are Kai Hughes and Eris Rayne—your "closest pair". Benjamin Hughes is another," he continued. "That reality throttled you in the face not so long ago, not that you would remember. You know what? Take a good, proper look around you. See for yourself." Leo threw his arms out from his sides and tipped his head back slightly, a look of defiance on his face.

Morrigan let out a breath, releasing a plume of dust out into the air with it. "I see," she said, taking a few steps towards us. Her hair tumbled in copper waves over her shoulders as she crouched down to look at Kai and me, or at least she seemed to; I could not see her feet anymore. "Well, at least I know your names, yes? Kai, and Eris." She met his gaze quickly, then mine. "Is it not terrific, that such tender little mites as you could hold such violence inside? Thank you both, darlings. You've won."

That would be all she said to us. She moved on with haste, out of the edge of my vision. I tried to twist my neck with the intention of following her, but found myself stuck, staring listlessly at not much at all.

[Kai]

Eris still had not moved an inch. I could not even attempt to imagine what went on inside her head, for how blank her face appeared. She might as well have been asleep.

That woman, Morrigan, now looked to say something to Fenrir, but he interrupted her first.

"So, I was never free from you. No matter what I did, it was all for *you.* You left me out there, just long enough. Let me live, just enough that I found reason to care, and now you are done, you're going to take it from me." His face gradually melted with each word he spat out. He looked somehow distorted.

Ben saw it, I could tell that much. He had stopped teetering on his toes and now seemed poised to launch himself at someone. I had never seen him on edge like this, which alone made me uneasy. I held no doubt in my mind that, were it not for the rent in his metal arm rendering it useless, it would once again have collided with what remained of Morrigan's face. His other fist functioned perfectly fine, though. He flinched slightly, however, when Fenrir shouted out.

"Now look what happened! No—no, I am not *yours*!" He trailed off, seemingly having run out of fuel.

Morrigan's hand rose as if to touch Fenrir's face, but stopped short. "Please, be at peace," she murmured, before she backed away from him. That was it. That was all she had to say to him.

Something had swept over her—her eyes shot wide and as quickly she returned, back to the same spot where she had originally fallen. She spoke hastily, fixated on a spot past my shoulder, as though a sand timer hung there that only she could see. "Know this," she said, "my Soul, the one that allowed me to get this far, it was called Ambition. It is gone now, poor thing. That Soul perished the instant it mutated into this creature. I cannot promise that will remain a fact indefinitely. In theory, Ambition could return, and in what form I cannot say. Although, that does not mean a thing such as this must happen again. Once again, fate is left out of our control. Perhaps that is the nature of things. How quaint." She sniggered to herself weakly, but for a fleeting moment, a certain darkness cloaked her face. Claws tore at my throat, and then it vanished. She dropped to the ground. "That's it," she concluded. "I'm done."

As she ground out her last words, more of her body fell away as dust. Her breath disturbed the tumbling cloud; it seemed to shine a little as it lingered under the low sunlight, barely creeping in through the open door.

The last thing to go was her amber-red hair.

Nobody moved. Blood and ash stuck in my mouth, but I barely noticed the pain anymore. This did not feel like victory. It did not feel like anything. I thanked the eventual crack in the vacuum, even if it had to be by Eris's quiet, choked sob. I ran to her.

[Eris]
Her bright curls had glowed like feathers of the phoenix. Caught, blazed, and expired, just for a second. It was enough. I had loved her, once.

The room heaved with invisible mist. My mind drifted amongst it. I could not focus on anything, could not hold on to any one thought. It was over. That was good, no? The anchor had floated away, and I had nowhere to go. I sank, lost again, grabbing around in the darkness for *something*. I made a pathetic, sad sound that stung in my chest.

"Hey." Kai knelt somewhere to the side of me. One rough hand hovered over my shoulder. It stirred up a brief memory from minutes ago, already too cluttered to properly decipher. How different he appeared now, and yet he was the same as always. Something tempered his voice, a tiny, strange laugh, maybe. "Why are you crying?" he said.

"I don't know."

I tried a smile, thankful, and started to pull myself back together again. A little patchwork always suited perfectly well. Kai did not look so convinced, himself. He frowned and dipped his head.

"Thank you, but please, do not concern yourself with me. It's nothing," I explained, wiping furiously at my face. "Just give me a minute; I'll be fine."

For a while, I imagined my feet dragging themselves out from under me and lifting me up off the ground. Once I actually got around to it though, I found my knees shuddered a little more than I would have liked. The room continued to spin even after I had already turned around.

There was a small commotion underway; Kai now grasped Benjamin's shattered arm in his hands, frantically twisting it and moving the joints in all ways, glancing across his back, before returning his attention to the innards of the broken machine. All the while, he muttered under his breath although, looking at the damage, I could quite easily guess what words flew out of his mouth in such rapid succession.

Then he exclaimed, loud enough to hear, "What the fuck did you do that for, Ben?"

Benjamin only vaguely acknowledged his brother, patting him on the shoulder, but not quite looking at his face. “I’ll fix it later,” he said.

“No, I can do that; what I meant was—” Kai hesitated. “Never mind.”

“Come on, let me try. I can take more time, you know, make it a bit more swish.”

“If that’s how you’re thinking, then you’re not touching it.”

“It’s my arm.”

As Kai readied a lungful of air to interject with, Tank stormed across the room, and snatched the metal wrist out of his hand.

“This it?” he said, mostly to himself, as he haphazardly examined Benjamin. “Hell, I reckon even I can sort that, now I’ve got my breath back.” Both watched him with the same dubious expression as he took hold of Benjamin in a sort of unenthusiastic half-embrace. “Go on then, you’ll have to clock me over the head or somethin’.”

Benjamin hung back, his battered and tired mind visibly struggling to work its way around Tank’s words. He only managed to say, “I’m not sure that—”

He was cut short by Kai, who hardly wavered at all. The exhaustion appeared to have a vastly different effect on him, and he pitched forward as if he had any strength left to spare, striking Tank across his cheek. He immediately stumbled, groaning, most likely with the sort of dull ache which occurred when the body could not decide which part should hurt the most. At least the old soldier caught him before he could fall, easing him back upright.

“Good shot, kid,” Tank noted, with a well-timed cough to disguise the bruising in his voice. Then, taking a look at his handiwork, he added, “There it is: fixed, like I said, see? Give it a go.”

Sure enough, as Benjamin lifted his right arm in front of him, the left moved also, and once it tilted into my view, I could see it truly restored. Shards of metal were still scattered around their feet, yet his contraption appeared to even shine, as if newly polished. The mechanisms behind what I saw did not settle in my mind until Benjamin spoke.

"Huh, what do you know? I had better apologise, sir. It seems I underestimated Durability's convenience."

"I reckon you did; thought it a little too complex for me, didn't you?" Tank said, in a feigned pompous accent. "I ain't kiddin' when I say anythin'. Just as long as it's made of metal, I'll put it back, exactly as it was before."

I wondered why the idea of Tank possessing a Soul had never occurred to me. No-one had ever mentioned it, and thus I never thought to bring it up. And yet, there still arose a sense of a little red brick dropping into place. Sights I had not thought to question at the time immediately made sense, even if I never previously realised that they were conundrums. From his improbable strength, to his excess of hefty armour, to our odd partnership, all were explained, giving me a new sense of understanding and closure. The colonel and a librarian were a terrible mismatch—Tank unwittingly made that glaringly obvious—but Durability and Fortitude were not. He noticed me staring, looming in the dim light like an apparition, and winked. I had to consider the possibility that he had deliberately kept this secret all this time, simply so he could make a spectacle of it, right at the very end.

Benjamin, however, did not seem to be paying much interest, far less anxious about the harm to himself than something else. Kai noticed, eventually, and pulled limply at Tank's arms until he understood the obstruction and stepped aside.

He continued to fix his eyes on the centre of the room, where Fenrir stood, alone. I was conscious that the latter bowed his head, so I could not see much of his appearance. But at the sound of shuffling feet approaching, he perked up enough that a bar of faint light caught his face.

"Fenrir, your eyes," I mumbled, in a voice scarcely audible even to me, yet enough to seize his attention, if only for a moment. He glanced in my direction, probably surprised to hear me address him in person. It gave me a better look at those eyes, but only briefly, before they were taken by Benjamin appearing in front of him.

They were no longer that sickly yellow colour I had come to expect. His irises still appeared to glisten, almost, but now with a bright, regal blue that reflected the light. They struck me as familiar, but at the same time, transcendentally pretty.

Seeing Benjamin seemed to trigger something in Fenrir, as he suddenly began to shake, his entire body trembling. He took quick, uneven gasps of breath, like his lungs had forgotten to work for him, and he was having to wilfully, and in great panic, think to do it himself. I felt an aching camaraderie with him, when I recognised that. Some murmuring I had not registered before now ceased, leaving the basement in silence, save for him.

"I should be dead," he managed, the scratchy sound starting low and rising into a shout, "or almost, at least. Soulless—all of us—are meant to disappear with their creator. I don't understand. I don't understand."

"Is that what you expected, all this time?" Kai called, over his brother's shoulder. "Explains a lot. You know, maybe you're not the same, not in the way you think."

"Or, perhaps, you were quite like the others. But at some point, you changed. From a Soul given a physical body—some sort of lifeless contraption of death—to a human body with a Soul," I said, rushing my words to keep up with my thoughts. "She said it herself: 'something has happened', something I don't believe she had anything to do with. Somewhere between the moment you were born, and the moment Morrigan Larsen died, you unearthed yourself, not just memory, but fear, sympathy, desire. You *became* human in your own right."

"Incredible." Medi wandered across the floor, to the spot where Morrigan had stood, and fell. She crouched down, picking up the rusted chain still nailed firmly under the floorboards, evidently mulling over her own conclusions. "She really could do it."

Fenrir did not seem to know what to make of the possibilities we had proposed, if he had even listened to any. The same could be said for Benjamin, who continued to observe the former's eyes with a rare kind of expression that drooped, without being necessarily sad. It was quiet. Ever so slowly, as though as to avoid startling him, Benjamin brought his hands—both of them—upward, and I watched him gently press two fingers against the side of Fenrir's neck, under the line of his jaw. He waited like that for some time, blinking slowly, then his shoulders dropped, and a delightful blend of a sigh, a laugh and a desperate cry burst from his chest. After that, he folded his arms over his front, and directed his gaze down into them.

There were emotions of hardly bearable magnitude filling him up inside; even I could hear that in the swollen sound he made. Yet he beat them down, patiently waiting for another time to reveal their actual nature. I found it unusual, to see a person of his character ardently insisting on keeping such a feeling so private. In my mind, whatever flowered there between those two, knotted up in the basic presence of a heartbeat, it became sacred—untouchable. A silent voice asked me politely to turn away.

Leo's command made the wood rumble under my shoes. "There are a couple of things I've got left to do down here. But you should head outside." I heard a scrape of slow, labouring movement, and the second General added, in a lower tone, "That was good of you, kid. Now never do anything like it again."

I lingered on the spot, contemplating those last words of his, when a tap on my arm caused me to sway.

"Come on, you too." Kai did not let go of my hand, practically lifting me up the stairs and out into the open air in a hollow trance.

The afternoon sun seared my skin, and the breeze stung against open cuts I was not aware I had. Benjamin and Fenrir had exited ahead of us and disappeared out of sight. I did not search around for them. Medi and Tank followed up behind and, before we could stray any further, Medi stopped us to let Empathy heal the worst of our wounds.

Time passed peculiarly. It could have been minutes or hours since we escaped the house. Eventually, we found a decent patch of grassy soil to collapse upon. Kai's fingers were still curled around my thumb.

[Fenrir]

The outside looked different now. Not literally—the crumbling walls appeared the same, giving no indication of the violence that had not long ended beneath. But the light cast shadows over them I had not noted previously, exposing the most delicate cracks and precipices in the discoloured clay. The vines, climbing up through every gap they could find, had leaves that brushed against the coarse surface and inside my ears. I thought I might have left Benjamin struggling behind. But he was here, a little way behind me, waiting to let out whatever he had been about to say.

I heard movement up the stairs, back inside the wreckage, and resolved to avoid them. Their words still repeated over and over at high speed, behind any actual sounds. I could not face either of them again, not yet. I was busy. I climbed around the walls until I found the back of the house, shrouded in shade.

"You should sit." As I expected, Benjamin had followed.

I did not have the energy to argue, and so set myself down first. A few bricks jutted out from the rest of the wall, into my back. I offered up my hand to use as a prop; it took him much more effort to drop to the ground on purpose. Eventually, he landed opposite me with an audible bump, resting the soles of his feet against the wall next to where I reclined.

After a while of me glaring at my hands curled up on my knees, he reached out and held them. "You shake still," he said, keeping a low voice, not quite a whisper. "Breathe. What's going on in your head?"

"I don't understand," I started.

"You're alive."

"I don't know what to do."

"You never planned for this, did you? I remember, you said to me before, you never even considered…"

"I'm sorry."

"For what?"

"Not sure. I needed to say it."

"It's okay, Fen. You're going to be alright."

"I don't see how."

"Do you trust me?"

I paused. I had not been asked such a thing before. "Obviously—that's an odd question."

"It's a big question, I suppose."

"Yes. I mean, yes, I do."

"Then you know you're going to be fine."

I suddenly faced the jabbing sense of having been tricked. I nudged him in the side with my toe. He chuckled at me.

"What happened to my eyes?" I finally thought to ask. "Eris said something about my eyes, and you haven't stopped glancing at them."

He gasped under his breath, like he only now realised I would not be aware, and turned the back of his hands up, directing his gaze toward the metal one, glossy as if it were new and unscathed.

"Take a look," he said.

I tipped his hand around in mine, until a curved and stretched distortion of my face appeared. I found where my eyes would be, and in place of yellow smudges, I saw blue instead.

"What were you going to say?" I asked. "When we were down there, you were about to speak, and then you didn't."

"Oh, yeah, I remember."

"Why did you stop yourself like that?"

"Huh, I guess something didn't feel right, down in that musty old basement. And, I went to say something before I realised I didn't actually know how to, you know, say it."

"Strange, that's normally my problem."

"Oh, how the tables have turned," he said, laughing again under his breath.

I felt his wandering gaze land on me again. He concentrated thoroughly, I surmised, from the squint about his face, and so I watched him at the edge of my vision. His mouth moved ineffectually for a few attempts, before he actually spoke any words.

"They're beautiful."

"Was that it?"

"Nah, not just that. They really are, though."

I failed to infer an appropriate reaction to that, since I could not see what he meant. I was still in the process of growing accustomed to my own appearance, and now it had changed colour slightly. Yet, hearing Benjamin repeat that long, redundant word did not irritate as much as it should have.

"Let's see," he mumbled. "It's only now kicking in that half of my body isn't real. But at the same time, you're alive; I'm alive. Kai's okay. We all made it out, alive. You're actually here. And you have beautiful eyes. What else?" He hummed some obscure tune for a little while, mindlessly rocking his hands, until I lost my dissolving reflection in the metal. Finally, he shrugged and said, "Nope, I can't think of anything. I'll get it later, probably."

"I'll wait."

"You've got time, right?"

"Everything looks different, Benjamin. All of this, around me, it's not the same as before I walked in there—before I knew."

"Better?"

"More."

As I thought, I brushed my palms over the cool carpet of grass that managed to grow upward, despite the sparse light. I idly savoured the tickle of the tiny stems between each of my fingers, while the rest of my mind tried to process too many different sensations, notions, recollections, all at once. Logical thought became impossible. Benjamin was too tired—he could not even compensate for my absence right now. He seemed content for the pair of us to continue to amble our way around this conversation, only somewhat consciously.

"You don't have to keep on talking to me, if you don't want. It's just nice to sit like this, without having to think too much about things. It has been a little while, hasn't it? I knew you were holding your distance, pretty much straight after you told me, you know, that you thought you were going to nip out of existence as soon as we killed Morrigan."

I folded into myself, until my forehead almost pressed the inside of my arms. "I know. I made an effort after that, kept my shoulder turned to you, avoided looking to your face. I thought about it, intentionally. Knowing what I did, I probably believed that, to pretend it affected nothing—to lie—would be heinously cruel, especially once you realised the truth." Gracefully, he ignored the discrepancies I made. My reasoning still had not adapted to the fact that I was, in reality, wrong—not dead. "It felt… repulsive. But I convinced myself I had to do it."

"It did hurt a bit, actually. But shit, I think that was, at least partly, because I knew you didn't want to. I blamed myself, in many ways. I thought: if only I had never taken you outside of those walls, never made eye contact even, it would've been better for the both of us." The temperature of the air seemed to suddenly drop. I looked down at my body, to discern whether the cold, and the paralysis, were genuine. "See?" Benjamin said. "It's not just you."

"But now the truth has changed. I'm not gone."

"No, you're not."

"So, what now? Do we go back?"

"Honestly, I can't say I ever went anywhere. So that's up to you."

His shoulders slumped to mark the end of that little stream of admissions. I took my turn to begin another.

"How badly are you injured? Your neck looks like it's bruising, where your arm trapped it."

"Ah, not really," he said, dabbed at the blotch with his fingers, and winced. "Little bit."

"I should have moved faster, realised what she was doing sooner. I don't know what went wrong in me."

"Don't say that. It was my own bloody fault for waltzing over there and hitting her. Man, it felt so good, though." He grinned at himself, and in doing so, appeared to notice a strange feeling he had missed previously. Curiously, he wiped the back of his knuckles under his nose, snorting with amusement at the dark streak of drying blood left on his hands. The crimson smear did not do much to spoil his countenance. If anything, his nonchalance towards it had a rather enhancing effect. "Besides," he said, "Medi will probably be quite eager to put me back together. She might even be trying to track us down already."

"Would it not be best to let her?"

"Most likely it would, but not yet. Do you mind?"

"No."

"There's something about the feeling of finally winning the fight. Even the bruises are kind of satisfying, in a painful, annoying way. Or, maybe it's just me, thinking like that."

"It's not."

A beat, and a thoughtful lean to one side, then he said, slowly, "What are you feeling now, Fen?"

"I'm still trying to understand all of this. I have a life. It's mine. But I don't know what I'm supposed to do with that, and there's nothing telling me anymore. There is so much."

He bent forward, holding on to his knees. "Look, I reckon you might be overcomplicating this. You're trying so hard to think, to understand every little thing your huge brain notices right this second, that you're not letting yourself actually feel. Life is going to happen to you. You can let it. Trust me."

"I already said I did."

"That's true."

"And yet I sense that the absence of due thought has brought you pain."

He seemed to quieten, to shrink a little before me. "You are absolutely correct. But, at the same time, you can logic yourself into some deep fucking pits. Nothing works always."

"So, there is always pain."

"There's always some pain. And there is so much time, all yours now. You can let go, for a while. You'll be okay."

I inhaled, and exhaled as steadily as I could, holding my gaze on a dirty spot on Benjamin's shirt. One brace had started to drop off of my left shoulder, which proved horribly distracting until I yanked it back straight. Deliberately emptying one's mind proved as difficult a task as it sounded. There were a few seconds, from down in the basement, which continued to return relentlessly. Eris mentions my eyes in her low, unobtrusive voice, but the surrounding room is silenced by her. Benjamin reaches out, finds blood still fluttering under my skin, and at that realisation he makes a sound as muddled as his face. I could relate to it, even if it could not explain it. I shook my head, having to force myself to stop struggling. The memory ended there. Some platitudes about being "different" and "human" followed me out of the door, and I ended up here.

Just let it, he said. Feel what is happening go ahead. His voice painted it to be so simple, and there seemed nothing left but to try. Using the wall, I shoved myself onto my knees, bringing Benjamin within reach. My hand first closed the gap, wavering for a while, before it came to rest in the middle of his chest, fingers disappearing under the silken lining of his waistcoat. Through the rigid defences of his ribcage, his heart thudded against my palm, as I already knew it would. Still, the sensation had an ability to make the ground seem more solid. Soothing, perhaps, was the correct term. Benjamin did not know, though. He had not known until he touched me, back there, that he would find anything but cold death within me. A warm breeze glanced over my face. It came from his lungs. I felt his pulse, initially in time with his breath, change, speed up inexplicably, and then subside again. His face had merged together before me, into an indistinct blur of colours without shape. I closed my useless eyes; I would not bother with them. He smelt faintly metallic. Earlier, as he had brushed his hands over his face, a trace of blood had smeared onto his lip. The salty taste nettled on my tongue.

"Fen, remember," he spoke into my mouth. "You have to breathe for me, alright?"

[Emery]

"Aria, we have to go."

She stood in the deepest darkness of the basement, staring down at the chains that still lay on a bed of black ash on the floor—all that remained of her. The object of our rage had gone, leaving behind nothing for us to keep fighting against. I hated her all the more for that, because we were forced to keep going, while she was allowed to escape. After what she did, she could just die. Watching her tighten her clenched fists, I knew that thought lingered in Aria's head too. We both stayed down there in the murk because, in our resentment, for a few selfish minutes longer, we believed the only thing we had left was each other.

But now we had to leave. Everyone else had already returned to the surface, even Leo, once he had collected everything he needed. I waited quietly for her to realise it too. She continued to stand, with her back facing me. I could never abandon her. If she demanded a battle of endurance, I would give her that. Eventually, she turned around, possibly to see if I had given up and disappeared without her noticing, somehow. Seeing me remain there, her expression shifted from unbending resolution to, more than anything, weariness.

I held out a hand to her. "Come on—we need to get out of this place."

After a moment of reluctance, she nodded silently and, threading our fingers together, allowed me to lead her up the narrow stairway and under the fallen beam positioned inconveniently at the top. At that point, she halted, tugging at my arm.

"Wait," she said.

Still holding on to my hand, she went back, ducking under the beam. I saw her stretch her arm into the passage, and pull the handle back, on what remained of the wooden door. She yanked at it until she heard the sound of the latch clicking shut. In a literal sense, it made next to no impact; the hole Benjamin had made in the door gaped wide enough for the average person to squeeze through.

"That's better," she proclaimed.

When she brought us out into the sun, it seemed impossibly hot for its place in the sky, not oppressively so, but it simmered inside me as if I had lived through most of my days in that dim cave. The front of the building had been deserted, save for us. A few steps toward the brow of the slope, however, revealed Medi, Tank, and the two apprentices all sat on the grass a little further down. Leo towered above them, a sizeable tin case swinging in his hands. His hand rested firmly on the shoulder of Tank, who had linked arms with Medi. He peered over, and momentarily caught my eye.

"Should we go?" I suggested. Aria had collected up her lance from the dust and now used it to lean against. She smiled, shooting one arm into the air to wave at the group.

[Kai]

There were only three of us who got on the train in the end: Eris, Ben, and myself. Even considering that, for the first hour or so of the journey, it took conscious effort to believe we were really going home.

Benjamin sat in the same cabin as us for a time, chattering away about nothing much, as though not one momentous thing had happened for weeks. Once enough of the other passengers had cleared off though, he excused himself, and wandered further down the train. I assumed he went to find another empty compartment, in which to be alone.

Eris and I fell quiet after that, save for the occasional comment on some mundane curiosity out of the window. *Ah, sheep, all the way up the hill. Yes. Doesn't that little one look like it's watching? Poor sod.* It seemed painfully clear that we struggled to keep this up without Ben. Thankfully now, the stinging white circle of the sun rose far enough above the window frame, no longer beaming relentlessly into every passenger's face. It left the cabin looking comparatively dull. I heard across from me a shallow, breathy sound, like a yawn. Glancing over, I saw Eris hunched oddly in her seat, her head being rocked slowly back and forth, propped against the wall beside her. I ducked down, to check her eyes, which were shut. She did not snore, exactly, but she came close. In her lap, her half-finished book lay still open. I watched it slide a little out of her hand's limp grip, before it suddenly slipped from her knees altogether, and I bent forward, catching it by the spine. She did not budge. Mindful, I snuck back into my seat, the book in my hands, and as I flipped it over, I found the cover read "*The Definitive Compendium of Espritian Myths: Volume One of Three*". The tinge of blue on the trim of its cover had seemed vaguely familiar. Looking inside, there were words underlined, some notes in the margins here and there, an eclectic mixture of handwriting. A faded blot of ink stained one edge of the book, causing that paper to contort into stiff ripples. Not in a sorry state, necessarily, well-loved was the kindest word for it I could think of.

Keeping one finger under the page at which Eris had left off, I turned back to the volume's beginning, and pulled my glasses from my front pocket.

[Eris]

The path back from the station felt shorter, fleeting even, compared to my memory of the journey there. Bags and cases rattling and clunking behind the three of us, we soon reached the point where every brown building and street corner became familiar. I was pondering the idea that two people, so recently strangers, could have existed so close to me, when the sound of wheels and boots on the pavement ceased abruptly. I looked up at the house before us. I had often admired this one; it had a porch out front, raised up on a wooden deck. Up there now, at the top of the stairs, a man, perhaps approaching middle-age, noticed us emerge from an alley behind the antique shop. I jumped at the height of the voices that erupted on either side of me.

"Dad!"

His face was much squarer than either of his sons, with a thick beard, and the shape of his features settled somewhere in between theirs, not quite matching one or the other. Passing him by chance on the street, I would not necessarily have placed him as the father of the Hughes family. The brothers approached a little faster now though, taking full strides rather than my half-steps, so I could hang back and look closer. They certainly inherited their impressive height from him, and at the top of his head, I could still make out the remnants of coal-coloured hair, to correspond with his eyes.

As he crossed the road, he sped almost to a run, and he might have tripped over if he had not, at that precise moment, fastened his arms around his sons' shoulders. Lagging behind as I did, I only arrived close enough to hear a fragment of their first exchange in what felt like a terribly long time.

"…at you. What have they done to my boys?"

The two of them held their father a little tighter, with murmurings of apologies, which he shook off. When he opened his scrunched eyes, he found me staring from some way opposite him. He appeared to experience a sudden epiphany, since he straightened himself, ironing out the front of his waistcoat with his hands. Making a subtle point in my general direction, he glanced at Kai, who also looked at me, and nodded knowingly. He reached past the boys, taking my gloved hand in both of his, and bowed at the waist, nearly touching my knuckles to his face.

"Welcome home, Eris," he said. "It's good to meet you." I stuttered, thrown off by this introduction, which he had evidently prepared for. "My sons did think to send me several letters between the pair of them, during this whole nightmare. Your name happened to crop up quite a bit. I have to thank you, for all you've done."

"That's alright, sir. I didn't do much of anything; I was just there."

"You were. Silas."

"Sorry?"

"That's me."

I heard sniggering behind him. Benjamin desperately bit down on his lip, while Kai's face was hidden in his hands.

"Apologies, Eris," Benjamin said, "our dad's pretty crap at this. He's not trying to put you off, I swear."

"What happened with your other mate, Ben?" his father called over his shoulder. "You did mention he would probably have to stick around in Interieur, but…"

"Yeah—yeah, it was the only way, really. He'll get on well, though, I'm sure. Emery will look after him."

Silas hummed in one long, gravelly breath, translating the melancholy droop in his son's eyes, regardless of the smile beneath them. He bent over to pick up a couple of the cases dotted around their feet.

"I'll help you get some of these inside," he insisted.

As the other two headed up onto the porch, Silas whispering something to Benjamin, Kai leaned forward and said quietly, "He likes you. You'll be alright."

"You make sure you tell her she's welcome any time. Marvellous girl!" The older man's voice boomed from inside the house.

[Fenrir]

I leaned on the windowsill, letting the air cool my face. I noticed a potted plant next to my elbow, left behind in the aftermath. It probably needed some water.

"Aha." Emery entered, tapping softly on the doorframe.

"Found him?" Aria called, some way down the hallway.

He leaned into her view and nodded. "I thought I might come across you in here," he said.

"He said I could take any room I wanted."

"Of course you can."

"And will you screw locks to this door as well?"

"No, Fenrir." He held out the bundle in his arms and dropped it on the end of the bed. "I brought these for you. They are a size too small for me now, but they should fit you well enough, at least for the time being, before we can get you a set measured up properly."

I rifled through the pile of clothes. This uniform had an identity attached to it. It could be all I had, for a long time. I laid each component out, trying to picture myself in this image.

Emery indicated with his hands. "These are a couple of pairs of trousers. Make sure you keep them pressed, but no pleats down the front. You've got a few shirts to keep you going. They are all white, yes, but you'll find you get much better at taking out stains. And your jacket should slip straight on. Don't worry about lacing up the back again, unless you want to." He glanced around him. "You have a set of drawers in here, right?"

"It's here," I said, taking the neatly folded pile already in his hands. "Benjamin decided to rearrange the furniture in this room after he arrived in it."

He laughed, and then coughed to smother it somewhat.

"What?" I questioned.

"It's only this." He motioned to his eyes, obviously referring to the strange transformation in my own. "I find it so bizarre how such a minute change can make a person appear so very different. What did Benjamin have to say about them? You had a lot to talk about after you got out of that house, didn't you?"

"He said they were—he said they were…" I could not force the word out of my mouth. I remembered exactly what I wanted to say, but something physically stopped me from producing it. A sleeve got caught in a drawer. I shook it to release it, yanked the fabric out and slammed it closed.

"It's okay. I understand," Emery said.

"I don't think you do, though. You will always have your Aria; in fact, she's waiting out there for you right now. How could you possibly understand?" I paused to collect my thoughts, before I slipped into a rampant outburst. "You were right," I admitted. "You were completely right, and I was wrong. And I hate you a little for that."

"That's fine; I probably would have hated me too. I think you need some time to be alone. Ben will be back, I promise you that much. You will be surprised how short that time seems, whether it's here, with us, or someplace else you prefer. But please, Fenrir, you need to give yourself time."

"That's the same as what he told me, you know, almost to the word. I suppose I should take it as the truth, then. I remember I wanted to cry, as far as I could tell. But I wouldn't, not in front of him, not while he still smiled for me. He told me how glad he was to be going home. I couldn't do that to him."

Emery crouched next to me, staring at the water rising in the corners of my eyes. "Oh no, you realise he wouldn't have cared a whit, right? Remember, he was a friend to me first, so I should like to believe I know him well enough." He took an arm and wrapped it around my shoulders, burying his nose in my hair. "You can cry now, Fen. Cry as much as you want, and after that, you've got to keep going, okay?"

As I tried to blink away the burning that had returned to my cheeks once again, I made out another figure entering the room, and setting themselves down on my other side. Aria did not announce her presence with words, but instead started to hum a melody that enflamed part of my brain. It must have been especially old, one of Morrigan's memories. Her skin felt cool compared to my own, when she squeezed my hands in hers.

I could not turn and run, or even dry my face. I did not even have the energy in me to make a sound. I seemed to fall asleep, almost, damp with tears, cocooned in Emery's arms, Aria's lullaby in my ears.

[Kai]

"Ah, I see, another Hughes. And what are you doing at my library?"

She must have been two feet shorter than me, at least. But the silent, unmoving manner with which she glared from under her brow at me made me baulk as if she towered high as an oak tree. From Eris's description, I had to assume this woman, who had appeared from behind the door, was Maud.

"I stepped out for some air. I had no place in particular to head, so I walked wherever until I ended up here, I guess."

"I was so very lost in the absence of your majesty, Maud; I simply had to hurry to this glorious bastion of literature as fast as I could. That would be the correct answer."

"Well, pardon me, I—"

"I'm joshing with you, lad. Here, in you come." She waved me into the building. "Getting some fresh daylight on your skin, were you? Well, maybe I did prod some sense into your father. You're still transparent, mind you. I am afraid madam isn't about at the minute. She fell asleep a little while ago."

"She did? Never mind, I won't disturb. She could do with the rest."

She leaned on an ancient-looking desk, one hand nestled on her hip and, looking down past some high bookshelves, nodded. "That's right," she said.

As I went to disappear, I caught a glimpse of movement, in the same direction as she stared. Out from between a pair of cases, a stout tabby cat appeared. It trotted along, against every vertical surface it could find, on its way to the old woman. But about halfway there, it suddenly froze, noticing the very obvious, unfamiliar member of its audience. The little creature arrested me with possibly the roundest, most disproportionately large pair of eyes I had seen. I watched it repetitively lift its left foot, before tentatively touching the pad against the floor again.

"Oh, don't mind him," she piped up. "That's only Enobarbus. You see what a nervy old lug he is, couldn't hurt a fly if he tried."

I crouched close to the floor and drummed on the glossy wooden board under my fingertips. Enticed by the sound, the cat made hesitant, painstaking steps in my direction; though, every time I happened to glance at its huge eyes, it would stop dead until I looked away again. Maud watched his progress from behind her monocle, the light from overhead reflecting off the glass, leaving a circular, white hollow on the right side of her face. Eventually, I felt the tickle of whiskers against my skin, a soft nudge across my knuckles. If I was subtle enough, I could watch him out of the corner of my eye, covering the burgundy of my shirt cuff pale with threads of hair. Both of his ears twisted around at the sound of me exhaling.

"I say every house should have a cat," Maud said, taking her seat to press on with some paperwork, as though she had forgotten I was there—which suited me fine.

Enobarbus had been distracted from me as well, by a faint thump across the other side of the library. Like him, I followed the sound as it seemed to move down from a floor above. Perhaps the cat could distinguish people by the weight of their stride, or something similar, since he went practically skipping over to a spiral staircase I had failed to notice before. He waited at the bottom, making chirping sounds clearly reserved for those he liked best. I could discern that much from who appeared, descending out of the shadows: Eris, looking pink and puffy around her eyelids. She kept a hand on the banister, leaning her weight on it now and again, as if she still had yet to recover her balance, having been forcibly woken from a decent sleep.

Spotting me kneeling on her floor, she glanced about herself, probably debating the likelihood that she had simply exited one dream and wandered into another. No, it was only me.

"Good morning," she called, her voice still wavering in some confusion.

"It is, only just," I said.

"Oh, I see the old man came to inspect you, then." She swept Enobarbus up in her arms, and he twisted to rest his chin on her shoulder. I could hear the low rumble he made, like a little motor engine, from all the way across the room.

"We've never had a cat at our place."

"Everywhere should have a cat."

She walked over tentatively, her shoeless feet making no sound against the floor now. I realised she had to peer down at me, on my knees, and leaped to my feet.

"Sorry, I didn't mean to fall back asleep," she said. "I had no idea you were visiting today."

"I didn't exactly plan on it."

"You're not a problem, lad. Madam will go get you a cup of something to drink. I can always find some work for you to do, if you're that worried."

"Yes, of course, it's just this way." She lowered her four-legged companion to the ground and headed back the way she came.

Seeing her in front of me—in a heavy skirt that bounced around her knees and a jumper with worn, baggy sleeves that probably smelled of dust and stale paper, leading me towards an antique spiral staircase—I realised she was at home here. Doubtless, the red stain of the battlefield suited her, but she had no desire to be there. This was the place she chose. I had previously thought I could never understand it, but perhaps this counted as a start.

[Eris]

Maud called across from her desk. "Are you nearly sorted?"

I dropped the last of the finished books onto the trolley, and fastened them with twine, knotted at the top. A pile of degraded, coverless volumes and loose stacks of pages still watched me from the corner of the room. The task had taken me somewhat longer than I had hoped. I would repair those ones too, in time, but for now I would take what I had to offer back to Interieur, where they belonged.

"Here, something for you," she said, plucking a cream-coloured envelope from under a paperweight. "Arrived with the post this morning."

"Oh, they seem early." I walked over and idly reached to take it from her outstretched hand.

"This doesn't look like the usual to me. Must have been delivered by hand if "Eris" is all that is written on it. Beautiful penmanship, whoever it is."

"Curious."

The letter opener was buried among some pens, in an empty ink bottle by Maud's elbow. I flipped the slice of silver between my fingers before pushing it under the seal.

"Nice paper, too," I noted, as it split apart in a neat line.

"Isn't it?"

I returned to my luggage, to lean on as I read.

"Dear Eris,

I heard from Leo that you would be stopping by in the next week. Unfortunately, as you know all too well, there is a fair chance that we will miss each other, so I decided to put this in writing for you. Lieutenant-Class postage tends to be faster, so this should reach you before you set off, should we be able to speak face-to-face.

To the point, I have some rather bizarre news to give you. Or rather, I believe I have information about you which might be of interest. I am not sure.

I am uncertain as to where to start, so perhaps the beginning is simply best. When you first arrived at our base in Interieur, I came to find you on the roof, if you remember. I told you I had sought you out so as to introduce myself. This was not a lie, but certainly not the entire truth, either. In fact, I knew your name, R, before I ever met you. I had heard it long before I was aware you existed. It struck a chord, somewhere in my memory, but I could not figure out where.

Now I can remember, and in this case, I resolved that late is better than never. Despite being young, and not involved in the business side of operations, I nevertheless had ears. Altair—that is, my father—had dealings with people called R. They were smugglers, as far as I can tell. Not unlike us, they were constantly on the move, travelling with trade and from the law. I know because the Rs had a bit of a reputation. They knew their craft; they were tactical, smart, had their wits about them. One might say conniving.

For a very long time, I have been trying, albeit with limited success, to disconnect myself from my past. What with very recently arresting my elder brother, much of it has returned to the surface. I had not realised to what extent I failed to move on from those experiences. I hope, at least, they might be useful to you.

Of course, there is every chance I am mistaken. Of the things I knew about the Rs, a child was not one of them. I leave it to your discretion, whether to ignore what I have written here. It also may or may not be in your interests to destroy this letter. Fire is best.

I hope that you are well, and that you find the time to be happy. May your Soul protect you. We will meet again soon.

Yours,

Emery.

P.S. Aria has asked that I attach her own note. She apologises in advance for any errors. I have been forbidden from reading it, so I am oblivious to its contents, but fairly certain that you will not need to burn this one."

I pulled the envelope open; inside, along with two matches, was a smaller leaf of the same paper, folded in half. The letters were round and stout, some crossed out or swapped around but, nonetheless, perfectly legible to my eye.

"Dear Eris,

I was so glad to hear you are coming with some of your books soon! I took a little glance in the library the other day, and it looks wonderful. Mama would be so very pleased with the work you have done for her.

I could tell from the way Emery was tapping his pen on the desk that his letter is rather serious. In case he did not repeat it enough, I shall say again that we would love for you to visit us soon, proper, I mean. You are most likely on your way as you read, but I dread to think that you may not get to see everyone. Of course, you did not learn this from me, but Tank is positively lost without you! I think it would do Emery some good too.

Anyway, I am seeking some advice. He and I are finally able to take that leave we missed out on so long ago. We have decided to spend the week in the Western District as was originally planned. Silly though it may sound, I would very much like to be a tourist for once. On that note, as someone who must know their way around, where would you recommend? Please let us know your thoughts!

All the best,

Aria."

"Anything interesting?" Maud said, as she noticed me tuck Aria's letter into my pocket.

"Not really."

I noticed her scrutinise what remained in my hands, briefly, before returning to her work. She opened a volume from the stack to her left, took a stamp from the ink pad beside it, and pushed it onto the front page with a dull thump.

Then I asked her, without thinking, "Did you know who I was?"

She nodded, not to me, but to herself, before touching her monocle and stamping another book. "You don't get to my age, madam," she said, "without knowing a lot of things."

"That makes three of us, then." I pulled out the matches.

"Some things make us better off for knowing, others make us worse. A lot of truths don't achieve either. They just are." She paused. "I suppose you had best be off, girl. You don't want to miss your train. You've got that appointment with the boy Hughes later on, haven't you?"

I felt around my skirt pocket for the silver chain of my watch, to check the time. Ever since he had given it to me, it had ticked away perfectly. I fell into such a habit of carrying it around that my clothes felt strange, too light, without it.

"What would you say," I started, as I manoeuvred the trolley down the front steps, "if I suggested I was not going to read any of the usual letters anymore, if I just shredded them up for compost?"

"Whatever helps." I heard the thump of the stamp.

As I leaned back inside to close the door, I quickly added, "Oh, and since you know so many things, what about touristy places over here in the West? Excluding this place, obviously. Have a think for me before this evening."

She cackled. "Over here? They'll be bloody lucky over this way. You want any help with that?"

"I should be alright." I still had plenty of time to get to the station, even lugging this load. "Yes, I think I'll be fine."

"Whatever you say—I forget sometimes, I fostered a solid little one with you. Go on, then, go. I'll be waiting when you get home."

End.

Printed in Great Britain
by Amazon